"I know you're not really asleep," Mia said.

Her hand felt good in his hair. Too good. Frisco reached up and caught her wrist as he opened his eyes, pushing her away from him. "That's right," he said. "I'm just shutting everything out."

She was gazing at him with eyes that were a perfect mixture of green and brown. "Well, before you shut me out again, I want you to know—I don't judge whether or not someone is a man based on his ability to beat an opponent into a pulp. And I wasn't running away from *you* on the beach today—"

Frisco shut his eyes again. "Look, you don't have to explain why you don't want to sleep with me. If you don't, then you don't. That's all I need to know."

"I was running away from myself," she said very softly.

SUZANNE BROCKMANN

FRISCO'S KID

MIRA

ISBN 1-55166-759-2

FRISCO'S KID

Copyright © 1997 by Suzanne Brockmann.

All rights reserved. Except for use in any review, the reproduction or
utilization of this work in whole or in part in any form by any electronic,
mechanical or other means, now known or hereafter invented, including
xerography, photocopying and recording, or in any information storage or
retrieval system, is forbidden without the written permission of the publisher,
MIRA Books, 225 Duncan Mill Road, Don Mills, Ontario, Canada M3B 3K9.

All characters in this book have no existence outside the imagination of the
author and have no relation whatsoever to anyone bearing the same name
or names. They are not even distantly inspired by any individual known or
unknown to the author, and all incidents are pure invention.

MIRA and the Star Colophon are trademarks used under license and registered
in Australia, New Zealand, Philippines, United States Patent and Trademark
Office and in other countries.

Visit us at www.mirabooks.com

Printed in U.S.A.

For my cousin, Elise Kramer,
who played with and loved my mother,
then me, and now my children, too,
as if we were her own kids.
With all my love, Elise, this one's for you.

1

Frisco's knee was on fire.

He had to lean heavily on his cane to get from the shower to the room he shared with three other vets, and still his leg hurt like hell with every step he took.

But pain was no big deal. Pain had been part of Navy Lt. Alan ''Frisco'' Francisco's everyday life since his leg had damn near been blown off more than five years ago during a covert rescue operation. The pain he could handle.

It was this cane that he couldn't stand.

It was the fact that his knee wouldn't—couldn't—support his full weight or fully extend that made him crazy.

It was a warm California day, so he pulled on a pair of shorts, well aware that they wouldn't hide the raw, ugly scars on his knee.

His latest surgery had been attempted only a few months ago. They'd cut him open all over again, trying, like Humpty Dumpty, to put all the pieces back together. After the required hospital stay, he'd been sent here, to this physical therapy center, to build up strength in his leg, and to see if the operation had worked—to see if he had more flexibility in his injured joint.

But his doctor had been no more successful than the legendary King's horses and King's men. The operation hadn't improved Frisco's knee. His doctor couldn't put Frisco together again.

There was a knock on the door, and it opened a crack.

''Yo, Frisco, you in here?''

It was Lt. Joe Catalanotto, the commander of SEAL Team Ten's Alpha Squad—the squad to which, an aeon of pain and frustration and crushed hopes ago, Frisco had once belonged.

"Where else would I be?" Frisco said.

He saw Joe react to his bitter words, saw the bigger man's jaw tighten as he came into the room, closing the door behind him. He could see the look in Joe's dark eyes—a look of wary reserve. Frisco had always been the optimist of Alpha Squad. His attitude had always been upbeat and friendly. Wherever they went, Frisco had been out in the street, making friends with the locals. He'd been the first one smiling, the man who'd make jokes before a high-altitude parachute jump, relieving the tension, making everyone laugh.

But Frisco wasn't laughing now. He'd stopped laughing five years ago, when the doctors had walked into his hospital room and told him his leg would never be the same. He'd never walk again.

At first he'd approached it with the same upbeat, optimistic attitude he'd always had. *He'd* never walk again? Wanna make a bet? He was going to do more than walk again. He was going to bring himself back to active duty as a SEAL. He was going to run and jump and dive. No question.

It had taken years of intense focus, operations and physical therapy. He'd been bounced back and forth from hospitals to physical therapy centers to hospitals and back again. He'd fought long and hard, and he *could* walk again.

But he couldn't run. He could do little more than limp along with his cane—and his doctors warned him against doing too much of that. His knee couldn't support his weight, they told him. The pain that he stoically ignored was a warning signal. If he wasn't careful, he'd lose what little use he did have of his leg.

And that wasn't good enough.

Because until he could run, he couldn't be a SEAL again.

Five years of disappointment and frustration and failure had worn at Frisco's optimism and upbeat attitude. Five years of itching to return to the excitement of his life as a Navy SEAL;

of being placed into temporary retirement with no real, honest hope of being put back into active duty; of watching as Alpha Squad replaced him—*replaced* him; of shuffling along when he *burned* to run. All those years had worn him down. He wasn't upbeat anymore. He was depressed. And frustrated. And angry as hell.

Joe Catalanotto didn't bother to answer Frisco's question. His hawklike gaze took in Frisco's well-muscled body, lingering for a moment on the scars on his leg. "You look good," Joe said. "You're keeping in shape. That's good. That's real good."

"Is this a social call?" Frisco asked bluntly.

"Partly," Joe said. His rugged face relaxed into a smile. "I've got some good news I wanted to share with you."

Good news. Damn, when was the last time Frisco had gotten *good* news?

One of Frisco's roommates, stretched out on his bed, glanced up from the book he was reading.

Joe didn't seem to mind. His smile just got broader. "Ronnie's pregnant," he said. "We're going to have a kid."

"No way." Frisco couldn't help smiling. It felt odd, unnatural. It had been too long since he'd used those muscles in his face. Five years ago, he'd have been pounding Joe on the back, cracking ribald jokes about masculinity and procreation and laughing like a damn fool. But now the best he could muster up was a smile. He held out his hand and clasped Joe's in a handshake of congratulations. "I'll be damned. Who would've ever thought *you'd* become a family man? Are you terrified?"

Joe grinned. "I'm actually okay about it. Ronnie's the one who's scared to death. She's reading every book she can get her hands on about pregnancy and babies. I think the books are scaring her even more."

"God, a *kid,*" Frisco said again. "You going to call him Joe Cat, Junior?"

"I want a girl," Joe admitted. His smile softened. "A redhead, like her mother."

"So what's the other part?" Frisco asked. At Joe's blank look, he added, "You said this was partly a social call. That means it's also partly something else. Why else are you here?"

"Oh. Yeah. Steve Horowitz called me and asked me to come sit in while he talked to you."

Frisco slipped on a T-shirt, instantly wary. Steve Horowitz was his doctor. Why would his doctor want *Joe* around when he talked to Frisco? "What about?"

Joe wouldn't say, but his smile faded. "There's an officer's lounge at the end of the hall," he said. "Steve said he'd meet us there."

A talk in the officer's lounge. This was even more serious than Frisco had guessed. "All right," he said evenly. It was pointless to pressure Joe. Frisco knew his former commander wouldn't tell him a thing until Steve showed up.

"How's the knee?" Joe asked as they headed down the corridor. He purposely kept his pace slow and easy so that Frisco could keep up.

Frisco felt a familiar surge of frustration. He hated the fact that he couldn't move quickly. Damn, he used to break the sprint records during physical training.

"It's feeling better today," he lied. Every step he took hurt like hell. The really stupid thing was that Joe knew damn well how much pain he was in.

He pushed open the door to the officer's lounge. It was a pleasant enough room, with big, overstuffed furniture and a huge picture window overlooking the gardens. The carpet was a slightly lighter shade of blue than the sky, and the green of the furniture upholstery matched the abundant life growing outside the window. The colors surprised him. Most of the time Frisco had spent in here was late at night, when he couldn't sleep. In the shadowy darkness, the walls and furniture had looked gray.

Steven Horowitz came into the room, a step behind them. "Good," he said in his brisk, efficient manner. "Good, you're here." He nodded to Joe. "Thank you, Lieutenant, for coming by. I know your schedule's heavy, too."

"Not too heavy for this, Captain," Joe said evenly.

"What exactly is 'this'?" Frisco asked. He hadn't felt this uneasy since he'd last gone out on a sneak-and-peek—an information-gathering expedition behind enemy lines.

The doctor gestured to the couch. "Why don't we sit down?"

"I'll stand, thanks." Frisco had sat long enough during those first few years after he'd been injured. He'd spent far too much time in a wheelchair. If he had his choice, he'd never sit again.

Joe made himself comfortable on the couch, his long legs sprawled out in front of him. The doctor perched on the edge of an armchair, his body language announcing that he wasn't intending to stay long.

"You're not going to be happy about this," Horowitz said bluntly to Frisco, "but yesterday I signed papers releasing you from this facility."

Frisco couldn't believe what he was hearing. "You did *what?*"

"You're out of here," the doctor said, not unkindly. "As of fourteen hundred hours today."

Frisco looked from the doctor to Joe and back. Joe's eyes were dark with unhappiness, but he didn't contradict the doctor's words. "But my physical therapy sessions—"

"Have ended," Horowitz said. "You've regained sufficient use of your knee and—"

"Sufficient for *what?*" Frisco asked, outraged. "For hobbling around? That's not good enough, dammit! I need to be able to run. I need to be able to—"

Joe sat up. "Steve told me he's been watching your chart for weeks," the commander of Alpha Squad told Frisco quietly. "Apparently, there's been no improvement—"

"So I'm in a temporary slump. It happens in this kind of—"

"Your therapist has expressed concern that you're overdoing it." Horowitz interrupted him. "You're pushing yourself too hard."

"Cut the crap." Frisco's knuckles were white as he gripped his cane. "My time is up. That's what this is about, isn't it?" He looked back at Joe. "Someone upstairs decided that I've had my share of the benefits. Someone upstairs wants my bed emptied, so that it can be filled by some other poor son of a bitch who has no real hope of a full recovery, right?"

"Yeah, they want your bed," Joe said, nodding. "That's certainly part of it. There's limited bed space in every VA facility. You know that."

"Your progress has begun to decline," the doctor added. "I've told you this before, but you haven't seemed to catch on. Pain is a signal from your body to your brain telling you that something is wrong. When your knee hurts, that does *not* mean push harder. It means back off. Sit down. Give yourself a break. If you keep abusing yourself this way, Lieutenant, you'll be back in a wheelchair by August."

"I'll *never* be back in a wheelchair. Sir." Frisco said the word *sir,* but his tone and attitude said an entirely different, far-less-flattering word.

"If you don't want to spend the rest of your life sitting down, then you better stop punishing a severely injured joint," Dr. Horowitz snapped. He sighed, taking a deep breath and lowering his voice again. "Look, Alan, I don't want to fight with you. Why can't you just be grateful for the fact that you can stand. You can *walk.* Sure, it's with a cane, but—"

"I'm going to run," Frisco said. "I'm not going to give up until I can run."

"You can't run," Steven Horowitz said bluntly. "Your knee won't support your weight—it won't even properly extend. The best you'll manage is an awkward hop."

"Then I need another operation."

"What you need is to get on with your life."

"My life requires an ability to run," Frisco said hotly. "I don't know too many active-duty SEALs hobbling around with a cane. Do you?"

Dr. Horowitz shook his head, looking to Joe for help.

But Joe didn't say a word.

"You've been in and out of hospitals and PT centers for five years," the doctor told Frisco. "You're not a kid in your twenties anymore, Alan. The truth is, the SEALs don't need you. They've got kids coming up from BUD/S training who could run circles around you even if you *could* run. Do you really think the top brass are going to want some old guy with a bum knee to come back?"

Frisco carefully kept his face expressionless. "Thanks a lot, man," he said tightly as he gazed sightlessly out of the window. "I appreciate your vote of confidence."

Joe shifted in his seat. "What Steve's saying is harsh—and not entirely true," he said. "Us 'old guys' in our thirties have experience that the new kids lack, and that usually makes us better SEALs. But he's right about something—you *have* been out of the picture for half a decade. You've got more to overcome than the physical challenge—as if that weren't enough. You've got to catch up with the technology, relearn changed policies...."

"Give yourself a break," Dr. Horowitz urged again.

Frisco turned his head and looked directly at the doctor. "No," he said. He looked at Joe, too. "No breaks. Not until I can walk without this cane. Not until I can run a six-minute mile again."

The doctor rolled his eyes in exasperation, standing up and starting for the door. "A six-minute mile? Forget it. It's *not* going to happen."

Frisco looked out the window again. "Captain, you also said I'd never walk again."

Horowitz turned back. "This is *different*, Lieutenant. The truth—whether you believe it or not—is that the kind of physical exertion you've been up to is now doing your knee more damage than good."

Frisco didn't turn around. He stood silently, watching bright pink flowers move gently in the breeze.

"There are other things you can do as a SEAL," the doctor said more gently. "There are office jobs—"

Frisco spun around, his temper exploding. "I'm an expert in ten different fields of warfare, and you want me to be some kind of damn pencil pusher?"

"Alan—"

Joe stood up. "You've at least got to take some time and think about your options," he said. "Don't say no until you think it through."

Frisco gazed at Joe in barely disguised horror. Five years ago they'd joked about getting injured and being sucked into the administrative staff. It was a fate worse than death, or so they'd agreed. "You want me to think about jockeying a desk?" he said.

"You could teach."

Frisco shook his head in disbelief. "That's just perfect, man. Can't you just see me writing on a blackboard...?" He shook his head in disgust. "I would've expected *you* of all people to understand why I could never do that."

"You'd still be a SEAL," Joe persisted. "It's that or accept your retirement as permanent. *Some*one's got to teach these new kids how to survive. Why can't you do it?"

"Because I've been in the middle of action," Frisco nearly shouted. "I know what it's like. I want to go back there, I want to *be* there. I want to be *doing,* not...teaching. *Damn!*"

"The Navy doesn't want to lose you," Joe said, his voice low and intense. "It's been five years, and there's *still* been nobody in the units who can touch you when it comes to strategic warfare. Sure, you can quit. You can spend the rest of your life trying to get back what you once had. You can lock yourself away and feel sorry for yourself. Or you can help pass your knowledge on to the next generation of SEALs."

"Quit?" Frisco said. He laughed, but there was no humor in it at all. "I can't quit—because I've already been kicked out. Right, Captain Horowitz? As of fourteen hundred hours, I'm outta here."

There was silence then—silence that settled around them all, heavy and still and thick.

"I'm sorry," the doctor finally said. "I've got to do what is best for you and for this facility. We need to use your bed for someone who really could use it. You need to give your knee a rest before you damage it further. The obvious solution was to send you home. Someday you'll thank me for this." The door clicked as it closed behind him.

Frisco looked at Joe. "You can tell the Navy that I'm not going to accept anything short of active duty," he said bluntly. "I'm not going to teach."

There was compassion and regret in the bigger man's dark eyes. "I'm sorry," Joe said quietly.

Frisco glared up at the clock that was set into the wall. It was nearly noon. Two more hours, and he'd have to pack up his things and leave. Two more hours, and he wouldn't be a Navy SEAL, temporarily off the active duty list, recovering from a serious injury. In two hours he'd be *former* Navy SEAL Lt. Alan Francisco. In two hours, he'd be a civilian, with nowhere to go, nothing to do.

Anger hit him hard in the gut. Five years ago, it was a sensation he'd rarely felt. He'd been calm, he'd been cool. But nowadays, he rarely felt anything besides anger.

But wait. He *did* have somewhere to go. The anger eased up a bit. Frisco had kept up the payments on his little condo in San Felipe, the low-rent town outside of the naval base. But...once he arrived in San Felipe, then what? He would, indeed, have nothing to do.

Nothing to do was worse than nowhere to go. What *was* he going to do? Sit around all day, watching TV and collecting disability checks? The anger was back, this time lodging in his throat, choking him.

"I can't afford to continue the kind of physical therapy I've been doing here at the hospital," Frisco said, trying to keep his desperation from sounding in his voice.

"Maybe you should listen to Steve," Joe said, "and give your leg a rest."

Easy for Joe to say. Joe was going to stand up and walk out of this hospital without a cane, without a limp, without his entire life shattered. Joe was going to go back to the home he shared with his beautiful wife—who was pregnant with their first child. He was going to have dinner with Veronica, and later he'd probably make love to her and fall asleep with her in his arms. And in the morning, Joe was going to get up, go for a run, shower, shave and get dressed, and go into work as the commanding officer of SEAL Team Ten's Alpha Squad.

Joe had everything.

Frisco had an empty condo in a bad part of town.

"Congratulations about the baby, man," Frisco said, trying as hard as he could to actually mean it. Then he limped out of the room.

2

There was a light on in condo 2C.

Mia Summerton stopped in the parking lot, her arms straining from the weight of her grocery bags, and looked up at the window of the second-floor condo that was next to her own. Apartment 2C had remained empty and dark for so many years, Mia had started to believe that its owner would never come home.

But that owner—whoever he was—was home tonight.

Mia knew that the owner of 2C was, indeed, a "he." She got a better grip on the handles of her cloth bags and started for the outside cement stairs that led up to the second story and her own condo. His name was Lt. Alan Francisco, U.S.N., Ret. She'd seen his name in the condo association owner's directory, and on the scattered pieces of junk mail that made it past the post office's forwarding system.

As far as Mia could figure out, her closest neighbor was a retired naval officer. With no more than his name and rank to go on, she had left the rest to her imagination. He was probably an older man, maybe even elderly. He had possibly served during the Second World War. Or perhaps he'd seen action in Korea or Vietnam.

Whatever the case, Mia was eager to meet him. Next September, her tenth graders were going to be studying American history, from the stock market crash through to the end of the Vietnam conflict. With any luck, Lt. Alan Francisco, U.S.N., Ret., would be willing to come in and talk to her class, tell his story, bring the war he'd served in down to a personal level.

And that was the problem with studying war. Until it could be understood on a personal level, it couldn't be understood at all.

Mia unlocked her own condo and carried her groceries inside, closing the door behind her with her foot. She quickly put the food away and stored her cloth grocery bags in the tiny broom closet. She glanced at herself in the mirror and adjusted and straightened the high ponytail that held her long, dark hair off her neck.

Then she went back outside, onto the open-air corridor that connected all of the second-floor units in the complex.

The figures on the door, 2C, were slightly rusted, but they still managed to reflect the floodlights from the courtyard, even through the screen. Not allowing herself time to feel nervous or shy, Mia pressed the doorbell.

She heard the buzzer inside of the apartment. The living room curtains were open and the light was on inside, so she peeked in.

Architecturally, it was the mirror image of her own unit. A small living room connected to a tiny dining area, which turned a corner and connected to a galley kitchen. Another short hallway led back from the living room to two small bedrooms and a bath. It was exactly the same as her place, except the layout of the rooms faced the opposite direction.

His furniture was an exact opposite of Mia's, too. Mia had decorated her living room with bamboo and airy, light colors. Lieutenant Francisco's was filled with faintly shabby-looking mismatched pieces of dark furniture. His couch was a dark green plaid, and the slipcovers were fraying badly. His carpeting was the same forest green that Mia's had been when she'd first moved in, three years ago. She'd replaced hers immediately.

Mia rang the bell again. Still no answer. She opened the screen and knocked loudly on the door, thinking if Lieutenant Francisco *was* an elderly man, he might be hard of hearing....

"Looking for someone in particular?"

Mia spun around, startled, and the screen door banged shut, but there was no one behind her.

"I'm down here."

The voice carried up from the courtyard, and sure enough, there was a man standing in the shadows. Mia moved to the railing.

"I'm looking for Lieutenant Francisco," she said.

He stepped forward, into the light. "Well, aren't you lucky? You found him."

Mia was staring. She knew she was staring, but she couldn't help herself.

Lt. Alan Francisco, U.S.N., Ret., was no elderly, little man. He was only slightly older than she was—in his early thirties at the most. He was young and tall and built like a tank. The sleeveless shirt he was wearing revealed muscular shoulders and arms, and did very little to cover his powerful-looking chest.

His hair was dark blond and cut short, in an almost boxlike military style. His jaw was square, too, his features rugged and harshly, commandingly handsome. Mia couldn't see what color his eyes were—only that they were intense, and that he examined her as carefully as she studied him.

He took another step forward, and Mia realized he limped and leaned heavily on a cane.

"Did you want something besides a look at me?' he asked.

His legs were still in the shadows, but his arms were in the light. And he had tattoos. One on each arm. An anchor on one arm, and something that looked like it might be a mermaid on the other. Mia pulled her gaze back to his face.

"I, um…' she said. "I just…wanted to say…hi. I'm Mia Summerton. We're next-door neighbors," she added lamely. Wow, she sounded like one of her teenage students, tongue-tied and shy.

It was more than his rugged good looks that was making her sound like a space cadet. It was because Lt. Alan Francisco was a career military man. Despite his lack of uniform, he was standing there in front of her, shoulders back, head held high—the Navy version of G.I. Joe. He was a warrior not by draft but by choice. He'd chosen to enlist. He'd chosen to perpetuate everything Mia's antiwar parents had taught her to believe was wrong.

He was still watching her as closely as she'd looked at him. "You were curious," he said. His voice was deep and accentless. He didn't speak particularly loudly, but his words carried up to her quite clearly.

Mia forced a smile. "Of course."

"Don't worry," he said. He didn't smile back. In fact, he hadn't smiled once since she'd turned to look over the railing at him. "I'm not loud. I don't throw wild parties. I won't disturb you. I'll stay out of your way and I hope you'll have the courtesy to do the same."

He nodded at her, just once, and Mia realized that she'd been dismissed. With a single nod, he'd just dismissed her as if she were one of his enlisted troops.

As Mia watched, the former Navy lieutenant headed toward the stairs. He used his cane, supporting much of his weight with it. And every step he took looked to be filled with pain. Was he honestly going to climb those stairs…?

But of course he was. This condo complex wasn't equipped with elevators or escalators or anything that would provide second-floor accessibility to the physically challenged. And this man was clearly challenged.

But Lieutenant Francisco pulled himself up, one painful step at a time. He used the cast-iron railing and his upper-body strength to support his bad leg, virtually hopping up the stairs. Still, Mia could tell that each jarring movement caused him no little amount of pain. When he got to the top, he was breathing hard, and there was a sheen of sweat on his face.

Mia spoke from her heart as usual, not stopping to think first. "There's a condo for sale on the ground floor," she said. "Maybe the association office can arrange for you to exchange your unit for the…one on the…"

The look he gave her was withering. "You still here?" His

voice was rough and his words rude. But as he looked up again, as for one brief moment he glanced into her eyes, Mia could see myriad emotions in his gaze. Anger. Despair. Shame. An incredible amount of shame.

Mia's heart was in her throat. "I'm sorry," she said, her gaze dropping almost involuntarily to his injured leg. "I didn't mean to—"

He moved directly underneath one of the corridor lights, and held up his right leg slightly. "Pretty, huh?" he said.

His knee was a virtual railroad switching track of scars. The joint itself looked swollen and sore. Mia swallowed. "What—" she said, then cleared her throat. "What... happened...?"

His eyes were an odd shade of blue, she realized, gazing up into the swirl of color. They were dark blue, almost black. And they were surrounded by the longest, thickest eyelashes she'd ever seen on a man.

Up close, even despite the shine of perspiration on his face, Mia had to believe that Lt. Alan Francisco was the single most attractive man she had ever seen in her entire twenty-seven years.

His hair was dark blond. Not average, dirty blond, but rather a shiny mixture of light brown with streaks and flashes of gold and even hints of red that gleamed in the light. His nose was big, but not too big for his face, and slightly crooked. His mouth was wide. Mia longed to see him smile. What a smile this man would have, with a generous mouth like that. There were laugh lines at the corners of his mouth and his eyes, but they were taut now with pain and anger.

"I was wounded," he said brusquely. "During a military op."

He had been drinking. He was close enough for Mia to smell whiskey on his breath. She moved back a step. "Military...op?"

"Operation," he said.

"That must have been...awful," she said. "But...I wasn't aware that the United States has been involved in any naval battles recently. I mean, someone like, oh, say…the *President* would let us all know if we were at war, wouldn't he?''

"I was wounded during a search-and-rescue counterterrorist operation in downtown Baghdad," Francisco said.

"Isn't Baghdad a little bit inland for a sailor?"

"I'm a Navy SEAL," he said. Then his lips twisted into a grim version of a smile. "*Was* a Navy SEAL," he corrected himself.

Frisco realized that she didn't know what he meant. She was looking up at him with puzzlement in her odd-colored eyes. They were a light shade of brown and green—hazel, he thought it was called—with a dark brown ring encircling the edges of her irises. Her eyes had a slightly exotic tilt to them, as if somewhere, perhaps back in her grandparents' generation, there was Asian or Polynesian blood. Hawaiian. That was it. She looked faintly Hawaiian. Her cheekbones were wide and high, adding to the exotic effect. Her nose was small and delicate, as were her graceful-looking lips. Her skin was smooth and clear and a delicious shade of tan. Her long, straight black hair was up in a ponytail, a light fringe of bangs softening her face. Her hair was so long, that if she wore it down, it would hang all the way to her hips.

His next-door neighbor was strikingly beautiful.

She was nearly an entire twelve inches shorter than he was, with a slender build. She was wearing a loose-fitting T-shirt and a pair of baggy shorts. Her shapely legs were that same light shade of brown and her feet were bare. Her figure was slight, almost boyish. Almost. Her breasts may have been small, but they swelled slightly beneath the cotton of her shirt in a way that was decidedly feminine.

At first glance, from the way she dressed and from her clean, fresh beauty, Frisco had thought she was a kid, a teenager. But up close, he could see faint lines of life on her face, along with a confidence and wisdom that no mere teenager could possibly exude. Despite her youthful appearance, this Mia Summerton was probably closer to his own age.

"Navy SEALs," he explained, still gazing into her remarkable hazel eyes, "are the U.S. military's most elite special operations group. We operate on sea, in the air and on land. SEa, Air, Land. SEAL."

"I get it," she said, with a smile. "Very cute."

Her smile was crooked and made her look just a little bit goofy. Surely she knew that her smile marred her perfect beauty, but that didn't keep her from smiling. In fact, Frisco was willing to bet that, goofy or not, a smile was this woman's default expression. Still, her smile was uncertain, as if she wasn't quite sure he deserved to be smiled at. She was ill at ease—whether that was caused by his injury or his imposing height, he didn't know. She *was* wary of him, however.

"'Cute' isn't a word used often to describe a special operations unit."

"Special operations," Mia repeated. "Is that kind of like the Green Berets or the Commandos?"

"Kind of," Frisco told her, watching her eyes as he spoke. "Only, smarter and stronger and tougher. SEALs are qualified experts in a number of fields. We're all sharpshooters, we're all demolitions experts—both underwater and on land—we can fly or drive or sail any jet or plane or tank or boat. We all have expert status in using the latest military technology."

"It sounds to me as if you're an expert at making war." Mia's goofy smile had faded, taking with it much of the warmth in her eyes. "A professional soldier."

Frisco nodded. "Yeah, that's right." She didn't like soldiers. *That* was her deal. It was funny. Some women went for military men in a very major way. At the same time, others went out of their way to keep their distance. This Mia Summerton clearly fell into the second category.

"What do you do when there's no war to fight? Start one of your own?"

Her words were purposely antagonistic, and Frisco felt himself bristle. He didn't have to defend himself or his former profession to this girl, no matter how pretty she was. He'd run into plenty of her type before. It was politically correct these days to be a pacifist, to support demilitarization, to support limiting funds for defense—without knowing the least little thing about the current world situation.

Not that Frisco had anything against pacifists. He truly believed in the power of negotiation and peace talks. But he followed the old adage: walk softly and carry a big stick. And the Navy SEALs were the biggest, toughest stick America could hope to carry.

And as for war, they were currently fighting a great big one—an ongoing war against terrorism.

"I don't need your crap." Frisco turned away as he used his cane to limp toward the door of his condo.

"Oh, my opinion is crap?" She moved in front of him, blocking his way. Her eyes flashed with green fire.

"What I *do* need is another drink," Frisco announced. "Badly. So if you don't mind moving out of my way...?"

Mia crossed her arms and didn't budge. "I'm sorry," she said. "I confess that my question *may* have sounded a bit hostile, but I don't believe that it was *crap.*"

Frisco gazed at her steadily. "I'm not in the mood for an argument," he said. "You want to come in and have a drink—please. Be my guest. I'll even find an extra glass. You want to spend the night—even better. It's been a long time since I've shared my bed. But I have no intention of standing here arguing with you."

Mia flushed, but her gaze didn't drop. She didn't look away. "Intimidation is a powerful weapon, isn't it?" she said. "But I know what you're doing, so it won't work. I'm not intimidated, Lieutenant."

He stepped forward, moving well into her personal space, backing her up against the closed door. "How about now?" he asked. "Now are you intimidated?"

She wasn't. He could see it in her eyes. She *was* angrier, though.

"How typical," she said. "When psychological attack doesn't work, resort to the threat of physical violence." She smiled at him sweetly. "I'm calling your bluff, G.I. Joe. What are you going to do now?"

Frisco gazed down into Mia's oval-shaped face, out of ideas, although he'd never admit that to her. She was *supposed* to have turned and run away by now. But she hadn't. Instead, she was still here, glaring up at him, her nose mere inches from his own.

She smelled amazingly good. She was wearing perfume— something light and delicate, with the faintest hint of exotic spices.

Something had stirred within him when she'd first given him one of her funny smiles. It stirred again and he recognized the sensation. Desire. Man, it had been a long time....

"What if I'm not bluffing?" Frisco said, his voice no more than a whisper. He was standing close enough for his breath to move several wisps of her hair. "What if I really do want you to come inside? Spend the night?"

He saw a flash of uncertainty in her eyes. And then she stepped out of his way, moving deftly around his cane. "Sorry, *I'm* not in the mood for casual sex with a jerk," she retorted.

Frisco unlocked his door. He should have kissed her. She'd damn near dared him to. But it had seemed wrong. Kissing her would have been going too far. But, Lord, he'd wanted to....

He turned to look back at her before he went inside. "If you change your mind, just let me know."

Mia laughed and disappeared into her own apartment.

3

"Yeah?" Frisco rasped into the telephone. His mouth was dry and his head was pounding as if he'd been hit by a sledge-hammer. His alarm clock read 9:36, and there was sunlight streaming in underneath the bedroom curtains. It was bright, cutting like a laser beam into his brain. He closed his eyes.

"Alan, is that you?"

Sharon. It was his sister, Sharon.

Frisco rolled over, searching for something, *any*thing with which to wet his impossibly dry mouth. There was a whiskey bottle on the bedside table with about a half an inch of amber liquid still inside. He reached for it, but stopped. No way was he going to take a slug of that. Hell, that was what his old man used to do. He'd start the day off with a shot—and end it sprawled, drunk, on the living room couch.

"I need your help," Sharon said. "I need a favor. The VA hospital said you were released and I just couldn't believe how lucky my timing was."

"How big a favor?" Frisco mumbled. She was asking for money. It wasn't the first time, and it wouldn't be the last. His older sister Sharon was as big a drunk as their father had been. She couldn't hold a job, couldn't pay her rent, couldn't support her five-year-old daughter, Natasha.

Frisco shook his head. He'd been there when Tasha was born, brought into the world, the offspring of an unknown father and an irresponsible mother. As much as Frisco loved his sister, he knew damn well that Sharon *was* irresponsible. She floated through life, drifting from job to job, from town to town, from man to man. Having a baby daughter hadn't rooted Sharon in any one place.

Five years ago, back when Natasha was born, back before his leg had damn near been blown off, Frisco had been an optimist. But even he hadn't been able to imagine much happiness in the baby's future. Unless Sharon owned up to the fact that she had a drinking problem, unless she got help, sought counseling and finally settled down, he'd known that little Natasha's life would be filled with chaos and disruption and endless change.

He'd been right about that.

For the past five years, Frisco had sent his sister money every month, hoping to hell that she used it to pay her rent, hoping Natasha had a roof over her head and food to fill her stomach.

Sharon had visited him only occasionally while he was in the VA hospital. She only came when she needed money, and she never brought Natasha with her—the one person in the world Frisco would truly have wanted to see.

"This one's a major favor," Sharon said. Her voice broke. "Look, I'm a couple of blocks away. I'm gonna come over, okay? Meet me in the courtyard in about three minutes. I broke my foot, and I'm on crutches. I can't handle the stairs."

She hung up before giving Frisco a chance to answer. Sharon broke her foot. Perfect. Why was it that people with hard luck just kept getting more and more of the same? Frisco rolled over, dropped the receiver back onto the phone, grabbed his cane and staggered into the bathroom.

Three minutes. It wasn't enough time to shower, but man, he needed a shower badly. Frisco turned on the cold water in the bathroom sink and then put his head under the faucet, both drinking and letting the water flow over his face.

Damn, he hadn't meant to kill that entire bottle of whiskey last night. During the more than five years he'd been in and out of the hospital and housed in rehabilitation centers, he'd never had more than an occasional drink or two. Even before his injury, he was careful not to drink too much. Some of the

guys went out at night and slammed home quantities of beer
and whiskey—enough to float a ship. But Frisco rarely did.
He didn't want to be like his father and his sister, and he
knew enough about it to know that alcoholism could be he-
reditary.

And last night? He'd meant to have one more drink. That
was all. Just one more to round down the edges. One more
to soften the harsh slap of his release from the therapy center.
But one drink had turned into two.

Then he'd started thinking about Mia Summerton, separated from him by only one very thin wall, and two had become three. He could hear the sound of her stereo. She was
listening to Bonnie Raitt. Every so often, Mia would sing
along, her voice a clear soprano over Bonnie's smoky alto.
And after three drinks, Frisco had lost count.

He kept hearing Mia's laughter, echoing in his head, the
way she'd laughed at him right before she'd gone into her
own condo. It had been laughter loaded with meaning. It had
been "a cold day in hell" kind of laughter, as in, it would be
a cold day in hell before she'd even deign to so much as *think*
about him again.

That was good. That was exactly what he wanted. Wasn't
it?

Yes. Frisco splashed more water on his face, trying to convince himself that that was true. He didn't want some neighbor lady hanging around, giving him those goddamned pitying
looks as he hobbled up and down the stairs. He didn't need
suggestions about moving to a lousy ground-floor condo as if
he were some kind of cripple. He didn't need self-righteous
soapbox speeches about how war is not healthy for children
and other living things. If anyone should know *that,* he sure
as hell should.

He'd been in places where bombs were falling. And, yes,
the bombs had military targets. But that didn't mean if a bomb
accidentally went off track, it would fail to explode. Even if
it hit a house or a church or a school, it was gonna go off.
Bombs had no conscience, no remorse. They fell. They ex-

ploded. They destroyed and killed. And no matter how hard
the people who aimed those bombs tried, civilians ended up
dead.

But if a team of SEALs was sent in before air strikes became necessary, those SEALs could conceivably achieve
more with fewer casualties. A seven-man team of SEALs such
as the Alpha Squad could go in and totally foul up the enemy's communication system. Or they could kidnap the enemy's military leader, ensuring chaos and possibly reopening
negotiations and peace talks.

But more often than not, because the top brass failed to
realize the SEALs' full potential, they weren't utilized until
it was too late.

And then people died. Children died.

Frisco brushed his teeth, then drank more water. He dried
his face and limped back into his bedroom. He searched for
his sunglasses to no avail, uncovered his checkbook, pulled
on a clean T-shirt and, wincing at the bright sunlight, he
headed outside.

The woman in the courtyard burst into tears.

Startled, Mia looked up from her garden. She'd seen this
woman walk in—a battered, worn-out-looking blonde on
crutches, awkwardly carrying a suitcase, followed by a very
little, very frightened red-haired girl.

Mia followed the weeping woman's gaze and saw Lieutenant Francisco painfully making his way down the stairs. Wow,
he looked awful. His skin had a grayish cast, and he was
squinting as if the brilliant blue California sky and bright sun-
shine were the devil's evil doing. He hadn't shaved, and the
stubble on his face made him look as if he'd just been rolled
from a park bench. His T-shirt looked clean, but his shorts
were the same ones he'd had on last night. Clearly he'd slept
in them.

He'd obviously had "another" drink last night, and quite
probably more than that afterward.

Fabulous. Mia forced her attention back to the flowers she

was weeding. She had been convinced beyond a shadow of a doubt that Lt. Alan Francisco was *not* the kind of man she even wanted to have for a friend. He was rude and unhappy and quite possibly dangerous. And now she knew that he drank way too much, too.

No, she was going to ignore condo 2C from now on. She would pretend that the owner was still out of town.

The blond woman dropped her crutches and wrapped her arms around Francisco's neck. "I'm sorry," she kept saying, "I'm sorry."

The SEAL led the blonde to the bench directly across from Mia's garden plot. His voice carried clearly across the courtyard—she couldn't help but overhear, even though she tried desperately to mind her own business.

"Start at the beginning," he said, holding the woman's hands. "Sharon, tell me what happened. From the beginning."

"I totaled my car," the blonde—Sharon—said, and began to cry again.

"When?" Francisco asked patiently.

"Day before yesterday."

"That was when you broke your foot?"

She nodded. Yes.

"Was anyone else hurt?"

Her voice shook. "The other driver is still in the hospital. If he dies, I'll be up on charges of vehicular manslaughter."

Francisco swore. "Shar, if he dies, he'll be dead. That's a little bit worse than where you'll be, don't you think?"

Blond head bowed, Sharon nodded.

"You were DUI." It wasn't a question, but she nodded again. DUI—driving under the influence. Driving drunk.

A shadow fell across her flowers, and Mia looked up to see the little red-haired girl standing beside her.

"Hi," Mia said.

The girl was around five. Kindergarten age. She had amazing strawberry blond hair that curled in a wild mass around her round face. Her face was covered with freckles, and her eyes were the same pure shade of dark blue as Alan Francisco's.

This had to be his daughter. Mia's gaze traveled back to the blonde. That meant Sharon was his...wife? Ex-wife? Girlfriend?

It didn't matter. What did she care if Alan Francisco had a *dozen* wives?

The red-haired girl spoke. "I have a garden at home. Back in the old country."

"Which old country is that?" Mia asked with a smile. Kindergarten-age children were so wonderful.

"Russia," the little girl said, all seriousness. "My real father is a Russian prince."

Her *real* father, hmm? Mia couldn't blame the little girl for making up a fictional family. With a mother up on DUI charges, and a father who was only a step or two behind...Mia could see the benefits of having a pretend world to escape to, filled with palaces and princes and beautiful gardens.

"Do you want to help me weed?" Mia asked.

The little girl glanced over at her mother.

"The bottom line is that I have no more options," Sharon was tearfully telling Alan Francisco. "If I voluntarily enter the detox program, I'll win points with the judge who tries my case. But I need to find someplace for Natasha to stay."

"No way," the Navy lieutenant said, shaking his head. "I'm sorry. There's no way in hell I can take her."

"Alan, please, you've got to help me out here!"

His voice got louder. "What do I know about taking care of a kid?"

"She's quiet," Sharon pleaded. "She won't get in the way."

"I don't want her." Francisco had lowered his voice, but it still carried clearly over to Mia. And to the little girl—to Natasha.

Mia's heart broke for the child. What an awful thing to overhear: Her own father didn't want her.

"I'm a teacher," Mia said to the girl, hoping she wouldn't hear the rest of her parents' tense conversation. "I teach older children—high school kids."

Natasha nodded, her face a picture of concentration as she imitated Mia and gently pulled weeds from the soft earth of the garden.

"I'm supposed to go into detox in an hour," Sharon said. "If you don't take her, she'll be a ward of the state—she'll be put into foster care, Alan."

"There's a man who works for my father the prince," Natasha told Mia, as if she, too, were trying desperately not to listen to the other conversation, "who only plants flowers. That's all he does all day. Red flowers like these. And yellow flowers."

On the other side of the courtyard, Mia could hear Alan Francisco cursing. His voice was low, and she couldn't quite make out the words, but it was clear he was calling upon his full sailor's salty vocabulary. He wasn't angry at Sharon—his words weren't directed at her, but rather at the cloudless California sky above them.

"My very favorites are the blue flowers," Mia told Natasha. "They're called morning glories. You have to wake up very early in the morning to see them. They close up tightly during the day."

Natasha nodded, still so seriously. "Because the bright sun gives them a headache."

"Natasha!"

The little girl looked up at the sound of her mother's voice. Mia looked up, too—directly into Alan Francisco's dark blue eyes. She quickly lowered her gaze, afraid he'd correctly read the accusations she knew were there. How could he ignore his own child? What kind of man could admit that he didn't want his daughter around?

"You're going to be staying here, with Alan, for a while," Sharon said, smiling tremulously at her daughter.

He'd given in. The former special operations lieutenant had given in. Mia didn't know whether to be glad for the little girl, or concerned. This child needed more than this man could give her. Mia risked another look up, and found his disturbingly blue eyes still watching her.

"Won't that be fun?" Sharon hopefully asked Natasha.

The little girl considered the question thoughtfully. "No," she finally said.

Alan Francisco laughed. Mia hadn't thought him capable, but he actually smiled and snorted with laughter, covering it quickly with a cough. When he looked up again, he wasn't smiling, but she could swear she saw amusement in his eyes.

"I want to go with you," Natasha told her mother, a trace of panic in her voice. "Why can't I go with you?"

Sharon's lip trembled, as if she were the child. "Because you can't," she said ineffectively. "Not this time."

The little girl's gaze shifted to Alan and then quickly back to Sharon. "Do we know him?" she asked.

"Yes," Sharon told her. "Of course we know him. He's your uncle Alan. You remember Alan. He's in the Navy...?"

But the little girl shook her head.

"I'm your mom's brother," Alan said to the little girl.

Her brother. Alan was Sharon's brother. Not her husband. Mia didn't want to feel anything at that news. She refused to feel relieved. She refused to feel, period. She weeded her garden, pretending she couldn't hear any of the words being spoken.

Natasha gazed at her mother. "Will you come back?" she asked in a very small voice.

Mia closed her eyes. But she did feel. She felt for this little girl; she felt her fear and pain. Her heart ached for the mother, too, God help her. And she felt for blue-eyed Alan Francisco. But what she felt for him, she couldn't begin to define.

"I always do," Sharon said, dissolving once more into tears as she enveloped the little girl in a hug. "Don't I?" But then she quickly set Natasha aside. "I've got to go. Be good. I love you." She turned to Alan. "The address of the detox center is in the suitcase."

Alan nodded, and with a creak of her crutches, Sharon hurried away.

Natasha stared expressionlessly after her mother, watching until the woman disappeared from view. Then, with only a very slight tightening of her lips, she turned to look at Alan.

Mia looked at him, too, but this time his gaze never left the little girl. All of the amusement was gone from his eyes, leaving only sadness and compassion.

All of his anger had vanished. All of the rage that seemed to burn endlessly within him was temporarily doused. His blue eyes were no longer icy—instead they seemed almost warm. His chiseled features looked softer, too, as he tried to smile at Natasha. He may not have wanted her—he'd said as much—but now that she was here, it seemed as if he were going to do his best to make things easier for her.

Mia looked up to see that the little girl's eyes had filled with tears. She was trying awfully hard not to cry, but one tear finally escaped, rolling down her face. She wiped at it fiercely, fighting the flood.

"I know you don't remember me," Alan said to Natasha, his voice impossibly gentle. "But we met five years ago. On January 4."

Natasha all but stopped breathing. "That's my birthday," she said, gazing across the courtyard at him.

Alan's forced smile became genuine. "I know," he said. "I was driving your mom to the hospital and..." He broke off, looking closely at her. "You want a hug?" he asked. "Because I could really use a hug right now, and I'd sure appreciate it if you could give me one."

Natasha considered his words, then nodded. She slowly crossed to him.

"You better hold your breath, though," Alan told her ruefully. "I think I smell bad."

She nodded again, then carefully climbed onto his lap. Mia tried not to watch, but it was nearly impossible not to look at the big man, with his arms wrapped so tentatively around the little girl, as if he were afraid she might break. But when

Natasha's arms went up and locked securely around his neck, Alan closed his eyes, holding the little girl more tightly.

Mia had thought his request for a hug had been purely for Natasha's sake, but now she had to wonder. With all of his anger and his bitterness over his injured leg, it was possible Alan Francisco hadn't let anyone close enough to give him the warmth and comfort of a hug in quite some time. And everyone needed warmth and comfort—even big, tough professional soldiers.

Mia looked away, trying to concentrate on weeding her last row of flowers. But she couldn't help but overhear Natasha say, "You don't smell bad. You smell like Mommy—when she wakes up."

Alan didn't look happy with that comparison. "Terrific," he murmured.

"She's grouchy in the morning," Natasha said. "Are you grouchy in the morning, too?"

"These days I'm afraid I'm grouchy all the time," he admitted.

Natasha was quiet for a moment, considering that. "Then I'll keep the TV turned down really quiet so it doesn't bother you."

Alan laughed again, just a brief exhale of air. Still, it drew Mia's eyes to his face. When he smiled, he transformed. When he smiled, despite the pallor of his skin and his heavy stubble and his uncombed hair, he became breathtakingly handsome.

"That's probably a good idea," he said.

Natasha didn't get off his lap. "I don't remember meeting you before," she said.

"You wouldn't," Alan said. He shifted painfully. Even Natasha's slight weight was too much for his injured knee, and he moved her so that she was sitting on his good leg. "When we first met, you were still inside your mom's belly. You decided that you wanted to be born, and you didn't want to wait. You decided you wanted to come into the world in the front seat of my truck."

"Really?" Natasha was fascinated.

Alan nodded. "Really. You came out before the ambulance could get there. You were in such a hurry, I had to catch you and hold on to you to keep you from running a lap around the block."

"Babies can't run," the little girl scoffed.

"Maybe not *regular* babies," Alan said. "But you came out doing the tango, smoking a cigar and hollering at everybody. Oh, baby, were you loud."

Natasha giggled. "Really?"

"Really," Alan said. "Not the tango and the cigar, but the loud. Come on," he added, lifting her off his lap. "Grab your suitcase and I'll give you the nickel tour of my condo. You can do…something…while I take a shower. Man, do I need a shower."

Natasha tried to pick up her suitcase, but it was too heavy for her. She tried dragging it after her uncle, but she was never going to get it up the stairs. When Alan turned back to see her struggle, he stopped.

"I better get that," he said. But even as he spoke, a change came over his face. The anger was back. Anger and frustration.

Mia was only one thought behind him, and she realized almost instantly that Alan Francisco was not going to be able to carry Natasha's suitcase up the stairs. With one hand on his cane, and the other pulling himself up on the cast-iron railing, it wasn't going to happen.

She stood up, brushing the dirt from her hands. However she did this, it was going to be humiliating for him. And, as with all painful things, it was probably best to do it quickly—to get it over with.

"I'll get that," she said cheerfully, taking the suitcase out of Natasha's hand. Mia didn't wait for Alan to speak or react. She swept up the stairs, taking them two at a time, and set the suitcase down outside the door to 2C.

"Beautiful morning, isn't it?" she called out as she went into her own apartment and grabbed her watering can.

She was outside again in an instant, and as she started down the stairs, she saw that Alan hadn't moved. Only the expression on his face had changed. His eyes were even darker and angrier and his face was positively stormy. His mouth was tight. All signs of his earlier smile were gone.

"I didn't ask for your help," he said in a low, dangerous voice.

"I know," Mia said honestly, stopping several steps from the bottom so she could look at him, eye to eye. "I figured you wouldn't ask. And if *I* asked, I knew you would get all mad and you wouldn't let me help. This way, you can get as mad as you want, but the suitcase is already upstairs." She smiled at him. "So go on. Get mad. Knock yourself out."

As Mia turned and headed back to her garden, she could feel Alan's eyes boring into her back. His expression hadn't changed—he *was* mad. Mad at her, mad at the world.

She knew she shouldn't have helped him. She should have simply let him deal with his problems, let him work things out. She knew she shouldn't get entangled with someone who was obviously in need.

But Mia couldn't forget the smile that had transformed Alan into a real human being instead of this rocky pillar of anger that he seemed to be most of the time. She couldn't forget the gentle way he'd talked to the little girl, trying his best to set her at ease. And she couldn't forget the look on his face when little Natasha had given him a hug.

Mia couldn't forget—even though she knew that she'd be better off if she could.

4

Frisco started to open the bathroom door, but on second thought stopped and wrapped his towel around his waist first.

He could hear the sound of the television in the living room as he leaned heavily on his cane and went into his bedroom, shutting the door behind him.

A kid. What the hell was he going to do with a kid for the next six weeks?

He tossed his cane on the unmade bed and rubbed his wet hair with his towel. Of course, it wasn't as if his work schedule were overcrowded. He'd surely be able to squeeze Natasha in somewhere between "Good Morning, America" and the "Late Show with David Letterman."

Still, little kids required certain specific attention—like food at regular intervals, baths every now and then, a good night's sleep that didn't start at four in the morning and stretch all the way out past noon. Frisco could barely even provide those things for himself, let alone someone else.

Hopping on his good leg, he dug through his still-packed duffel bag, searching for clean underwear. Nothing.

It had been years since he'd had to cook for himself. His kitchen skills were more geared toward knowing which cleaning solutions made the best flammable substances when combined with other household products.

He moved to his dresser, and found only a pair of silk boxers that a lady friend had bought him a lifetime ago. He pulled on his bathing suit instead.

There was nothing to eat in his refrigerator besides a lemon and a six-pack of Mexican beer. His kitchen cabinets contained only shakers of moisture-solidified salt and pepper and an ancient bottle of tabasco sauce.

The second bedroom in his condo was nearly as bare as his cabinets. It had no furniture, only several rows of boxes neatly stacked along one wall. Tasha was going to have to crash on the couch until Frisco could get her a bed and whatever other kind of furniture a five-year-old girl needed.

Frisco pulled on a fresh T-shirt, throwing the clothes he'd been wearing onto the enormous and ever-expanding pile of dirty laundry in the corner of the room…some of it dating from the last time he'd been here, over five years ago. Even the cleaning lady who'd come in yesterday afternoon hadn't dared to touch it.

They'd kicked him out of the physical therapy center before laundry day. He'd arrived here yesterday with two bags of gear and an enormous duffel bag filled with dirty laundry. Somehow he was going to have to figure out a way to get his dirty clothes down to the laundry room on the first floor— and his clean clothes back up again.

But the first thing he had to do was make sure his collection of weapons were all safely locked up. Frisco didn't know much about five-year-olds, but he was certain of one thing— they didn't mix well with firearms.

He quickly combed his hair and, reaching for the smooth wood of his cane, he headed toward the sound of the TV. After he secured his private arsenal, he and Tasha would hobble on down to the grocery store on the corner and pick up some chow for lunch and…

On the television screen, a row of topless dancers gyrated. Frisco lunged for the off switch. Hell! His cable must've come with some kind of men's channel—the Playboy Channel or something similar. He honestly hadn't known.

"Whoa, Tash. I've got to program that off the remote control," he said, turning to the couch to face her.

Except she wasn't sitting on the couch.

His living room was small, and one quick look assured him

that she wasn't even in the room. Hell, that was a relief. He limped toward the kitchen. She wasn't there, either, and his relief turned to apprehension.

"Natasha...?" Frisco moved as quickly as he could down the tiny hallway toward the bedrooms and bathroom. He looked, and then he looked again, even glancing underneath his bed and in both closets.

The kid was gone.

His knee twinged as he used a skittering sort of hop and skip to propel himself back into the living room and out the screen door.

She wasn't on the second-floor landing, or anywhere in immediate view in the condo courtyard. Frisco could see Mia Summerton still working, crouched down among the explosion of flowers that were her garden, a rather silly-looking floppy straw hat covering the top of her head.

"Hey!"

She looked up, startled and uncertain as to where his voice had come from.

"Up here."

She was too far away for him to see exactly which shade of green or brown her eyes were right now. They were wide though. Her surprise quickly changed to wariness.

He could see a dark V of perspiration along the collar and down the front of her T-shirt. Her face glistened in the morning heat, and she reached up and wiped her forehead with the back of one arm. It left a smudge of dirt behind.

"Have you seen Natasha—you know, the little girl with red hair? Did she come down this way?"

Mia rinsed her hands in a bucket of water and stood up. "No—and I've been out here since you went upstairs."

Frisco swore and started down past his condo door, toward the stairs at the other side of the complex.

"What happened?" Mia came up the stairs and caught up with him easily.

"I got out of the shower and she was gone," he told her curtly, trying to move as quickly as he could. Damn, he didn't want to deal with this. The morning sun had moved high into the sky and the brightness still made his head throb—as did every jarring step he took. It was true that living with him wasn't going to be any kind of party, but the kid didn't have to run away, for God's sake.

But then he saw it.

Sparkling and deceptively pure looking, the alluring blue Pacific Ocean glimmered and danced, beckoning in the distance. The beach was several blocks away. Maybe the kid was like him and had salt water running through her veins. Maybe she caught one look at the water and headed for the beach. Maybe she wasn't running away. Maybe she was just exploring. Or maybe she was pushing the edge of the obedience envelope, testing him to see just what she could get away with.

"Do you think she went far? Do you want me to get my car?" Mia asked.

Frisco turned to look at her and realized she was keeping pace with him. He didn't want her help, but dammit, he needed it. If he was going to find Tasha quickly, four eyes were definitely better than two. And a car was far better than a bum knee and a cane when it came to getting someplace fast.

"Yeah, get your car," he said gruffly. "I want to check down at the beach."

Mia nodded once then ran ahead. She'd pulled her car up at the stairs that led to the parking lot before he'd even arrived at the bottom of them. She reached across the seat, unlocking the passenger's side door of her little subcompact.

Frisco knew he wasn't going to fit inside. He got in anyway, forcing his right knee to bend more than it comfortably could. Pain and its accompanying nausea washed over him, and he swore sharply—a repetitive, staccato chant, a profane mantra designed to bring him back from the edge.

He looked up to find Mia watching him, her face carefully expressionless.

"Drive," he told her, his voice sounding harsh to his own ears. "Come on—I don't even know if this kid can swim."

She put the car into first gear and it lurched forward. She took the route the child might well have taken if she was, indeed, heading for the beach. Frisco scanned the crowded sidewalks. What exactly had the kid been wearing? Some kind of white shirt with a pattern on it...balloons? Or maybe flowers? And a bright-colored pair of shorts. Or was she wearing a skirt? Was it green or blue? He couldn't remember, so he watched for her flaming red hair instead.

"Any sign of her?" Mia asked. "Do you want me to slow down?"

"No," Frisco said. "Let's get down to the water and make sure she's not there first. We can work our way back more slowly."

"Aye, aye, sir." Mia stepped on the gas, risking a glance at Alan Francisco. He didn't seem to notice her military-style affirmative. He was gripping the handle up above the passenger window so tightly that his knuckles were white. The muscles in his jaw were just as tight, and he kept watching out the window, searching for any sign of his tiny niece in the summertime crowd.

He'd shaved, she noticed, glancing at him again. He looked slightly less dangerous without the stubble—but only slightly.

He'd hurt his knee getting into her car, and Mia knew from the paleness of his face underneath his tan that it hurt him still. But he didn't complain. Other than his initial explosion of profanity, he hadn't said a word about it. Finding his niece took priority over his pain. Obviously it took priority, since finding Natasha was important enough for him to call a temporary truce with Mia and accept her offer of help.

She was signaling to make the left into the beach parking lot when the man finally spoke.

"There she is! With some kid. At two o'clock—"

"Where?" Mia slowed, uncertain.

"Just stop the car!"

Francisco opened the door, and Mia slammed on the brakes,

afraid he would jump out while the car was still moving. And then she saw Natasha. The little girl was at the edge of the parking lot, sitting on the top of a picnic table, paying solemn attention to a tall African-American teenage boy who was standing in front of her. Something about the way he wore his low-riding, baggy jeans was familiar. The kid turned, and Mia saw his face.

"That's Thomas King," she said. "That boy who's with Natasha—I know him."

But Francisco was already out of the car, moving as fast as he could with his limp and his cane toward the little girl.

There was nowhere to park. Mia watched through the windshield as the former Navy lieutenant descended upon his niece, pulling her none-too-gently from the table and setting her down on the ground behind him. She couldn't hear what he was saying, but she could tell that it wasn't a friendly greeting. She saw Thomas bristle and turn belligerently toward Francisco, and she threw on her hazard lights and left the car right where it was in the middle of the lot as she jumped out and ran toward them.

She arrived just in time to hear Thomas say, "You raise one hand to that girl and I'll clean the street with your face."

Alan Francisco's blue eyes had looked deadly and cold when Mia first ran up, but now they changed. Something shifted. "What are you talking about? I'm not going to *hit* her." He sounded incredulous, as if such a thing would never have occurred to him.

"Then why are you shouting at her as if you are?" Thomas King was nearly Francisco's height, but the former SEAL had at least fifty pounds of muscle over him. Still, the teenager stood his ground, his dark eyes flashing and narrowed, his lips tight.

"I'm not—"

"Yes, you are," Thomas persisted. He mimicked the older man. "'What the hell are you doing here? Who the hell gave you permission to leave...' I thought you were going to slam her—and *she* did, too."

Frisco turned to look at Natasha. She had scurried underneath the picnic table, and she looked back at him, her eyes wide. "Tash, you didn't think…"

But she had thought that. He could see it in her eyes, in the way she was cowering. Man, he felt sick.

He crouched down next to the table as best he could. "Natasha, did your mom hit you when she was angry?" He couldn't believe softhearted Sharon would hurt a defenseless child, but liquor did funny things to even the gentlest of souls.

The little girl shook her head no. "Mommy didn't," she told him softly, "but Dwayne did once and I got a bloody lip. Mommy cried, and then we moved out."

Thank God Sharon had had that much sense. Damn Dwayne to hell, whoever he was. What kind of monster would strike a five-year-old child?

What kind of monster would scare her to death by shouting at her the way he just had?

Frisco sat down heavily on the picnic table bench, glancing up at Mia. Her eyes were soft, as if she could somehow read his mind.

"Tash, I'm sorry," he said, rubbing his aching, bleary eyes. "I didn't mean to scare you."

"This some kind of *friend* of yours?" the black kid said to Mia, his tone implying she might want to be more selective in her choice of friends in the future.

"He's in 2C," Mia told the boy. "The mystery neighbor— Lt. Alan Francisco." She directed her next words to Frisco. "This is Thomas King. He's a former student of mine. He lives in 1N with his sister and her kids."

A former…student? That meant that Mia Summerton was a teacher. Damn, if he had had teachers who looked like her, he might've actually gone to high school.

She was watching him now with wariness in her eyes, as if he were a bomb on a trick timer, ready to blow at any given moment.

"Lieutenant," Thomas repeated. "Are you the badge?"

"No, I'm not a cop," Frisco said, tearing his eyes away

from Mia to glance at the kid. "I'm in the Navy...." He caught himself, and shook his head, closing his eyes briefly. "I *was* in the Navy."

Thomas had purposely crossed his arms and tucked both hands underneath them to make sure Frisco knew he had no intention of shaking hands.

"The lieutenant was a SEAL," Mia told Thomas. "That's a branch of special operations—"

"I *know* what a SEAL is," the kid interrupted. He turned to run a bored, cynical eye over Frisco. "One of those crazy freaks that ride the surf and crash their little rubber boats into the rocks down by the hotel in Coronado. Did *you* ever do that?"

Mia was watching him again, too. Damn but she was pretty. And every time she looked at him, every time their eyes met, Frisco felt a very solid slap of mutual sexual awareness. It was almost funny. With the possible exception of her exotic fashion-model face and trim, athletic body, everything about the woman irritated him. He didn't want a nosy neighbor poking around in his life. He didn't need a helpful do-gooder getting in his face and reminding him hourly of his limitations. He had no use for a disgustingly cheerful, flower-planting, antimilitary, unintimidatable, fresh-faced girl-next-door type.

But every single time he looked into her hazel eyes, he felt an undeniable surge of physical attraction. Intellectually, he may have wanted little more than to hide from her, but physically... Well, his body apparently had quite a different agenda. One that included moonlight gleaming on smooth, golden tanned skin, long dark hair trailing across his face, across his chest and lower.

Frisco managed a half smile, wondering if she could read his mind now. He couldn't look away from her, even to answer Thomas's question. "It's called rock portage," he said, "and, yeah. I did that during training."

She didn't blush. She didn't look away from him. She just steadily returned his gaze, slightly lifting one exotic eyebrow.

Frisco had the sense that she did, indeed, know exactly what he was thinking. *Cold day in hell.* She hadn't said those exact words last night, but they echoed in his mind as clearly as if she had.

It was just as well. He was having a pure, raw-sex reaction to her, but she wasn't the pure, raw type. He couldn't picture her climbing into his bed and then slipping away before dawn, no words spoken, only intense pleasure shared. No, once she got into his bed, she would never get out. She had "girl-friend" written all over her, and that was the last thing he needed. She would fill his apartment with flowers from her garden and endless conversation and little notes with smiley faces on them. She'd demand tender kisses and a clean bathroom and heart-to-heart revelations and a genuine interest in her life.

How could he begin to be interested in *her* life, when he couldn't even muster up the slightest enthusiasm for his own?

But he was getting *way* ahead of himself here. He was assuming that he'd have no trouble getting her into his bed in the first place. That might've been true five years ago, but he wasn't exactly any kind of prize anymore. There was no way a girl like Mia would want to be saddled with a man who could barely even walk.

Cold day in hell. Frisco looked out at the blinding blueness of the ocean, feeling his eyes burn from the glare.

"What's a SEAL doing with a kid who can't swim?" Thomas asked. Most of the anger had left the teenager's eyes, leaving behind a cynical disdain and a seemingly ancient weariness that made him look far older than his years. He had scars on his face, one bisecting one of his eyebrows, the other marking one of his high, pronounced cheekbones. That, combined with the fact that his nose had been broken more than once, gave him a battle-worn look that erased even more of his youth. But except for a few minor slang expressions, Thomas didn't speak the language of the street. He had no discernible accent of any kind, and Frisco wondered if the kid had worked as hard to delete that particular tie with his past and his parents as he himself had.

"Natasha is the lieutenant's niece," Mia explained. "She's going to stay with him for a few weeks. She just arrived today."

"From Mars, right?" Thomas looked under the table and made a face at Natasha.

She giggled. "Thomas thinks I'm from Mars 'cause I didn't know what that water was." Natasha slithered on her belly out from underneath the table. The sand stuck to her clothes, and Frisco realized that she was wet.

"A little Martian girl is the only kind of girl I can think of who hasn't seen the ocean before," Thomas said. "She didn't even seem to know kids shouldn't go into the water alone."

Mia watched a myriad of emotions cross Alan Francisco's face. The lifeguard's flag was out today, signaling a strong undertow and dangerous currents. She saw him look at Thomas and register the fact that the teenager's jeans were wet up to his knees.

"You went in after her," he said, his low voice deceptively even.

Thomas was as nonchalant. "I've got a five-year-old niece, too."

Francisco pulled himself painfully up with his cane. He held out his hand to Thomas. "Thanks, man. I'm sorry about before. I'm...new at this kid thing."

Mia held her breath. She knew Thomas well, and if he'd decided that Alan Francisco was the enemy, he'd never shake his hand.

But Thomas hesitated only briefly before he clasped the older man's hand.

Again, a flurry of emotions flickered in Francisco's eyes, and again he tried to hide it all. Relief. Gratitude. Sorrow. Always sorrow and always shame. But it was all gone almost before it was even there. When Alan Francisco tried to hide his emotions, he succeeded, tucking them neatly behind the ever-present anger that simmered inside of him.

He managed to use that anger to hide everything quite nicely—everything except the seven-thousand-degree nuclear-powered sexual attraction he felt for her. That he put on display, complete with neon signs and million-dollar-a-minute advertising.

Good grief, last night when he'd made that crack about wanting her to share his bed, she'd thought he'd been simply trying to scare her off.

She had been dead wrong. The way he'd looked at her just minutes ago had nearly singed her eyebrows off.

And the *truly* stupid thing was that the thought of having a physical relationship with this man didn't send her running for her apartment and the heavy-duty dead bolt that she'd had installed on her door. She couldn't figure out why. Lt. Alan Francisco was a real-life version of G.I. Joe, he was probably a male chauvinist, he drank so much that he still looked like hell at noon on a weekday *and* he carried a seemingly permanent chip on his shoulder. Yet for some bizarre reason, Mia had no trouble imagining herself pulling him by the hand into her bedroom and melting together with him on her bed.

It had nothing to do with his craggy-featured, handsome face and enticingly hard-muscled body. Well, yes, okay, so she wasn't being completely honest with herself. It had at least a *little* bit to do with that. It was true—the fact that the man looked as if he should have his own three-month segment in a hunk-of-the-month calendar was not something she'd failed to notice. And notice, and notice and notice.

But try as she might, it was the softness in his eyes when he spoke to Natasha and his crooked, painful attempts to smile at the little girl that she found hard to resist. She was a sucker for kindness, and she suspected that beneath this man's outer crust of anger and bitterness, and despite his sometimes crude language and rough behavior, there lurked the kindest of souls.

"Here's the deal about the beach," Alan Francisco was saying to his niece. "You never come down here without a grown-up, and you never, *ever* go into the water alone."

"That's what Thomas said," Tasha told him. "He said I might've drownded."

"Thomas is right," Francisco told her.

"What's drownded?"

"Drowned," he corrected her. "You ever try to breathe underwater?"

Tash shook her head no, and her red curls bounced.

"Well, don't try it. People can't breathe underwater. Only fish can. And you don't look like a fish to me."

The little girl giggled, but persisted. "What's drownded?"

Mia crossed her arms, wondering if Francisco would try to sidestep the issue again, or if he would take the plunge and discuss the topic of death with Natasha.

"Well," he said slowly, "if someone goes into the water, and they can't swim, or they hurt themselves, or the waves are too high, then the water might go over their head. Then they can't breathe. Normally, when the water goes over your head it's no big deal. You hold your breath. And then you just swim to the surface and stick your nose and mouth out and take a breath of air. But like I said, maybe this person doesn't know how to swim, or maybe their leg got a cramp, or the water's too rough, so they can't get up to the air. And if there's no air for them to breathe...well, they'll die. They'll drown. People need to breathe air to live."

Natasha gazed unblinkingly at her uncle, her head tilted slightly to one side. "I don't know how to swim," she finally said.

"Then I'll teach you," Francisco said unhesitatingly. "Everyone should know how to swim. But even when you *do* know how to swim, you still don't swim alone. That way, if you *do* get hurt, you got a friend who can save you from drowning. Even in the SEALs we didn't swim alone. We had something called swim buddies—a friend who looked out for you, and you'd look out for him, too. You and me, Tash, for the next few weeks, we're going to be swim buddies, okay?"

"I'm outta here, Ms. S. I don't want to be late for work."

Mia turned to Thomas, glad he'd broken into her reverie.

She'd been standing there like an idiot, gazing at Alan Francisco, enthralled by his conversation with his niece. "Be careful," she told him.

"Always am."

Natasha crouched down in the sand and began pushing an old Popsicle stick around as if it were a car. Thomas bent over and ruffled her hair. "See you later, Martian girl." He nodded to Francisco. "Lieutenant."

The SEAL pulled himself up and off the bench. "Call me Frisco. And thanks again, man."

Thomas nodded once more and then was gone.

"He works part-time as a security guard at the university," Mia told Francisco. "That way he can audit college courses in his spare time—spare time that doesn't exist because he also works a full day as a landscaper's assistant over in Coronado."

He was looking at her again, his steel blue eyes shuttered and unreadable this time. He hadn't told *her* she could call him Frisco. Maybe it was a guy thing. Maybe SEALs weren't allowed to let women call them by their nicknames. Or maybe it was more personal than that. Maybe Alan Francisco didn't want her as a friend. He'd certainly implied as much last night.

Mia looked back at her car, still sitting in the middle of the parking lot. "Well," she said, feeling strangely awkward. She had no problem holding her own with this man when he came on too strong or acted rudely. But when he simply stared at her like this, with no expression besides the faintest glimmer of his ever-present anger on his face, she felt off balance and ill at ease, like a schoolgirl with an unrequited crush. "I'm glad we found—*you* found Natasha..." She glanced back at her car again, more to escape his scrutiny than to reassure herself it was still there. "Can I give you a lift back to the condo?"

Frisco shook his head. "No, thanks."

"I could adjust the seat, see if I could make it more comfortable for you to—"

"No, we've got some shopping to do."

"But Natasha's all wet."

"She'll dry. Besides, I could use the exercise."

Exercise? Was he kidding? "What you could use is a week or two off your feet, in bed."

Just like that, he seemed to come alive, his mouth twisting into a sardonic half smile. His eyes sparked with heat and he lowered his voice, leaning forward to speak directly into her ear. "Are you volunteering to keep me there? I knew sooner or later you'd change your mind."

He knew nothing of the sort. He'd only said that to rattle and irritate her. Mia refused to let him see just how irritated his comment had made her. Instead, she stepped even closer, looking up at him, letting her gaze linger on his mouth before meeting his eyes, meaning to make him wonder, and to make him squirm before she launched her attack.

But she launched nothing as she looked into his eyes. His knowing smile had faded, leaving behind only heat. It magnified, doubling again and again, increasing logarithmically as their gazes locked, burning her down to her very soul. She knew that he could see more than just a mere reflection of his desire in her eyes, and she knew without a doubt that she'd given too much away. This fire that burned between them was not his alone.

The sun was beating down on them and her mouth felt parched. She tried to swallow, tried to moisten her dry lips, tried to walk away. But she couldn't move.

He reached out slowly. She could see it coming—he was going to touch her, pull her close against the hard muscles of his chest and cover her mouth with his own in a heated, heart-stopping, nuclear meltdown of a kiss.

But he touched her only lightly, tracing the path of a bead of sweat that had trailed down past her ear, down her neck and across her collarbone before it disappeared beneath the collar of her T-shirt. He touched her gently, only with one finger, but in many ways it was far more sensual, far more intimate than even a kiss.

The world seemed to spin and Mia almost reached for him. But sanity kicked in, thank God, and instead she backed away.

"When I change my mind," she said, her voice barely louder than a whisper, "it'll be a cold day in July."

She turned on legs that were actually trembling—*trembling*—and headed toward her car. He made no move to follow, but as she got inside and drove away, she could see him in the rearview mirror, still watching her.

Had she convinced him? She doubted it. She wasn't sure she'd even managed to convince herself.

5

"Okay, Tash," Frisco called down from the second-floor landing where he'd finally finished lashing the framework to the railing. "Ready for a test run?"

She nodded, and he let out the crank and lowered the rope down to her.

The realization had come to him while they were grocery shopping. He wasn't going to be able to carry the bags of food he bought up the stairs to his second-floor condominium. And Tasha, as helpful as she tried to be when she wasn't wandering off, couldn't possibly haul all the food they needed up a steep flight of stairs. She could maybe handle one or two lightweight bags, but certainly no more than that.

But Frisco had been an expert in unconventional warfare for the past ten years. He could come up with alternative, creative solutions to damn near any situation—including this one. Of course, this wasn't war, which made it that much easier. Whatever he came up with, he wasn't going to have to pull it off while underneath a rain of enemy bullets.

It hadn't taken him long to come up with a solution. He and Tasha had stopped at the local home building supply store and bought themselves the fixings for a rope-and-pulley system. Frisco could've easily handled just a rope to pull things up to the second-floor landing, but with a crank and some pulleys, Natasha would be able to use it, too.

The plastic bags filled with the groceries they'd bought were on the ground, directly underneath the rope to which he'd attached a hook.

"Hook the rope to one of the bags," Frisco commanded his niece, leaning over the railing. "Right through the handles—that's right."

Mia Summerton was watching him.

He'd been hyperaware of her from the moment he and Tash had climbed out of the taxi with all of their groceries. She'd been back in her garden again, doing God knows what and watching him out of the corner of her eye.

She'd watched as he'd transferred the frozen food and perishables into a backpack he'd bought and carried them inside. She'd watched as he'd done the same with the building supplies and set them out on the second-floor landing. She'd watched as he awkwardly lowered himself down to sit on the stairs with his tool kit and began to work.

She'd watched, but she'd been careful never to let him catch her watching.

Just the same, he felt her eyes following him. And he could damn near smell her awareness.

Man, whatever it was that they'd experienced back on the beach… He shook his head in disbelief. Whatever it was, he wanted some more. A whole lot of more. She'd looked at him, and he'd been caught in an amazing vortex of animal magnetism. He hadn't been able to resist touching her, hadn't been able to stop thinking about exactly where that droplet of perspiration had gone after it had disappeared from view beneath her shirt. It hadn't taken much imagination to picture it traveling slowly between her breasts, all the way down to her softly indented belly button.

He'd wanted to dive in after it.

It had been damn near enough to make him wonder if he'd seriously underrated smiley-face-endowed notes.

But he'd seen the shock in Mia's eyes. She hadn't expected the attraction that had surged between them. She didn't want it, didn't want him. Certainly not for a single, mind-blowing sexual encounter, and *definitely* not for anything longer term. That was no big surprise.

"I can't get it," Natasha called up to him, her face scrunched with worry.

Mia had kept to herself ever since they'd arrived home. Her offers to help had been noticeably absent. But now she stood up, apparently unable to ignore the note of anxiety in Tasha's voice.

"May I help you with that, Natasha?" She spoke directly to the little girl. She didn't even bother to look up at Frisco.

Frisco wiped the sweat from his face as he watched Tasha step back and Mia attach the hook to the plastic handles of the grocery bags. It had to be close to ninety degrees in the shade, but when Mia finally did glance up at him there was a definite wintry chill in the air.

She was trying her damnedest to act as if she had not even the slightest interest in him. Yet she'd spent the past hour and a half watching him. Why?

Maybe whatever this was that constantly drew his eyes in her direction, whatever this was that had made him hit his thumb with his hammer more times than he could count, whatever this was that made every muscle in his body tighten in anticipation when he so much as *thought* about her, whatever this uncontrollable sensation was—maybe she felt it, too.

It was lust and desire, amplified a thousandfold, mutated into something far more powerful.

He didn't want her. He didn't want the trouble, didn't want the hassle, didn't want the grief. And yet, at the same time, he wanted her desperately. He wanted her more than he'd ever wanted any woman before.

If he'd been the type to get frightened, he would've been terrified.

"We better stand back," Mia warned Tasha as Frisco began turning the crank.

It went up easily enough, the bag bulging and straining underneath the weight. But then, as if in slow motion, the bottom of the plastic bag gave out, and its contents went plummeting to the ground.

Frisco swore loudly as a six-pack shattered into pieces of

brown glass, the beer mixing unappetizingly with cranberry juice from a broken half-gallon container, four flattened tomatoes and an avocado that never again would see the light of day. The loaf of Italian bread that had also been in the bag had, thankfully, bounced free and clear of the disaster.

Mia looked down at the wreckage, and then up at Alan Francisco. He'd cut short his litany of curses and stood silently, his mouth tight and his eyes filled with far more despair than the situation warranted.

But she knew he was seeing more than a mess on the courtyard sidewalk as he looked over the railing. She knew he was seeing his life, shattered as absolutely as those beer bottles.

Still he took a deep breath, and forced himself to smile down into Natasha's wide eyes.

"We're on the right track here," he said, lowering the rope again. "We're definitely very close to outrageous success." Using his cane, he started down the stairs. "How about we try double bagging? Or a paper bag inside of the plastic one?"

"How about cloth bags?" Mia suggested.

"Back away, Tash—that's broken glass," Alan called warningly. "Yeah, cloth bags would work, but I don't have any."

Alan, Mia thought. When had he become Alan instead of Francisco? Was it when he looked down at his niece and made himself smile despite his pain, or was it earlier, at the beach parking lot, when he'd nearly lit Mia on fire with a single look?

Mia ran up the stairs past him, suddenly extremely aware that he'd taken off his shirt nearly an hour ago. His smooth tanned skin and hard muscles had been hard to ignore even from a distance. Up close it was impossible for Mia not to stare.

He wore only a loose-fitting, bright-colored bathing suit, and it rode low on his lean hips. His stomach was a washboard of muscles, and his skin gleamed with sweat. And that other tattoo on his bicep was a sea serpent, not a mermaid, as she'd first thought.

"I've got some bags," Mia called out, escaping into the coolness of her apartment, stopping for a moment to take a long, shaky breath. What was it about this man that made her heart beat double time? He was intriguing; she couldn't deny that. And he exuded a wildness, a barely tamed sexuality that constantly managed to captivate her. But so what? He was sexy. He was gorgeous. He was working hard to overcome a raftload of serious problems, making him seem tragic and fascinating. But these were not the criteria she usually used to decide whether or not to enter into a sexual relationship with a man.

The fact was that she *wasn't* going to sleep with him, she told herself firmly. Definitely probably not. She rolled her eyes in self-disgust. Definitely *probably* ...?

It had to be the full moon making her feel this way. Or—as her mother might say—maybe her astrological planets were lined up in some strange configuration, making her feel restless and reckless. Or maybe as she neared thirty, her body was changing, releasing hormones in quantities that she could no longer simply ignore.

Whatever the reason—mystical or scientific—the fact remained that she would *not* have sex with a stranger. Whatever happened between them, it wasn't going to happen until she'd had a chance to get to know this man. And once she got to know him and his vast collection of both physical and psychological problems, she had a feeling that staying away from him wasn't going to be so very difficult.

She took her cloth grocery bags from the closet and went back outside. Alan was crouched awkwardly down on the sidewalk, attempting to clean up the mess.

"Alan, wait. Don't try to pick up the broken glass," she called down to him. "I've got work gloves and a shovel you can use to clean it up." She didn't dare offer to do the work for him. She knew he would refuse. "I'll get 'em. Here—catch."

She threw the bags over the railing, and he caught them with little effort as she turned to go back inside.

Frisco looked at the printed message on the outside of the bags Mia had tossed him and rolled his eyes. Of course it had to be something political. Shaking his head, he sat down on the grass and began transferring the undemolished remainder of the groceries into the cloth bags.

"'Wouldn't it be nice if we fully funded education, and the government had to hold a bake sale to buy a bomber?'" he quoted from the bags when Mia came back down the stairs.

She was holding a plastic trash bag, a pair of work gloves and what looked rather suspiciously like a pooper-scooper. She gave him a crooked smile. "Yeah," she said. "I thought you would like that."

"I'd be glad to get into a knock-down, drag-out argument about the average civilian's ignorance regarding military spending some other time," he told her. "But right now I'm not really in the mood."

"How about if I pretend you didn't just call me ignorant, and *you* pretend I don't think you're some kind of rigid, militaristic, dumb-as-a-stone professional soldier?" she said much too sweetly.

Frisco had to laugh. It was a deep laugh, a belly laugh, and he couldn't remember the last time he'd done that. He was still smiling when he looked up at her. "That sounds fair," he said. "And who knows—maybe we're both wrong."

Mia smiled back at him, but it was tentative and wary.

"I didn't get to thank you for helping me this morning," he said. "I'm sorry if I was..."

Mia gazed at him, waiting for him to finish his sentence. Unfriendly? Worried? Upset? Angry? Inappropriate? Too sexy for words? She wondered exactly what he was apologizing for.

"Rude," he finally finished. He glanced over at Natasha. She was lying on her back in the shade of a palm tree, staring up at the sky through both her spread fingers and the fronds, singing some unintelligible and probably improvised song. "I'm in way over my head here," he admitted with another crooked smile. "I don't know the first thing about taking care of a kid, and..." He shrugged. "Even if I did, these days I'm not exactly in the right place psychologically, you know?"

"You're doing great."

The look he shot her was loaded with amusement and disbelief. "She was under my care for not even thirty minutes and I managed to lose her." He shifted his weight, trying to get more comfortable, wincing slightly at the pain in his leg. "While we were walking home, I talked to her about setting up some rules and regs—basic stuff, like she has to tell me if she's going outside the condo, and she's got to play inside the courtyard. She looked at me like I was speaking French." He paused, glancing back at the little girl again. "As far as I can tell, Sharon had absolutely no rules. She let the kid go where she pleased, when she pleased. I'm not sure anything I said sunk in."

He pulled himself up with his cane, and carried one of the filled cloth bags toward the hook and rope, sidestepping the puddle of broken glass, sodden cardboard and cranberry juiced-beer.

"You've got to give her time, Alan," Mia said. "You've got to remember that living here without her mom around has to be as new and as strange to her as it is to you."

He turned to look back at her as he attached the hook to the cloth handles. "You know," he said, "generally people don't call me Alan. I'm Frisco. I've been Frisco for years." He started up the stairs. "I mean, Sharon—my sister—she calls me Alan, but everyone else calls me Frisco, from my swim buddy to my CO...."

Frisco looked down at Mia. She was standing in the courtyard, watching him and not trying to hide it this time. Her gardening clothes were almost as filthy as his, and several strands of her long, dark hair had escaped from her ponytail. How come he felt like a sweat-sodden reject from hell, while she managed to look impossibly beautiful?

"CO?" she repeated.

"Commanding Officer," he explained, turning the crank.

The bag went up, and this time it made it all the way to the second floor.

Mia applauded and Natasha came over to do several clumsy forward rolls in the grass in celebration.

Frisco reached over the railing and pulled the bag up and onto the landing next to him.

"Lower the rope. I'll hook up the next one," Mia said.

It went up just as easily.

"Come on, Tash. Come upstairs and help me put away these supplies," Frisco called, and the little girl came barreling up the stairs. He turned back to look down at Mia. "I'll be down in a minute to clean up that mess."

"Alan, you know, I don't have anything better to do and I can—"

"Frisco," he interrupted her. "Not Alan. And *I'm* cleaning it up, not you."

"Do you mind if I call you Alan? I mean, after all, it is your *name*—"

"Yeah, I mind. It's not my name. Frisco's my name. Frisco is who I became when I joined the SEALs." His voice got softer. "Alan is nobody."

Frisco woke to the sound of a blood-chilling scream.

He was rolling out of bed, onto the floor, reaching, searching for his weapon, even before he was fully awake. But he had no firearm hidden underneath his pillow or down alongside his bed—he'd locked them all up in a trunk in his closet. He wasn't in the jungle on some dangerous mission, catching a combat nap. He was in his bedroom, in San Felipe, California, and the noise that had kicked him out of bed came from the powerful vocal cords of his five-year-old niece, who was supposed to be sound asleep on the couch in the living room.

Frisco stumbled to the wall and flipped on the light. Reaching this time for his cane, he opened his bedroom door and staggered down the hallway toward the living room.

He could see Natasha in the dim light that streamed down

the hallway from his bedroom. She was crying, sitting up in a tangle of sheets on the couch, sweat matting her hair.

"Hey," Frisco said. "What the h...uh... What's going on, Tash?"

The kid didn't answer. She just kept on crying.

Frisco sat down next to her, but all she did was cry.

"You want a hug or something?" he asked, and she shook her head no and kept on crying.

"Um," Frisco said, uncertain of what to do, or what to say.

There was a tap on the door.

"You want to get that?" Frisco asked Natasha.

She didn't respond.

"I guess I'll get it then," he said, unlocking the bolt and opening the heavy wooden door.

Mia stood on the other side of the screen. She was wearing a white bathrobe and her hair was down loose around her shoulders. "Is everything all right?"

"No, I'm not murdering or torturing my niece," Frisco said flatly and closed the door. But he opened it again right away and pushed open the screen. "You wouldn't happen to know where Tash's On/Off switch is, would you?"

"It's dark in here," Mia said, stepping inside. "Maybe you should turn on all the lights so that she can see where she is."

Frisco turned on the bright overhead light—and realized he was standing in front of his neighbor and his niece in nothing but the new, tight-fitting, utilitarian white briefs he'd bought during yesterday's second trip to the grocery store. Good thing he'd bought them, or he quite possibly would have been standing there buck naked.

Whether it was the sudden light or the sight of him in his underwear, Frisco didn't know, but Natasha stopped crying, just like that. She still sniffled, and tears still flooded her eyes, but her sirenlike wail was silenced.

Mia was clearly thrown by the sight of him—and determined to act as if visiting with a neighbor who was in his underwear was the most normal thing in the world. She sat down on the couch next to Tasha and gave her a hug. Frisco excused himself and headed down the hall toward his bedroom and a pair of shorts.

It wasn't really that big a deal—Lucky O'Donlon, Frisco's swim buddy and best friend in the SEAL unit, had bought Frisco a tan-through French bathing suit from the Riviera that covered far less of him than these briefs. Of course, the minuscule suit wasn't something he'd ever be caught dead in....

He threw on his shorts and came back out into the living room.

"It must've been a pretty bad nightmare," he heard Mia saying to Tasha.

"I fell into a big, dark hole," Tash said in a tiny voice in between a very major case of hiccups. "And I was screaming and screaming and *screaming,* and I could see Mommy way, way up at the top, but she didn't hear me. She had on her mad face, and she just walked away. And then water went up and over my head, and I knew I was gonna drownd."

Frisco swore silently. He wasn't sure he could relieve Natasha's fears of abandonment, but he would do his best to make sure she didn't fear the ocean. He sat down next to her on the couch and she climbed into his lap. His heart lurched as she locked her little arms around his neck.

"Tomorrow morning we'll start your swimming lessons, okay?" he said gruffly, trying to keep the emotion that had suddenly clogged his throat from sounding in his voice.

Natasha nodded. "When I woke up, it was so dark. And someone turned off the TV."

"I turned it off when I went to bed," Frisco told her.

She lifted her head and gazed up at him. The tip of her nose was pink and her face was streaked and still wet from her tears. "Mommy always sleeps with it on. So she won't feel lonely."

Mia was looking at him over the top of Tasha's red curls. She was holding her tongue, but it was clear that she had something to say.

"Why don't you make a quick trip to the head?" he said to Tasha.

She nodded and climbed off his lap. "The head is the bathroom on a boat," she told Mia, wiping her runny nose on her hand. "Before bedtime, me and Frisco pretended we were on a pirate boat. He was the cap'n."

Mia tried to hide her smile. So *that* was the cause of the odd sounds she'd heard from Frisco's apartment at around eight o'clock.

"We also played Russian Princess," the little girl added.

Frisco actually blushed—his rugged cheekbones were tinged with a delicate shade of pink. "It's after 0200, Tash. Get moving. And wash your face and blow your nose while you're in there."

"Yo ho ho and a bottle of rum," Mia said to him as the little girl disappeared down the hallway.

The pink tinge didn't disappear, but Frisco met her gaze steadily. "I'm doomed, aren't I?" he said, resignation in his voice. "You're going to tease me about this until the end of time."

Mia grinned. "I *do* feel as if I've been armed with a powerful weapon," she admitted, adding, "Your Majesty. Oh, or did you let Natasha take a turn and be the princess?"

"Very funny."

"What I would give to have been a fly on the wall...."

"She's five years old," he tried to explain, running his hand through his disheveled blond hair. "I don't have a single toy in the house. Or any books besides the ones I'm reading—which are definitely inappropriate. I don't even have paper and pencils to draw with—"

She'd gone too far with her teasing. "You don't have to explain. Actually, I think it's incredibly sweet. It's just... surprising. You don't really strike me as the make-believe type."

Frisco leaned forward.

"Look, Tash is gonna come back out soon. If there's something you want to tell me without her overhearing, you better say it now.''

Mia was surprised again. He hadn't struck her as being extremely perceptive. In fact, he always seemed to be a touch self-absorbed and tightly wrapped up in his anger. But he was right. There *was* something that she wanted to ask him about the little girl.

''I was just wondering,'' she said, ''if you've talked to Natasha about exactly where her mother is right now.''

He shook his head.

''Maybe you should.''

He shifted his position, obviously uncomfortable. ''How do you talk about things like addiction and alcoholism to a five-year-old?''

''She probably knows more about it than you'd believe,'' Mia said quietly.

''Yeah, I guess she would,'' he said.

''It might make her feel a little bit less as if she's been deserted.''

He looked up at her, meeting her eyes. Even now, in this moment of quiet, serious conversation, when Mia's eyes met his, there was a powerful burst of heat.

His gaze slipped down to the open neckline of her bathrobe, and she could see him looking at the tiny piece of her nightgown that was exposed. It was white, with a narrow white eyelet ruffle.

He wanted to see the rest of it—she knew that from the hunger in his eyes. Would he be disappointed if he knew that her nightgown was simple and functional? It was plain, not sexy, made from lightweight cotton.

He looked into her eyes again. No, he wouldn't be disappointed, because if they ever were in a position in which he would see her in her nightgown, she would only be wearing it for all of three seconds before he removed it and it landed in a pile on the floor.

The bathroom door opened, and Frisco finally looked away as their pint-size chaperon came back into the living room.

"I'd better go." Mia stood up. "I'll just let myself out."

"I'm hungry," the little girl said.

Frisco pulled himself to his feet. "Well, let's go into the kitchen and see what we can find to eat." He turned to look back at Mia. "I'm sorry we woke you."

"It's all right." Mia turned toward the door.

"Hey, Tash," she heard Frisco say as she let herself out through the screen door, "did your mom talk to you at all about where she was going?"

Mia shut the door behind her and went back into her own apartment.

She took off her robe and got into bed, but sleep was elusive. She couldn't stop thinking about Alan Francisco.

It was funny—the fact that Mia had found out he'd been kind enough to play silly make-believe games with his niece made him blush, yet he'd answered the door dressed only in his underwear with nary a smidgen of embarrassment.

Of course, with a body like his, what was there to be embarrassed about?

Still, the briefs he'd been wearing were brief indeed. The snug-fitting white cotton left very little to the imagination. And Mia had a *very* vivid imagination.

She opened her eyes, willing that same imagination not to get too carried away. Talk about make-believe games. She could make believe that she honestly wasn't bothered by the fact that Alan had spent most of his adult life as a professional soldier, and *Alan* could make believe that he wasn't weighed down by his physical challenge, that he was psychologically healthy, that he wasn't battling depression and resorting to alcohol to numb his unhappiness.

Mia rolled over onto her stomach and switched on the lamp on her bedside table. She was wide-awake, so she would read. It was better than lying in the dark dreaming about things that would never happen.

Frisco covered the sleeping child with a light blanket. The television provided a flickering light and the soft murmur of voices. Tasha hadn't fallen asleep until he'd turned it on, and he knew better now than to turn it off.

He went into the kitchen and poured himself a few fingers of whiskey and took a swallow, welcoming the burn and the sensation of numbness that followed. Man, he needed that. Talking to Natasha about Sharon's required visit to the detox center had *not* been fun. But it had been necessary. Mia had been right.

Tash had had no clue where her mother had gone. She'd thought, in fact, that Sharon had gone to jail. The kid had heard bits and pieces of conversations about the car accident her mother had been involved in, and thought Sharon had been arrested for running someone over.

Frisco had explained how the driver of the car Sharon had struck was badly hurt and in the hospital, but not dead. He didn't go into detail about what would happen if the man were to die—she didn't need to hear that. But he did try to explain what a detox center was, and why Sharon couldn't leave the facility to visit Natasha, and why Tash couldn't go there to visit her.

The kid had looked skeptical when Frisco told her that when Sharon came out of detox, she wouldn't drink anymore. Frisco shook his head. A five-year-old cynic. What was the world coming to?

He took both his glass and the bottle back through the living room and outside onto the dimly lit landing. The sterile environment of air-conditioned sameness in his condo always got to him, particularly at this time of night. He took a deep breath of the humid, salty air, filling his lungs with the warm scent of the sea.

He sat down on the steps and took another sip of the whiskey. He willed it to make him relax, to put him to sleep, to carry him past these darkest, longest hours of the early morning. He silently cursed the fact that here it was, nearly 0300 again, and here he was, wide awake. He'd been so certain when he'd climbed into bed tonight that his exhaustion would carry him through and keep him sound asleep until the morning. He hadn't counted on Tasha's 0200 reveille. He drained his glass and poured himself another drink.

Mia's door barely made a sound as it opened, but he heard it in the quiet. Still, he didn't move as she came outside, and he didn't speak until she stood at the railing, looking down at him.

"How long ago did your dog die?" he asked, keeping his voice low so as not to wake the other condo residents.

She stood very, very still for several long seconds. Finally she laughed softly and sat down next to him on the stairs. "About eight months ago," she told him, her voice velvety in the darkness. "How did you know I had a dog?"

"Good guess," he murmured.

"No, really... Tell me."

"The pooper-scooper you lent me to clean up the mess in the courtyard was a major hint," he said. "And your car had—how do I put this delicately?—a certain canine perfume."

"Her name was Zu. She was about a million years old in dog years. I got her when I was eight."

"*Z-o-o?*" Frisco asked.

"*Z-u,*" she said. "It was short for Zu-zu. I named her after a little girl in a movie—"

"*It's a Wonderful Life,*" he said.

Mia gazed at him, surprised again. "You've seen it?"

He shrugged. "Hasn't everybody?"

"Probably. But most people don't remember the name of George Bailey's youngest daughter."

"It's a personal favorite." He gave her a sidelong glance. "Amazing that I should like it, huh? All of the war scenes in it are incidental."

"I didn't say that...."

"But you were thinking it." Frisco took a sip of his drink. It was whiskey. Mia could smell the pungent scent from where she was sitting. "Sorry about your dog."

"Thanks," Mia said. She wrapped her arms around her knees. "I still miss her."

"Too soon to get another, huh?" he said.

She nodded.

"What breed was she? No, let me guess." He shifted slightly to face her. She could feel him studying her in the darkness, as if what he could see would help him figure out the answer.

She kept her eyes averted, suddenly afraid to look him in the eye. Why had she come out here? She didn't usually make a habit of inviting disaster, and sitting in the dark a mere foot away from this man was asking for trouble.

"Part lab, part spaniel," Frisco finally said, and she did look up.

"You're half-right—although cocker spaniel was the only part I could ever identify. Although sometimes I thought I saw a bit of golden retriever." She paused. "How did you know she was a mix?"

He lowered his eyebrows in a look of mock incredulousness. "Like you'd ever get a dog from anywhere but the pound...? And probably from death row at the pound, too, right?"

She had to smile. "Okay, obviously you've figured me out completely. There's no longer any mystery in our relationship—"

"Not quite. There's one last thing I need you to clear up for me."

He was smiling at her in the darkness, flirting with her, indulging in lighthearted banter. Mia would have been amazed, had she not learned by now that Alan Francisco was full of surprises.

"What are you doing still awake?" he asked.

"I could ask the same of you," she countered.

"I'm recovering from my talk with Tasha." He looked down into his glass, the light mood instantly broken. "I'm not sure I helped any. She's pretty jaded when it comes to her mom." He laughed, but there was no humor in it. "She has every right to be."

Mia looked over toward Frisco's condo. She could see the

flicker of the television through a gap in the curtains. "She's not still up, is she?"

He sighed, shaking his head no. "She needs the TV on to sleep. I wish *I* could find a solution to not sleeping that's as easy."

Mia looked down at the drink in his hand. "That's probably not it."

Frisco didn't say anything—he just looked at her. To Mia's credit, she didn't say another word. She didn't preach, didn't chastise, didn't lecture.

But after several long moments when he didn't respond, she stood up.

"Good night," she said.

He didn't want her to leave. Oddly enough, the night wasn't so damned oppressive when she was around. But he didn't know what to say to make her stay. He could've told her that he wasn't like Sharon, that he could stop drinking when and if he wanted to, but that would have sounded exactly like a problem drinker's claim.

He could've told her he was strong enough to stop—he just wasn't strong enough right now to face the fact that the Navy had quit on him.

Instead, he said nothing, and she quietly went inside, locking her door behind her.

And he poured himself another drink.

6

Mia's legs burned as she rounded the corner onto Harris Avenue. She was nearly there, down to the last quarter mile of her run, so she put on a burst of speed.

There was construction going on just about a block and a half from the condo complex. Someone was building another fast-food restaurant—just what this neighborhood needed, she thought.

They'd poured the concrete for the foundation, and the project was at a temporary standstill while the mixture hardened. The lot was deserted. Several A&B Construction Co. trucks were parked at haphazard angles among huge hills of displaced dirt and broken asphalt.

A little girl sat digging on top of one of those hills, her face and clothing streaked with dirt, her red hair gleaming in the sunlight.

Mia skidded to a stop.

Sure enough, it was Natasha. She was oblivious to everything around her, digging happily in the sun-hardened dirt, singing a little song.

Mia tried to catch her breath as she ducked underneath the limp yellow ribbon that was supposed to warn trespassers off the construction sight.

"Natasha?"

The little girl looked down at her and smiled. "Hi, Mia."

"Honey, does your uncle know where you are?"

"He's asleep," Tasha said, returning to her digging. She'd found a plastic spoon and a discarded paper cup and was filling it with dirt and stirring the dirt as if it were coffee. She had mud covering close to every inch of her exposed skin— which was probably good since the morning sun was hot enough to give her a bad sunburn. "It's still early. He won't be up 'til later."

Mia glanced at her watch. "Tash, it's nearly ten. He's got to be awake by now. He's probably going crazy, looking for you. Don't you remember what he told you—about not leaving the courtyard, and not even going out of the condo without telling him?"

Tasha glanced up at her. "How can I tell him when he's asleep?" she said matter of factly. "Mommy always slept until after lunchtime."

Mia held out her hands to help Tasha down from the dirt pile. "Come on. I'll walk you home. We can check to see if Frisco's still asleep."

The little girl stood up and Mia swung her down to the ground.

"You *are* dirty, aren't you?" she continued as they began walking toward the condo complex. "I think a bath is in your immediate future."

Tasha looked at her arms and legs. "I already had a bath— a mud bath. Princesses always have mud baths, and they never have more than one bath a day."

"Oh?" Mia said. "I thought princesses always had bubble baths right after their mud baths."

Tasha considered that thoughtfully. "I never had a bubble bath."

"It's very luxurious," Mia told her. What a sight they must've made walking down the street—a mud-encrusted child and an adult literally dripping with perspiration. "The bubbles go right up to your chin."

Natasha's eyes were very wide. "Really?"

"Yeah, and I just happen to have some bubble-bath soap," Mia told her. "You can try it out when we get home—unless you're absolutely certain you don't want a second bath today...?"

"No, princesses can only have one *mud* bath a day," Tasha told her in complete seriousness. "It's okay if they have a mud bath *and* a bubble bath."

"Good." Mia smiled as they entered the condo courtyard.

The complex was still pretty quiet. Most of the residents had left for work hours ago. Still, it was summer vacation for the few kids who lived in the building. Mia could hear the distant strains of television sets and stereo systems. Tasha followed her up the stairs to unit 2C.

The door was ajar and Mia knocked on the screen. "Hello?" she called, but there was no answer. She leaned on the bell. Still nothing.

Mia looked at the mud caked on Natasha's body and clothes. "You better wait out here," she told the little girl.

Tasha nodded.

"*Right* here," Mia said in her best teacher's voice, pointing to the little spot of concrete directly in front of Frisco's door. "Sit. And don't go *any*where, do you understand, miss?"

Tasha nodded again and sat down.

Feeling very much like a trespasser, Mia opened the screen door and went inside. With the curtains closed, the living room was dim. The television was on, but the volume was set to a low, barely discernible murmur. The air was cool, almost cold, as if the air conditioner had been working over-time to compensate for the slightly opened door. Mia turned off the TV as she went past.

"Hello?" Mia called again. "Lieutenant Francisco…?"

The condo was as silent as a tomb.

"He's gonna be grumpy if you wake him up," Tasha said, up on her knees with her nose pressed against the screen.

"I'll take my chances," Mia said, starting down the hall toward the bedrooms.

She *was* tiptoeing, though. When she reached the end of the hall, she glanced quickly into the bathroom and the smaller of the two bedrooms. Both were empty. The larger bedroom's door was half-closed, and she crept closer. Taking a deep breath, she pushed it open as she knocked.

The double bed was empty.

In the dimness, she could see that the sheets were twisted into a knot. The blanket had been kicked onto the floor, and the pillows were rumpled, but Alan Francisco was not still lying there.

There was not much furniture in the room—just the bed, a bedside table and a dresser. The setup was Spartan. The top of his dresser held only a small pile of loose change. There were no personal items, no knickknacks, no souvenirs. The sheets on the bed were plain white, the blanket a light beige. The closet door hung open, as did one of the drawers in the modest-size dresser. Several duffel bags sagged nearby on the floor. The whole place had a rather apathetic feel, as if the person living here didn't care enough to unpack, or to hang pictures on the wall and make the place his own.

There was nothing that gave any sense of personality to the resident of the room, with the exception of an enormous pile of dirty laundry that seemed to glower from one dark corner. That and a nearly empty bottle of whiskey standing on Frisco's bedside table were the only telling things. And the bottle, at least, certainly told quite a bit. It was similar to the bottle he'd had outside last night—except *that* bottle had been nearly full.

No wonder Tasha hadn't been able to wake him.

But eventually he *had* awakened and found the little girl gone. He was probably out searching for her right now, worried near out of his mind.

The best thing *they* could do was stay put. Eventually, Frisco would come back to see if Natasha had returned.

But the thought of hanging out in Frisco's condo wasn't extremely appealing. His belongings may have been impersonal to the point of distastefulness, but she felt as if by being there, she was invading his privacy.

Mia turned to leave when a gleam of reflected light from the closet caught her eye. She switched on the overhead light.

It was amazing. She'd never seen anything like it in her entire life. A naval uniform hung in the closet, bright white and crisply pressed. And on the upper left side of the jacket were row after row after row after row of colorful medals. And above it—the cause of that reflected light—was a pin in the shape of an eagle, wings outspread, both a gun and a trident clasped in its fierce talons.

Mia couldn't imagine the things Frisco had done to get all of those medals. But because there were so many of them there was one thing that she suddenly did see quite clearly. Alan Francisco had a dedication to his job unlike anyone she'd ever met. These medals told her that as absolutely as if they could talk. If he had had one or two medals—sure, that would have told her he was a brave and capable soldier. But there had to be more than ten of these colorful bars pinned to his uniform. She counted them quickly with her finger. Ten...*eleven*. Eleven medals surely meant that Frisco had gone above and beyond the call of duty time after time.

She turned, and in the new light of her discovery, his bedroom had an entirely different look to it. Instead of being the room of a someone who didn't care enough to add any personal touches, it became the room of a man who'd never taken the time to have a life outside of his dangerous career.

Even the whiskey bottle looked different. It looked far more sad and desperate than ever before.

And the room *wasn't* entirely devoid of personal items. There was a book on the floor next to the bed. It was a collection of short stories by J. D. Salinger. *Salinger.* Who would've thought...?

"Mia?"

Natasha was calling her from the living room door.

Mia turned off the light on her way out of Frisco's room. "I'm here, hon, but your uncle's not," she said, coming into the living room.

"He's not?" Tasha scrambled to her feet to get out of the way of the opening screen door.

"What do you say we go next door and see about that bubble-bath soap of mine?" Mia continued, shutting the heavy wooden door to unit 2C tightly behind her. "I'll write a note for your uncle so that he knows you're at my place when he gets back.''

She'd call Thomas, too. If he was home, he might be willing to go out looking for the Navy lieutenant, to tell him Natasha was safe.

"Let's go right into the bathroom," Mia told Tasha as she opened her screen door and unlocked the dead bolt to her condo. "We'll pop you directly into the tub, okay?"

Natasha hung back, her eyes very wide in her mud-streaked face. "Is Frisco gonna be mad at me?"

Mia gazed at the little girl. "Would you blame him very much if he was?"

Tasha's face fell as she shook her head, her lips stretching into that unmistakable shape children's mouths made when they were about to cry. "He was asleep."

"Just because he's sleeping doesn't mean you can break his rules," Mia told her.

"I was gonna come home before he woke up...."

Aha. Mia suddenly understood. Natasha's mother had frequently slept off her alcoholic binges until well past noon, unknowing and perhaps even uncaring of her daughter's private explorations. It was tantamount to neglect, and obviously Tasha expected the same treatment from Frisco.

Something was going to have to change.

"If I were you," Mia advised her, "I'd be good and ready to say I'm sorry the moment Frisco gets home."

Frisco saw the note on his door from down in the courtyard. It was a pink piece of paper taped to the outside of the screen, and it lifted in the first stirrings of a late-morning breeze. He hurried up the stairs, ignoring the pain in his knee, and pulled the note from the door.

"Found Natasha," it said in clean, bold printing. Thank *God.* He closed his eyes briefly, grateful beyond belief. He'd searched the beach for nearly an hour, terrified his niece had broken his rule and gone down to the ocean again. Hell, if she would break his rule about leaving the condo, she could just as well have broken his rule about never swimming alone.

He'd run into a lifeguard who'd told him he'd heard a rumor that a kid's body had washed up on the beach early in the morning. Frisco's heart had damn near stopped beating. He'd waited for nearly forty-five minutes at a pay phone, trying to get through to the shore patrol, trying to find out if the rumor was true.

It turned out that the body that had washed up in the surf had been that of a baby seal. And with that relief had come the knowledge that he'd wasted precious time. And the search had started again.

Frisco opened his eyes and found he had crumpled the pink paper. He smoothed it out to read the rest. "Found Natasha. We're at my place. Mia."

Mia Summerton. Saving the day again.

Leaning on his cane, he went toward Mia's door, catching his reflection in his living room window. His hair was standing straight up, and he looked as if he were hiding from the sunlight behind his dark sunglasses. His T-shirt looked slept in, and his shorts *were* slept in. He looked like hell and he *felt* worse. His head had been pounding from the moment he'd stumbled out into the living room and found that Natasha was gone again. No, strike that. His head had been pounding from the moment he'd opened his eyes. It had risen to a nearly unbearable level when he'd discovered Tash was AWOL. It was still just shy of intolerable.

He rang the doorbell anyway, well aware that in addition to the not-so-pretty picture he made, he didn't smell too damn good, either. His shirt reeked of a distillery. He hadn't been too picky when he snatched it off the floor of his room this morning on his way out the door to search for Tash. Just his luck, he'd grabbed the one he'd used to mop up a spilled glass of whiskey last night.

The door swung open, and Mia Summerton stood there, looking like something out of a sailor's fantasy. She was wearing running shorts that redefined the word *short*, and a midriff-baring athletic top that redefined the word *lust*. Her hair was back in a single braid, and still damp from perspiration.

"She's here, she's safe," Mia said in way of greeting. "She's in the tub, getting cleaned up."

"Where did you find her?" His throat felt dry and his voice came out raspy and harsh.

Mia looked back into her condo unit and raised her voice. "How you doing in there, Tasha?"

"Fine," came a cheery reply.

She opened the screen door and stepped outside. "Harris Avenue," she told Frisco. "She was over on Harris Avenue, playing in the dirt at that construction site—"

"*Dammit!* What the *hell* does she think she's doing? She's five years old! She shouldn't be walking around by herself or—God!—playing on a *construction* site!" Frisco ran one hand down his face, fighting to control his flare of anger. "I know that yelling at the kid's not going to help...." He forced himself to lower his voice, to take a deep breath and try to release all of the frustration and anger and worry of the past several hours. "I don't know what to do," he admitted. "She blatantly disobeyed my orders."

"That's not the way she sees it," Mia told him.

"The rule was for her to tell me when she went outside. The rule was to stay in the courtyard."

"In her opinion, all bets are off if Mom—or Uncle Frisco—can't drag themselves out of bed in the morning." Mia fixed him with her level gaze. Her eyes were more green than brown in the bright morning sun. "She told me she thought she'd be back before you even woke up."

"A rule is a rule," Frisco started.

"Yeah, and *her* rule," Mia interrupted, "is that if you climb into a bottle, she's on her own."

Frisco's headache intensified. He looked away, unable to meet her gaze. It wasn't that she was looking at him accusingly. There was nothing even remotely accusative in her eyes. In fact, her eyes were remarkably gentle, softening the harshness of her words.

"I'm sorry," she murmured. "That was uncalled for."

He shook his head, uncertain as to whether he was agreeing with her or disagreeing with her.

"Why don't you come inside?" Mia said, holding open the screen door for him.

Mia's condo might as well have been from a different planet than his. It was spacious and open, with unspotted, light brown carpeting and white painted bamboo-framed furniture. The walls were freshly painted and clean, and potted plants were everywhere, their vines lacing across the ceiling on a system of hooks. Music played softly on the stereo. Frisco recognized the smoky Texas-blues-influenced vocals of Lee Roy Parnell.

Pictures hung on the wall—gorgeous blue and green watercolors of the ocean, and funky, quirkily colorful figures of people walking along the beach.

"My mother's an artist," Mia said, following his gaze. "Most of this is her work."

Another picture was that of the beach before a storm. It conveyed all of the dangerous power of the wind and the water, the ominous, darkening sky, the rising surf, the palm trees whipped and tossed—nature at her most deadly.

"She's good," Frisco said.

Mia smiled. "I know." She raised her voice. "How's it going in bubbleland, Natasha?"

"Okay."

"While she was out playing in the dirt, she gave herself a Russian princess mud bath." With a wry smile, she led Frisco into the tiny kitchen. It was exactly like his—and nothing like his. Magnets of all shapes and sizes covered the refrigerator, holding up photos of smiling people, and notes and coupons and theater schedules. Fresh fruit hung in wire baskets that were suspended from hooks on the ceiling. A coffee mug in the shape of a cow wearing a graduate's cap sat on the counter next to the telephone, holding pencils and pens. The entire room was filled with little bits and pieces of Mia. "I managed to convince her that true royalty always followed a mud bath with a bubble bath."

"Bless you," Frisco said. "And thank you for bringing her home."

"It was lucky I ran that way." Mia opened the refrigerator door. "I usually take a longer route, but I was feeling the heat this morning." She looked up at Frisco. "Ice tea, lemonade or soda?"

"Something with caffeine, please," Frisco told her.

"Hmm," Mia said, reaching into the back of the fridge and pulling out a can of cola. She handed it to him. "And would you like that with two aspirin or three?"

Frisco smiled. It was crooked but it was a smile. "Three. Thanks."

She motioned to the small table that was in the dining area at the end of the kitchen, and Frisco lowered himself into one of a pair of chairs. She had a napkin holder in the shape of a pig and tiny airplanes for salt and pepper shakers. There were plants everywhere in here, too, and a fragile wind chime directly over his head, in front of a window that looked out over the parking lot. He reached up and brushed the wind chime with one finger. It sounded as delicate and ghostly as it looked.

The doors to her kitchen cabinets had recently been replaced with light, blond wood. The gleaming white countertop looked new, too. But he only spared it half a glance, instead watching Mia as she stood on tiptoes to reach up into one of the cabinets for her bottle of aspirin. She was a blinding mixture of muscles and curves. He couldn't look away, even when she turned around. Great, just what she needed. Some loser leering at her in her own kitchen. He could see her apprehension and discomfort in her eyes.

She set the bottle of aspirin down in front of him on the table and disappeared, murmuring some excuse about checking on Natasha.

Frisco pressed the cold soda can against his forehead. When

Mia returned, she was wearing a T-shirt over her running gear. It helped, but not a lot.

He cleared his throat. A million years ago, he had been so good at small talk. "So...how far do you run?" Cripes, he sounded like some kind of idiot.

"Usually three miles," she answered, opening the refrigerator again and taking out a pitcher of ice tea. She poured herself a glass. "But today I only went about two and a half."

"You gotta be careful when it's hot like this." Man, could he sound any more lame? *Lame?* Yeah, that was the perfect word to describe him, in more ways than one.

She nodded, turning to look at him as she leaned back against the kitchen counter and took a sip of her tea.

"So...your mother's an artist."

Mia smiled. Damn, she had a beautiful smile. Had he really thought that it was goofy-looking just two days ago?

"Yeah," she said. "She has a studio near Malibu. That's where I grew up."

Frisco nodded. This was where he was supposed to counter by telling her where he came from. "I grew up right here in San Felipe, the armpit of California."

Her smile deepened. "Armpits have their purpose—not that I agree with you and think that San Felipe is one."

"You're entitled to your opinion," he said with a shrug. "To me, San Felipe will always be an armpit."

"So sell your condo and move to Hawaii."

"Is that where your family's from?" he asked.

She looked down into her glass. "To tell you the truth, I'm not really sure. I think I must have some Hawaiian or Polynesian blood, but I'm not certain."

"Your parents don't know?"

"I was adopted from an overseas agency. The records were extremely sketchy." She looked up at him. "I went through a phase, you know, when I tried to find my birth parents."

"Birth parents aren't always worth finding. I would've been better off without knowing mine."

"I'm sorry," Mia said quietly. "There was a time when I

might've said that you can't possibly mean that, or that that couldn't possibly be true. But I've been teaching at an urban high school for over five years, and I'm well aware that most people didn't have the kind of childhood or the kind of parents that I did.'' Her eyes were a beautiful mixture of brown and green and compassion. ''I don't know what you might have gone through, but...I *am* sorry.''

''I've heard that teaching high school is a pretty dangerous job these days, what with guns and drugs and violence,'' Frisco said, trying desperately to bring the conversation out of this dark and ultrapersonal area. ''Did they give you any special kind of commando training when you took the job?''

Mia laughed. ''No, we're on our own. Thrown to the wolves naked, so to speak. Some of the teachers have compensated by becoming real drill sergeants. I've found that positive reinforcement works far better than punishment.'' She took another sip of her ice tea, gazing at him speculatively over the top of her glass. ''In fact, you might want to consider that when you're dealing with Natasha.''

Frisco shook his head. ''What? Give her a cookie for running away? I don't think so.''

''But what kind of punishment will possibly get through to her?'' Mia persisted. ''Think about it. The poor kid's already been given the ultimate punishment for a five-year-old—her mommy's gone. There's probably nothing else that you can take away from her that will matter. You can yell at her and make her cry. You can even frighten her and make her afraid of you, and maybe even give her worse nightmares. But if you reward her when she *does* follow your rules, if you make a really big deal about it and make her feel as if she's worth a million bucks, well, she'll catch on much more quickly.''

He ran his fingers through his hair. ''But I can't just ignore what she did this morning.''

''It's difficult,'' Mia admitted. ''You have to achieve a balance between letting a child know her behavior is unacceptable, and not wanting to reward the child's bad behavior by giving her too much attention. Kids who crave attention often misbehave. It's the easiest way to get a parent or teacher to notice them.''

Frisco pushed his mouth up into another smile. ''I know some so-called grown-ups who operate on the same principle.''

Mia gazed at the man sitting at her kitchen table. It was amazing. He looked as if he'd been rolled from a park bench, yet she still found him attractive. What would he look like, she wondered, shiny clean and dressed in that uniform she'd found in his closet?

He'd probably look like someone she'd go out of her way to avoid. She'd never been impressed by men in uniform. It wasn't likely that she'd be impressed now.

Still, all those medals…

Mia set her empty glass down and pushed herself off the counter. ''I'll get Tasha out of the tub,'' she told Frisco. ''You probably have things to do—she told me you promised to take her shopping for furniture for her bedroom.''

''Yeah.'' Frisco nodded and pulled himself clumsily to his feet. ''Thanks again for bringing her home.''

Mia smiled and slipped down the hall toward the bathroom. Considering their rocky start, they'd actually achieved quite a nice, neighborly relationship.

Nice and neighborly—that's exactly where they were going to leave it, too. Despite the fact that this man had the ability to make her blood heat with a single look, despite the fact that she genuinely liked him more and more each time they met, she *was* going to be careful to keep her distance.

Because the more Mia found out about her neighbor, the more she was convinced that they were absolute polar opposites.

7

It was pink. It was definitely, undeniably pink. Its back was reminiscent of a scallop shell, and its arms were scrolled. Its cushions were decorated with shiny silver buttons that absolutely, positively could not have been comfortable to sit upon.

It was far too fancy to be called a couch or even a sofa. It was advertised as a "settee."

For Natasha, it was love at first sight.

Fortunately for Frisco, she didn't spot it until they were on their way *out* of the furniture store.

She sat down on it and went into Russian princess mode. Frisco was so tired, and his knee and head ached so badly, he sat down, too.

"Kneel in front of the Russian princess," Tash commanded him sternly.

Frisco put his head back and closed his eyes. "Not a chance, babe," he mumbled.

After Tash's bath at Mia's place, he'd taken her home, then they'd both suited up and headed to the beach for the kid's first swimming lesson. The current had still been quite strong, and he'd kept his fingers solidly locked on Tash's bathing suit the entire time.

The kid was fearless. Considering that she hadn't even seen the ocean before yesterday, she was entirely enthusiastic about the water. At the end of the week, she'd be well on her way to swimming like a fish.

Frisco shook his head. How on earth had Sharon's kid managed to live to the ripe old age of five without having even *seen* the ocean? Historically, the Franciscos were coastline people. His old man had worked on a fishing boat for years. Vacations were spent at the water. Frisco and his two older brothers had loved the beach. But not Sharon, he remembered suddenly. Sharon had damn near drowned when she was hardly any older than Natasha was now. As an adult, Sharon moved inland, spending much of her time in Las Vegas and Reno. Tash had been born in Tucson, Arizona. Not much beachfront property there.

After the swimming lesson and a forty-five-minute lecture on why Tash had to follow Frisco's rules, they'd dragged themselves home, had lunch, changed and gone shopping for furniture for Frisco's second bedroom.

They'd found this particular store in the Yellow Pages. It was right around the corner, and—the advertisement boasted—it had free, same-day delivery. Frisco had picked out a simple mattress, box spring and metal-framed bed, and Tash had chosen a pint-size bright yellow chest of drawers. Together, they'd found a small desk and chair and a petite bookshelf.

"Can we get this, Frisco?" Tash now asked hopefully.

He snorted as he opened his eyes. "A *pink* couch? Man, are you kidding?"

As usual, she answered his rhetorical question as if he'd asked it seriously. "No."

"Where the hell would we put it?" He glanced at the price tag. It was supposedly on sale, marked down to a mere small fortune.

"We could put it where that other icky one is."

"Great. Just what that condo needs." Shaking his head, Frisco pulled himself to his feet. "Come on. If we don't hurry, the delivery truck is going to beat us home. We don't want them to deliver your new furniture to some other kid."

That got Tasha moving, but not without one final lovelorn glance at the pink sofa.

They were only two blocks from home, but Frisco flagged down a cab. The sun was merciless, and his knee was damn near making him scream with pain. His head wasn't feeling too great, either.

There was no sign of Mia out in her garden in the condo courtyard. Her door was tightly shut, and Frisco found himself wondering where she had gone.

Bad mistake, he told himself. She had been making it clear that she didn't want to be anything more than a neighbor. She didn't want the likes of him sniffing around her door.

Mia actually thought he was a drunk, like his old man and his sister. It was entirely possible that if he wasn't careful, she would be proven right.

No more, he vowed, pulling himself up the stairs. Tonight, if insomnia struck, he'd tough it out. He'd face the demons who were at their ugliest in the wee hours of the morning by spitting in their faces. If he awoke in the middle of the night, he'd spend the time working out, doing exercises that would strengthen his leg and support his injured knee.

He unlocked the door to his condo and Tasha went inside first, dashing through the living room and down the hall to the bedrooms.

Frisco followed more slowly, each painful step making him grit his teeth. He needed to sit down and get his weight off his knee, elevate the damn thing and ice the hell out of it.

Tasha was in her bedroom, lying down on the wall-to-wall carpeting. She was flat on her back on the floor, staring up at the ceiling.

As Frisco stood in the doorway and watched, she scrambled to her feet and then lay down on the floor in another part of the room.

"What are you doing?" he asked as she did the exact same thing yet a third time.

"I'm picking where to put the bed," Tash told him from her position on the floor.

Frisco couldn't hide his smile. "Good idea," he said. "Why don't you work on that for a while? I'm gonna chill for a few minutes before the delivery truck comes, okay?"

"'Kay."

He headed back into the kitchen and grabbed an ice pack from the freezer. He moved into the living room and sat on his old plaid couch, swinging his injured leg up and onto the cushions. The ice felt good, and he put his head back and closed his eyes.

He had to figure out a way to move those boxes out of Tash's room. There were a half a dozen of them, and they were all too ungainly for him to carry with only one arm. But he could drag 'em, though. That would work. He could use a blanket or sheet, and wrestle the boxes on top of it, one at a time. With the box firmly trapped in the sheet like a fish in a fishing net, he could pull the sheet, sliding the box along the rug out of Tash's room and into his own and...

Frisco held his breath. He'd sensed more than heard the movement of Tasha crossing the living room floor, but now he heard the telltale squeak of the front door being opened.

He opened his eyes and sat up, but she was already out the door.

"Natasha! *Damn* it!"

His cane had slipped underneath the couch and he scrambled for it, grabbing it and moving quickly to the door.

"Tash!"

He supported himself on the railing near his rope and pulley setup. Natasha looked up at him from the courtyard, eyes wide.

"Where the *hell* are you going?" he growled.

"To see if Thomas is home."

She didn't get it. Frisco could tell just from looking at the little girl that she honestly didn't understand why he was upset with her.

He took a deep breath and forced his racing pulse to slow. "You forgot to tell me where you were going."

"You were asleep."

"No, I wasn't. And even if I was, that doesn't mean you can just break the rules."

She was silent, gazing up at him.

Frisco went down the stairs. "Come here." He gestured

with his head toward one of the courtyard benches. He sat down and she sat next to him. Her feet didn't touch the ground, and she swung them back and forth. "Do you know what a rule is?" he asked.

Tasha chewed on her lower lip. She shook her head.

"Take a guess," Frisco told her. "What's a rule?"

"Something you want me to do that I don't want to do?" she asked.

It took all that he had in him not to laugh. "It's more than that," he said. "It's something that you *have* to do, whether or not you want to. And it's always the same, whether I'm asleep or awake."

She didn't get it. He could see her confusion and disbelief written clearly on her face.

He ran one hand down his face, trying to clear his cobweb-encrusted mind. He was tired. He couldn't think how to explain to Natasha that she *had* to follow his rules all of the time. He couldn't figure out how to get through to her.

"Hi, guys."

Frisco looked up to see Mia Summerton walking toward them. She was wearing a summery, sleeveless, flower-print dress with a long, sweeping skirt that reached almost all the way to the ground. She had sandals on her feet and a large-brimmed straw hat on her head and a friendly smile on her pretty face. She looked cool and fresh, like a long-awaited evening breeze in the suffocating late-afternoon heat.

Where had she been, all dressed up like that? On a lunch date with some boyfriend? Or maybe she wasn't coming, maybe she was going. Maybe she was waiting for her dinner date to arrive. Lucky bastard. Frisco scowled, letting himself hate the guy, allowing himself that small luxury.

"There's a furniture truck unloading in the driveway," Mia said, ignoring his dark look. In fact, she was ignoring him completely. She spoke directly to Tash. "Does that pretty yellow dresser belong to you, by any chance?"

Natasha jumped up, their conversation all but forgotten.

"Me," she said, dashing toward the parking lot. "It belongs to me!"

"Don't run too far ahead," Frisco called out warningly, pulling himself to his feet. He tightened his mouth as he put his weight on his knee, resisting the urge to wince, not wanting to show Mia how much he was hurting. "And do not step off that sidewalk."

But Mia somehow knew. "Are you all right?" she asked him, no longer ignoring him, her eyes filled with concern. She followed him after Natasha, back toward the parking lot.

"I'm fine," he said brusquely.

"Have you been chasing around after her all day?"

"I'm fine," he repeated.

"You're allowed to be tired," she said with a musical laugh. "I baby-sat a friend's four-year-old last week, and I practically had to be carried out on a stretcher afterward."

Frisco glanced at her. She gazed back at him innocently. She was giving him an out, pretending that the lines of pain and fatigue on his face were due to the fact that he wasn't used to keeping up with the high energy of a young child, rather than the result of his old injury.

"Yeah, right."

Mia knew better than to show her disappointment at Frisco's terse reply. She wanted to be this man's friend, and she'd assumed they'd continue to build a friendship on the shaky foundation they'd recently established. But whatever understanding they'd reached this morning seemed to have been forgotten. The old, angry, tight-lipped Frisco had returned with a vengeance.

Unless...

It was possible his knee was hurting worse than she thought.

A delivery man approached. "You Alan Francisco?" he asked, not waiting for a reply before he held out his clipboard. "Sign at the *X*."

Frisco signed. "It's going up to Unit 2C. It's right at the top of the stairs—"

"Sorry, pal, this is as far as I go." The man didn't sound even remotely apologetic. "My instructions are to get it off the truck. You've got to take it from here."

"You're kidding." Frisco's voice was flat, unbelieving. The furniture was standing there on the asphalt, next to the delivery vehicle.

The man closed the sliding back door of his truck with a crash. "Read the small print on your receipt. It's free delivery—and you got exactly what you paid for."

How was Frisco supposed to get all this up a flight of stairs? Mia saw the frustration and anger in his eyes and in the tight set of his mouth.

The man climbed into the cab and closed the door behind him.

"I bought this stuff from your store because you advertise a free delivery," Frisco said roughly. "If you're not going to deliver it, you can damn well load it up and take it back."

"First of all, it's not *my* store," the man told him, starting the engine with a roar and grinding the gears as he put it into first, "and secondly, you already signed for it."

It was all Frisco could do to keep himself from pulling himself up on the running board and slamming his fist into the man's surly face. But Tash and Mia were watching him. So he did nothing. He stood there like a damned idiot as the truck pulled away.

He stared after it, feeling helpless and impotent and frustrated beyond belief.

And then Mia touched his arm. Her fingers felt cool against his hot skin. Her touch was hesitant and light, but she didn't pull away even when he turned to glare down at her.

"I sent Tasha to see if Thomas is home," she said quietly. "We'll get this upstairs."

"I hate this," he said. The words were out of his mouth before he could stop them. They were dripping with despair and shame. He hadn't meant to say it aloud, to reveal so much of himself to her. It wasn't a complaint, or even self-pity. It was a fact. He hated his limitations.

Her brown-green eyes grew warmer, more liquid. She slid her hand all the way down to his, and intertwined their fingers. "I know," she said huskily. "I'm so sorry."

He turned to look at her then, to *really* look at her. "You don't even like me," he said. "How can you stand to be so nice?"

"I *do* like you," she said, trying to step back, away from the intensity of his gaze. But he wouldn't let go of her hand. "I want to be your friend."

Friend. She tugged again, and this time he released her. She wanted to be his friend. He wanted so much more....

"Yo, Frisco!"

Frisco turned. The voice was as familiar to him as breathing. It was Lucky O'Donlon. He'd parked his motorcycle in one of the visitor's spaces, and now sauntered toward them. He was wearing his blue dress uniform and looked to be one hundred percent spit and polish. Frisco knew better.

"Hey, guy, having a tag sale or something?" Lucky's wide smile and warm blue eyes traveled lazily over the furniture, Frisco's damned cane, and Mia. He took an especially long time taking in Mia. "You gonna introduce me to your friend?"

"Do I have a choice?"

Lucky held out his hand to Mia. "I'm Lt. Luke O'Donlon, U.S. Navy SEALs. And you are...?"

Mia smiled. Of course she would smile. No one could resist Lucky. "Mia Summerton. I'm Frisco's neighbor."

"I'm his swim buddy."

"*Former* swim buddy."

Lucky shook his head. "No such thing." He looped his arm around Frisco's neck and smiled at Mia. "We went through BUD/S together. That makes you swim buddies for life."

"BUD/S is basic training for SEALs," Frisco translated for her, pushing Lucky away from him. "Where are you going, dressed like that?"

"Some kind of semiformal affair at the OC. A shindig for

some top brass pencil pusher who's being promoted." He grinned at Frisco, but his gaze kept returning to Mia. "I thought maybe you'd want to come along."

Frisco snorted. "Dream on, man. I hated those parties when I was required to go."

"Please?" Lucky begged. "I need someone to keep me company or I'll spend all night dancing with the admiral's wife, trying to keep her from grabbing my butt." He smiled at Mia and winked.

"Even if I wanted to," Frisco told him, "which I *don't*, I couldn't. I'm taking care of my sister's kid for the next six weeks." He gestured to the furniture. "This is supposed to be for her bedroom."

"The kid's either fond of the outdoors, or you got yourself some kind of snafu here."

"Number two," Frisco said.

"Yo, neighbor babe," Lucky said, picking up one end of the mattress. "You look healthy. Grab the other end."

"Her name is Mia," Frisco said.

"Excuse me," Lucky said. "Mia babe, grab the other end."

Mia was laughing, thank God. As Frisco watched, she and Lucky carried the mattress into the courtyard. He could hear Mia's laughter long after they moved out of sight.

As Frisco picked up the lightweight bookcase and carried it slowly toward the courtyard, he could also hear Tasha's excited chirping, and Thomas King's rich voice coming toward him.

"Hey, Navy." Thomas nodded a greeting as he passed. He knew better than to offer to take the bookcase from Frisco on his way out to the parking lot.

"Thanks for helping out, man," Frisco said to him.

"No problem," the teenager replied.

No problem. It was possible that this whole deal wasn't a problem for anybody—except Frisco.

He set the bookcase down at the bottom of the stairs, and looked up to see Lucky come out of his condo, with Tasha in his arms. He was tickling the little girl, and she was giggling. Mia was right behind them, and she was laughing, too.

He'd never seen Mia look so beautiful or relaxed. Lucky leaned toward her and said something into her ear, and she laughed again. She started down the stairs, and Lucky watched her go, his eyes following the movement of her hips.

Frisco had to look away. He couldn't blame Lucky. At one time, the two of them had been so much alike. They still were alike in so many ways. It didn't surprise him that his best friend would be attracted to Mia, too.

It took all of ten minutes to transport Tasha's furniture into her bedroom and to move the boxes that were in there into Frisco's room.

Thomas headed off to work, and Mia made her excuses and disappeared into her condo—after smiling at the big deal Lucky made out of shaking her hand once again.

"She, uh, said you guys were just friends, huh?" Lucky said much too casually as Frisco walked him to his bike.

Frisco was silent, wondering what he could possibly say to that statement. If he agreed, then Lucky would be dropping by all the time, asking Mia out, working his famous O'Donlon charm and persistence until she gave in. And she would give in. No one could resist Lucky. And then Frisco would have to watch as his best friend dated and probably seduced this woman that he wanted so badly.

It was true. He wanted Mia. And dammit, he was going to do everything in his power to get her.

"She's wrong," he told Lucky. "We're more than friends. She just doesn't know it yet."

If Lucky was disappointed, he hid it well. And it didn't take long for his disappointment to turn into genuine pleasure. "This is great. This means you're coming back," he said.

"To the SEALs?" Frisco shook his head. "Man, haven't you heard, I'm—"

"No," Lucky interrupted. "I meant to the world of the living."

Frisco gazed at his friend. He didn't understand. He was

alive. He'd had five years of pain and frustration to prove that.

"Call me sometime," Lucky said, strapping on his motorcycle helmet. "I miss you, man."

Frisco awoke to the sound of an electronic buzzer. It was loud as hell and it was right in his ear and...

He sat up, wide-awake.

It was the sound of the booby trap he'd rigged to the front door last night before he went to bed. Tasha was AWOL again, dammit.

He pulled on a pair of shorts as he rolled out of bed, and grabbed his cane from the floor.

Oh, Lord, he was tired. He may have gone to bed last night, but he hadn't gone to sleep. It couldn't have been more than two hours ago that he'd finally closed his eyes. But he'd done it. He'd stared down the night without even a sip of whiskey to help him along.

He may have been exhausted, but he wasn't hung over.

And that was damn good, because if he had been, the sound of this blasted buzzer would have taken the top of his head clear off.

He quickly disconnected it. It was a simple system, designed for the circuit to break if the door was open. If the circuit was broken, the buzzer would sound.

He pulled the door the rest of the way open and...

Tasha, with Mia directly behind her, stood on the other side of the screen door.

Tash was still wearing her pajamas. Mia was wearing her bathing suit underneath a pair of shorts and a T-shirt. Frisco could see the brightly colored strap that tied up and around her neck.

"Good morning," she said.

Frisco glared at Tash. "Where the h—"

Mia cut him off. "Tasha was coming over to visit me," she told Frisco, "but she remembered that she was supposed to tell you first where she was going.'' She looked down at the little girl. ''Right, Tash?''

Tasha nodded.

Tasha remembered? Mia remembered was more like it.

Mia mouthed ''Positive reinforcement'' over Tasha's head.

Frisco swallowed his frustration. All right. If Mia thought he could get through to Tasha this way, he'd give it a shot. Somehow he mustered up far more enthusiasm than he felt. ''Excellent job remembering,'' he said to the little girl, opening the screen door and letting both Tasha and Mia inside.

He forced himself to smile, and Natasha visibly brightened. Jeez, maybe there *was* something to this.

He scooped the little girl into his arms and awkwardly spun her around until she began to giggle, then collapsed with her onto the couch. ''In fact,'' he continued, ''you are so *amazingly* excellent, I think you should probably get a medal. Don't you?''

She nodded, her eyes wide. ''What's a medal?''

''It's a very special pin that you get for doing something really great—like remembering my rules,'' Frisco told her. He dumped her off his lap and onto the soft cushions of the couch. ''Wait right here—I'll get it.''

Mia was standing near the door, and as she watched, Frisco pushed himself off the couch and headed down the hall to his bedroom.

''Getting a medal is a really big deal.'' Frisco raised his voice so they could hear him in the living room. ''It requires a very special ceremony.''

Tasha was bouncing up and down on the couch, barely able to contain her excitement. Mia had to smile. It seemed that Frisco understood the concept of positive reinforcement.

''Here we go,'' he said, coming back into the living room. He caught Mia's eye and smiled. He looked like hell this morning. He looked more exhausted than she'd ever seen him. He'd clearly been sound asleep mere moments ago. But somehow he seemed more vibrant, his eyes more clear. And the smile that he'd sent her was remarkably sweet, almost shy.

Mia's heart was in her throat as she watched him with his little niece.

"For the remarkable remembering of my rules and regs, including rule number one—'Tell Frisco where you're going before you leave the condo,'" he intoned, "I award Natasha Francisco this medal of honor."

He pinned one of the colorful bars Mia had seen attached to his dress uniform onto Tasha's pajama shirt.

"Now I salute you and you salute me," he whispered to the little girl after he attached the pin.

He stood at sharp attention, and snapped a salute. Tasha imitated him remarkably well.

"The only time SEALs ever salute is when someone gets a medal," Frisco said with another glance in Mia's direction. He pulled Tasha back to the couch with him. "Here's the deal," he told her. "In order to keep this medal, you have to remember my rules all day today. Do you remember the rules?"

"Tell you when I want to go outside...."

"Even when I'm asleep. You have to wake me up, okay? And what else?"

"Stay here...."

"In the courtyard, right. And...?"

"No swimming without my buddy."

"Absolutely, incredibly correct. Gimme a high five."

Natasha giggled, slapping hands with her uncle.

"Here's the rest of the deal," he said. "Are you listening, Tash?"

She nodded.

"When you get enough of these medals, you know what happens?"

Tasha shook her head no.

"We trade this thing in," Frisco told her, smacking the back of the couch they were sitting on with one hand, "for a certain pink sofa."

Mia thought it was entirely possible that the little girl was going to explode with pleasure.

"You're going to have to work really hard to follow the rules," Frisco was telling her. "You've got to remember that the reason I want you to obey these rules is because I want you to be safe, and it really gets me upset when I don't know for certain that you're safe. You have to think about that and remember that, because I know you don't want to make me feel upset, right?"

Tasha nodded. "Do you have to follow *my* rules?"

Frisco was surprised, but he hid it well. "What are *your* rules?"

"No more bad words," the little girl said without hesitation.

Frisco glanced up at Mia again, chagrin in his eyes. "Okay," he said, looking back at Tasha. "That's a tough one, but I'll try."

"More playing with Mia," Tasha suggested.

He laughed nervously. "I'm not sure we can make that a rule, Tash. I mean, things that concern you and me are fine, but..."

"I'd love to play with you," Mia murmured.

Frisco glanced up at her. She couldn't possibly have meant that the way it sounded. No, she was talking to Natasha. Still... He let his imagination run with the scenario. It was a very, *very* good one.

"But we don't have to make a rule about it," Mia added.

"Can you come to the beach with us for my swimming lesson?" Tasha asked her.

Mia hesitated, looking cautiously across the room at Frisco. "I don't want to get in the way."

"You've already got your bathing suit on," he pointed out.

She seemed surprised that he'd noticed. "Well, yes, but..."

"Were you planning to go to a different beach?"

"No... I just don't want to...you know..." She shrugged and smiled apologetically, nervously. "Interfere."

"It wouldn't be interfering," Frisco told her. Man, he felt as nervous as she sounded. When had this gotten so hard? He used to be so good at this sort of thing. "Tasha wants you to come with us." Perfect. Now he sounded as if he wanted her to come along as a playmate for his niece. That wasn't it at all. "And I...I do, too," he added.

Jeez, his heart was in his mouth. He swallowed, trying to make it go back where it belonged as Mia just gazed at him.

"Well, okay," she finally said. "In that case, I'd love to come. If you want, I could pack a picnic lunch...?"

"Yeah!" Tasha squealed, hopping around the room. "A picnic! A picnic!"

Frisco felt himself smile. A picnic on the beach with Mia. He couldn't remember the last time he'd felt such anticipation. And his anticipation was for more than his wanting to see what her bathing suit looked like, although he was feeling plenty of that, too. "I guess that's a yes. But it shouldn't be just up to you to bring the food."

"I'll make sandwiches," Mia told him, opening the door. "You guys bring something to drink. Soda. Or beer if you want it."

"No beer," Frisco said.

She paused, looking back at him, her hand on the handle of the screen door.

"It's another one of the rules I'm going to be following from now on," he said quietly. Natasha had stopped dancing around the room. She was listening, her eyes wide. "No more drinking. Not even beer."

Mia stepped away from the door, her eyes nearly as wide as Tasha's. "Um, Tash, why don't you go put on your bathing suit?"

Silently Tasha vanished down the hallway.

Frisco shook his head. "It's not that big a deal."

Mia clearly thought otherwise. She stepped closer to him, lowering her voice for privacy from Tasha's sensitive ears. "You know, there are support groups all over town. You can find a meeting at virtually any time of day—"

Did she honestly think his drinking was *that* serious a problem? "Look, I can handle this," he said gruffly. "I went overboard for a couple of days, but that's all it was. I didn't drink at all while I was in the hospital—right up 'til two days ago. These past few days—you haven't exactly been seeing me at my best.''

"I'm sorry," she murmured. "I didn't mean to imply..."

"It's no big deal."

She touched his arm, her fingers gentle and cool and so soft against his skin. "Yes, it is," she told him. "To Natasha, it's a *very* big deal."

"I'm not doing it for Tash," he said quietly, looking down at her delicate hand resting on the corded muscles of his forearm, wishing she would leave it there, but knowing she was going to pull away. "I'm doing it for myself."

8

"Is Thomas really a king?"

Mia looked up from the sand castle she was helping Tasha build. The little girl was making dribble turrets on the side of the large mound using wet sand and water from a plastic pail that Mia had found in her closet. She had remarkable dexterity for a five-year-old, and managed to make most of her dribbles quite tall and spiky.

"Thomas's last name is King," Mia answered. "But here in the United States, we don't have kings and queens."

"Is he a king somewhere else? Like I'm a princess in Russia?"

"Well," Mia said diplomatically, "you might want to check with Thomas, but I think King is just his last name."

"He looks like a king." Natasha giggled. "He thinks I'm from Mars. I'm gonna marry him."

"Marry who?" Frisco asked, sitting down in the sand next to them.

He'd just come out of the ocean, and water beaded on his eyelashes and dripped from his hair. He looked more relaxed and at ease than Mia had ever seen him.

"Thomas," Tasha told him, completely serious.

"Thomas." Frisco considered that thoughtfully. "I like him," he said. "But you're a little young to be getting married, don't you think?"

"Not now, silly," she said with exasperation. "When I'm a grown-up, of course."

Frisco tried to hide his smile. "Of course," he said.

"You can't marry my mom cause you're her brother, right?" she asked.

"That's right," Frisco told her. He leaned back in the sand on his elbows. Mia tried not to stare at the way the muscles in his arms flexed as they supported his weight. She tried to pull her gaze away from his broad shoulders and powerful chest and smooth, tanned skin. This wasn't the first time she'd seen him without a shirt, after all. She should be getting used to this....

"Too bad," Tash said with a sigh. "Mommy's always looking for someone to marry, and I like you."

Frisco's voice was husky. "Thanks, Tash. I like you, too."

"I didn't like Dwayne," the little girl said. "He scared me, but Mommy liked living in his house."

"Maybe when your mom comes back, the two of you could live a few doors down from me," Frisco said.

"You could marry Mia," Tasha suggested. "And move in with her. And we could live in your place."

Mia glanced up. Frisco met her eyes, clearly embarrassed. "Maybe Mia doesn't want to get married," he said.

"Do you?" the little girl asked, looking up from her handiwork to gaze at Mia with those pure blue eyes that were so like Frisco's.

"Well," she said carefully. "Someday I'd like to get married and have a family, but—"

"She does," Tasha informed her uncle. "She's pretty and she makes good sandwiches. You should ask her to marry you." She stood up and, taking her bucket, went down to the edge of the water, where she began to chase waves up the sand.

"I'm sorry about that," Frisco said with a nervous laugh. "She's...you know, *five*. She's heavily into happily ever after."

"It's all right," Mia said with a smile. "And don't worry. I won't hold you to any promises that Tasha makes on your behalf." She brushed the sand from her knees and moved back onto the beach blanket she'd spread out.

Frisco moved to join her. "That's good to know." He turned to look at Mia, his warm gaze skimming up her legs, lingering on her red two-piece bathing suit and the enormous amount of skin it exposed, before settling on her face. "She's right, though. You *are* pretty, and you make damn good sandwiches."

Mia's pulse was racing. When had it started to matter so much whether or not this man thought that she was pretty? When had the urge disappeared—the urge to cover herself up with a bulky T-shirt every time he looked at her with that heat in his eyes? When had her heart started to leap at his crooked, funny smiles? When had he crossed that boundary that defined him as more than a mere friend?

It had started days ago, with that very first hug he had given Natasha in the courtyard. He was so gentle with the child, so patient. Mia's attraction to him had been there from the start, yet now that she had come to know more of him, it was multilayered, existing on more complicated levels than just basic, raw sexual magnetism.

It was crazy. Mia knew it was crazy. This was not a man with whom she could picture herself spending the rest of her life. He'd been trained as a killer—a professional soldier. And if that wasn't enough, he had barrels of anger and frustration and pain to work through before he could be considered psychologically and emotionally healthy. And if *that* wasn't enough, there was the fact of his drinking.

Yes, he'd vowed to stop, but Mia's experience as a high school teacher had made her an expert on the disease of alcoholism. The best way to fight it was not to face it alone, but to seek help. He seemed hell-bent on handling it himself, and more often than not, such a course would end in failure.

No, if she were smart, she'd pack up her beach bag right now and get the heck out of there.

Instead, she put more sunblock on her face. "I went into your kitchen to help Natasha load the cooler with soda," she said. "And I noticed you had only one thing stuck onto your refrigerator. A list."

He glanced at her, his expression one of wariness. "Yeah?"

"I wasn't sure," she said, "but...it looked like it might've been a list of things that you have difficulty doing with your injured knee."

The list had included things like run, jump, skydive, bike, and climb stairs.

He gazed out at the ocean, squinting slightly in the brightness. "That's right."

"You forgot to include that you're no longer able to play on the Olympic basketball team, so I added that to the bottom," she said, her tongue firmly in her cheek.

He let loose a short burst of air that might've been called a laugh if he'd been smiling. "Very funny. If you'd looked carefully, you'd have noticed that the word *walk* was at the top. I crossed it off when I could walk. I intend to do the same with the rest of those things on that list."

His eyes were the same fierce shade of blue as the sky.

Mia rolled onto her stomach and propped her chin up in her hands. "Tell me about this amazing pink couch," she said. "What's that all about?"

This time Frisco *did* laugh, and the lines around his eyes crinkled with genuine amusement. He stretched out next to her on the blanket, making sure he could still see Tasha from where they lay. "Oh, that," he said. "It's gonna look great in my living room, don't you think? Dirt brown and ugly green go real well with pink and silver."

Mia smiled. "You'll have to redecorate. Maybe a white carpet and lots of Art Deco type mirrors on the walls would work."

"And it would be so me," he said, deadpan.

"Seriously, though," Mia said. "If anything will give Tasha incentive to follow your rules, that will. She's only mentioned it five thousand times today already."

"Tell me the truth," Frisco said, supporting his head with one hand as he gazed at her. "Did I go too far? Did I cross the line from positive reinforcement into sheer bribery?"

Mia shook her head, caught in the intense blue of his eyes. "You're giving her the opportunity to earn something that she truly wants, along with learning an important lesson about following rules. That's not bribery."

"I feel like I'm taking the point and heading into totally uncharted territory," Frisco admitted.

Mia didn't understand. "Taking the point...?"

"If you take the point, if you're the pointman," he explained, "that means you lead the squad. You're the first guy out there—the first guy either to locate or step on any booby traps or land mines. It's a pretty intense job."

"At least you know that Natasha's not suddenly going to explode."

Frisco smiled. "Are you sure about that?"

With amusement dancing in his eyes, a smile softening his face and the ocean breeze gently ruffling his hair, Frisco looked like the kind of man Mia would go far out of her way to meet. He looked charming and friendly and pleasant and sinfully handsome.

"You're doing a wonderful job with Tasha," she told him. "You're being remarkably consistent in dealing with her. I know how hard it is not to lose your temper when she disobeys you—I've seen you swallow it, and I know that's not easy. And giving her that medal—that was brilliant." She sat up, reaching for the T-shirt Tasha had been wearing over her bathing suit. "Look." She held it up so he could see. "She's so proud of that medal, she asked me to pin it onto this shirt for her so she could wear it to the beach. If you keep this up, it's only a matter of time before she'll remember to follow your rules."

Frisco had rolled over onto his back and was shielding his eyes from the glare of the sun with one hand as he looked up at her. He sat up now, in one smooth effortless motion, glancing back at Natasha, checking briefly to be sure the little girl was safe.

She was crouched in the sand halfway between the blanket and the water, starting a new dribble castle.

"I'm doing a wonderful job and I'm brilliant?" he said with a half smile. "Sounds like you're giving *me* a little positive reinforcement here."

Natasha's T-shirt was damp and Mia spread it out on top of the cooler to dry in the sun. "Well...maybe," she admitted with a sheepish smile.

He touched her gently under her chin, pulling her head up so that she was forced to look at him.

His smile had faded, and the amusement in his eyes was gone, replaced by something else entirely, something hot and dangerous and impossible to turn away from.

"I like my positive reinforcement delivered a little differently," he told her, his voice no more than a husky whisper.

His gaze flickered down to her mouth, then up again to meet her eyes, and Mia knew that he was going to kiss her. He leaned forward slowly, giving her plenty of time to back away. But she didn't move. She couldn't move. Or maybe she just plain didn't want to move.

She felt him sigh as his lips met hers. His mouth was warm and sweet, and he kissed her so softly. He touched her lips gently with his tongue, waiting until she granted him access before he deepened the kiss. And even then, even as she opened herself to him, he kissed her breathtakingly tenderly.

It was the sweetest kiss she'd ever shared.

He pulled back to look into her eyes, and she could feel her heart pounding. But then he smiled, one of his beautiful, heart-stoppingly perfect crooked smiles, as if he'd just found gold at the end of a rainbow. And this time she reached for him, wrapping her arms up around his neck, pressing herself against him, stabbing her fingers up into the incredible softness of his hair as she kissed him again.

This time it was pure fire. This time he touched her with more than just his lips, pulling her even harder against his chest, running his hands along the bare skin of her back, through her hair, down her arms as he met her tongue in a kiss of wild, bone-melting intensity.

"Frisco! Frisco! The ice-cream truck is here! Can I get an ice cream?"

Mia pushed Frisco away from her even as he released her. He was breathing as hard as she was, and he looked thoroughly shaken. But Natasha was oblivious to everything but the ice-cream truck that had pulled into the beach parking lot.

"Please, please, please, please, please," she was saying, running in circles around and around the beach blanket.

Frisco looked up toward the end of the beach, where the ice-cream truck was parked, and then back at Mia. He looked as shocked and as stunned as she felt. "Uh," he said. He leaned toward her and spoke quickly, in a low voice. "Can you take her? I can't."

"Of course." She quickly pulled on her T-shirt. God, her hands were shaking. She glanced up at him. "Is your knee all right?"

He dug a five-dollar bill out of his wallet and handed it to her with a weak grin. "Actually, it has nothing to do with my knee."

Suddenly Mia understood. She felt her cheeks heat with a blush. "Come on, Tasha," she said, pulling her hair out from the collar of her T-shirt as she led the little girl up the beach.

What had she just done?

She'd just experienced both the sweetest and the most arousing kisses of her entire life—with a man she'd vowed to stay away from. Mia stood in line with Tasha at the ice-cream truck, trying to figure out her next move.

Getting involved with Frisco was entirely out of the question. But, oh, those kisses... Mia closed her eyes. Mistake, she told herself over and over. She'd already made the mistake—to continue in this direction would be sheer foolishness. So okay. He was an amazing mixture of sweetness and sexiness. But he was a man who needed saving, and she knew better than to think she could save him. To become involved would only pull her under, too. Only he could save himself from his unhappiness and despair, and only time would tell if he'd succeed.

She'd have to be honest with him. She'd have to make sure he understood.

In a fog, she ordered Tasha's ice cream and two ice bars for herself and Frisco. The trek back to the blanket seemed endlessly long. The sand seemed hotter than before and her feet burned. Tasha went back to her sand castle, ice cream dripping down her chin.

Frisco was sitting on the edge of the blanket, soaking wet, as if he'd thrown himself into the ocean to cool down. That was good. Mia wanted him cooled down, didn't she?

She handed him the ice pop and tried to smile as she sat down. "I figured we could all use something to cool us off, but you beat me to it."

Frisco looked at Mia, sitting as far from him as she possibly could on the beach blanket, and then down at the ice bar in his hands. "I kind of liked the heat we were generating," he said quietly.

Mia shook her head, unable even to look him in the eye. "I have to be honest. I hardly even know you and…"

He stayed silent, just waiting for her to go on.

"I don't think we should… I mean, I think it would be a mistake to…" She was blushing again.

"Okay." Frisco nodded. "That's okay. I…I understand." He couldn't blame her. How could he blame her? She wasn't the type who went for short-term ecstasy. If she played the game, it would be for keeps, and face it, he wasn't a keeper. He was not the kind of man Mia would want to be saddled with for the rest of her life. She was so full of life, and he was forced to move so slowly. She was so complete; he was less than whole.

"I should probably get home," she said, starting to gather up her things.

"We'll walk you back," he said quietly.

"Oh, no—you don't have to."

"Yeah, we do, okay?"

She glanced up at him, and something she saw in his eyes or on his face made her know not to argue. "All right."

Frisco stood up, reaching for his cane. "Come on, Tash, let's go into the water one last time and wash that ice cream off your face."

He tossed the unopened ice pop into a garbage can as he walked Natasha down to the ocean. He stared out at the water and tried his damnedest not to think about Mia as Tasha rinsed the last of her ice cream from her face and hands. But he couldn't do it. He could still taste her, still feel her in his arms, still smell her spicy perfume.

And for those moments that he'd kissed her, for those incredible few minutes that she'd been in his arms, for the first time since the last dose of heavy-duty pain medication had worn off five years ago, he'd actually forgotten about his injured knee.

Natasha didn't seem to notice the awkward silence. She chattered on, to Mia, to Frisco, to no one in particular. She sang snatches of songs and chanted bits of rhymes.

Mia felt miserable. Rejection was never fun, from either the giving or the receiving end. She knew she'd hurt Frisco by backing away. But her worst mistake had been to let him kiss her in the first place.

She wished she'd insisted that they take her car to the beach, rather than walk. Frisco was a master at hiding his pain, but she could tell from the subtle changes in the way he held himself and the way he breathed that he was hurting.

Mia closed her eyes briefly, trying not to care, but she couldn't. She *did* care. She cared far too much.

"I'm sorry," she murmured to Frisco as Natasha skipped ahead of them, hopping over the cracks in the sidewalk.

He turned and looked at her with those piercing blue eyes that seemed to see right through to her very soul. "You really are, aren't you?"

She nodded.

"I'm sorry, too," he said quietly.

"Frisco!" Natasha launched herself at him, nearly knocking him over.

"Whoa!" he said, catching her in his left arm while he used his right to balance both of their weight with his cane. "What's wrong, Tash?"

The little girl had both of her arms wrapped tightly around his waist, and she was hiding her face in his T-shirt.

"Tash, what's going on?" Frisco asked again, but she didn't move. Short of yanking the child away from himself, he couldn't get her to release him.

Mia crouched down next to the little girl. "Natasha, did something scare you?"

She nodded yes.

Mia pushed Tasha's red curls back from her face. "Honey, what scared you?"

Tasha lifted her head, looking at Mia with tear-filled eyes. "Dwayne," she whispered. "I saw Dwayne."

Mia looked up at Frisco, frowning her confusion. "Who…?"

"One of Sharon's old boyfriends." He pulled Natasha up and into his arms. "Tash, you probably just saw someone who reminded you of him."

Natasha shook her head emphatically as Mia stood up. "I saw Dwayne," she said again, tears overflowing onto her cheeks and great gulping sobs making her nearly impossible to understand. "I saw him."

"What would he be doing here in San Felipe?" Frisco asked the little girl.

"He'd be looking for Sharon Francisco," a low voice drawled. "That's what he'd be doing here."

Natasha was suddenly, instantly silent.

Mia gazed at the man standing directly in front of them. He was a big man, taller and wider even than Frisco, but softer and heavily overweight. He was wearing a dark business suit that had to have been hand tailored to fit his girth, and lizard-skin boots that were buffed to a gleaming shine. His shirt was dark gray—a slightly lighter shade of the same black of his suit, and his tie was a color that fell somewhere between the two. His hair was thick and dark, and it tumbled forward into is eyes in a style reminiscent of Elvis Presley. His face was ifty pounds too heavy to be called handsome, with a distinctive hawklike nose and deep-set eyes that were now lost among the puffiness of his excess flesh.

In one big, beefy hand, he held a switchblade knife that he opened and closed, opened and closed, with a rhythmic hiss of metal on metal.

"My sister's not here," Frisco said evenly.

Mia felt him touch her shoulder, and she turned toward him. His eyes never left Dwayne and the knife in the man's right hand as he handed her Natasha. "Get behind me," he murmured. "And start backing away."

"I can see that your sister's not here," the heavy man had a thick New Orleans accent. The gentlemanly old South politeness of his speech somehow made him seem all the more frightening. "But since you have the pleasure of her daughter's company, I must assume you know of her whereabouts."

"Why don't you leave me your phone number," Frisco suggested, "and I'll have her call you."

Dwayne flicked his knife open again, and this time he didn't close it. "I'm afraid that's unacceptable. You see, she owes me a great deal of money." He smiled. "Of course, I could always take the child as collateral...."

Frisco could still sense Mia's presence behind him. He heard her sharp intake of breath. "Mia, take Tash into the deli on the corner and call the police," he told her without turning around.

He felt her hesitation and anxiety, felt the coolness of her fingers as she touched his arm. "Alan..."

"Do it," he said sharply.

Mia began backing away. Her heart was pounding as she watched Frisco smile pleasantly at Dwayne, always keeping his eyes on that knife. "You know I'd die before I'd let you even touch the girl," the former SEAL said matter-of-factly. Mia knew that what he said was true. She prayed it wouldn't come to that.

"Why don't you just tell me where Sharon is?" Dwayne

asked. "I'm not interested in beating the hell out of a poor, pathetic cripple, but I will if I have to."

"The same way you had to hit a five-year-old?" Frisco countered. Everything about him—his stance, his face, the look in his eyes, the tone of his voice—was deadly. Despite the cane in his hand, despite his injured knee, he looked anything but poor and pathetic.

But Dwayne had a knife, and Frisco only had his cane—which he needed to use to support himself.

Dwayne lunged at Frisco, and Mia turned and ran for the deli.

Frisco saw Mia's sudden movement from the corner of his eye. Thank God. It would be ten times easier to fight this enormous son of a bitch knowing that Mia and Tash were safe and out of the way.

Dwayne lunged with the knife again, and Frisco sidestepped him, gritting his teeth against the sudden screaming pain as his knee was forced to twist and turn in ways that it no longer could. He used his cane and struck the heavyset man on the wrist, sending the sharp-bladed knife skittering into the street.

He realized far too late that he had played right into Dwayne's hand. With his cane up and in the air, he couldn't use it to support himself. And Dwayne came at him again, spinning and turning with the graceful agility of a much smaller, lighter man. Frisco watched, almost in slow motion, as his opponent aimed a powerful karate kick directly at his injured knee.

He saw it coming, but as if he, too, were caught in slow motion, he couldn't move out of the way.

And then there was only pain. Sheer, blinding, excruciating pain. Frisco felt a hoarse cry rip from his throat as he went down, hard, onto the sidewalk. He fought the darkness that threatened to close in on him as he felt Dwayne's foot connect violently with his side, this time damn near launching him into the air.

Somehow he held on to the heavy man's leg. Somehow he

brought his own legs up and around, twisting and kicking and tripping, until Dwayne, too, fell onto the ground.

There were no rules. One of Dwayne's elbows landed squarely in Frisco's face, and he felt his nose gush with blood. He struggled to keep the bigger man's weight off of him, trying to keep Dwayne pinned as he hit him in the face again and again.

Another, smaller man would've been knocked out, but Dwayne was like one of those pop-up punching bag dolls. He just kept coming. The son of a bitch went for his knee again. There was no way he could miss, and again pain ripped into Frisco like a freight train. He grabbed hold of Dwayne's head and slammed it back against the sidewalk.

There were sirens in the distance—Frisco heard them through waves of nausea and dizziness. The police were coming.

Dwayne should have been out for the count, but he scrambled up and onto his feet.

"You tell Sharon I want that money back," he said through bruised and bleeding lips before he limped away.

Frisco tried to go after him, but his knee crumbled beneath his weight, sending another wave of searing pain blasting through him. He felt himself retch and he pressed his cheek against the sidewalk to make the world stop spinning.

A crowd had gathered, he suddenly realized. Someone pushed through the mob, running toward him. He tensed, moving quickly into a defensive position.

"Yo, Lieutenant! Whoa, back off, Navy, it's me, *Thomas.*"

It was. It was Thomas. The kid crouched down next to Frisco on the sidewalk.

"Who ran *you* over with a truck? My God..." Thomas stood up again, looking into the crowd. "Hey, someone call an ambulance for my friend! *Now!*"

Frisco reached for Thomas.

"Yeah, I'm here, man. I'm here, Frisco. I saw this big guy running away—he looked only a little bit better than you do,"

Thomas told him. "What happened? You make some kind of uncalled-for fat joke?"

"Mia," Frisco rasped. "She's got Natasha...at the deli. Stay with them...make sure they're okay."

"You're the one who looks like you need help—"

"I'm *fine*," Frisco ground out between clenched teeth. "If you won't go to them, I will." He searched for his cane. Where the hell was his cane? It was in the street. He crawled toward it, dragging his injured leg.

"God," Thomas said. His eyes were wide in amazement that Frisco could even move. For once he actually looked only eighteen years old. "You stay here, I'll go find them. If it's that important to you..."

"Run," Frisco told him.

Thomas ran.

9

The hospital emergency room was crowded. Mia was ignored by the nurses at the front desk, so she finally gave up and simply walked into the back. She was stepped around, pushed past and nearly knocked over as she searched for Frisco.

"Excuse me, I'm looking for—"

"Not now, dear," a nurse told her, briskly moving down the hallway.

Mia heard him before she saw him. His voice was low, and his language was abominable. It was definitely Alan Francisco.

She followed the sound of his voice into a big room that held six beds, all filled. He was sitting up, his right leg stretched out in front of him, his injured knee swollen and bruised. His T-shirt was covered with blood, he had a cut on his cheekbone directly underneath his right eye and his elbows and other knee looked abraded and raw.

A doctor was examining his knee. "That hurt, too?" he asked, glancing up at Frisco.

Yes, was the gist of the reply, minus all of the colorful superlatives. A new sheen of sweat had broken out on Frisco's face, and he wiped at his upper lip with the back of one hand as he braced himself for the rest of the examination.

"I thought you promised Tasha no more bad words."

Startled, he looked up, and directly into her eyes. "What are you doing here? Where's Tash?"

Mia had surprised him. And not pleasantly, either. She

could see a myriad of emotions flicker across his face. Embarrassment. Shame. Humiliation. She knew he didn't want her to see him like this, looking beaten and bloodied.

"She's with Thomas," Mia told him. "I thought you might want…" What? She thought he might want a hand to hold? No, she already knew him well enough to know he wouldn't need or want that. She shook her head. She'd come here purely for herself. "*I* wanted to make sure you were all right."

"I'm fine."

"You don't look fine."

"Depends on your definition of the word," he said. "In my book, it means I'm not dead."

"Excuse me, miss, but is Mr. Francisco a friend of yours?" It was the doctor. "Perhaps you'll be able to convince him to take the pain medication we've offered him."

Mia shook her head. "No, I don't think I'll be able to do that. He's extremely stubborn—and it's Lieutenant, not Mr. If he's decided that he doesn't want it—"

"Yes, he *has* decided he doesn't want it," Frisco interjected. "And he also *hates* being talked about as if he weren't in the room, so do you mind…?"

"The medication would make him rest much more comfortably—"

"Look, all I want you to do is X-ray my damn knee and make sure it's not broken. Do you think *maybe* you can do that?"

"He's a lieutenant in which organization?" the doctor asked Mia.

"Please ask him directly," she said. "Surely you can respect him and not talk over his head this way."

"I'm with the Navy SEALs—*was* with the SEALs," Frisco said.

The doctor snapped closed Frisco's patient clipboard. "Perfect. I should have known. Nurse!" he shouted, already striding away. "Send this man to X-ray, and then arrange a transfer over to the VA facility up by the naval base.…"

Frisco was watching Mia, and when she turned to look at him, he gave her a half smile. "Thanks for trying."

"Why don't you take the pain medicine?" she asked.

"Because I don't want to be stoned and drooling when Dwayne comes back for round two."

Mia couldn't breathe. "Comes back?" she repeated. "Why? Who was he anyway? And what did he want?"

Frisco shifted his weight, unable to keep from wincing. "Apparently my darling sister owes him some money."

"How much money?"

"I don't know, but I'm going to find out." He shook his head. "I'm gonna pay Sharon a little visit in the morning—to hell with the detox center's rules."

"When I saw that knife he was holding..." Mia's voice shook and she stopped. She closed her eyes, willing back the sudden rush of tears. She couldn't remember the last time she'd been that scared. "I didn't want to leave you there alone."

She opened her eyes to find him watching her, the expression on his face unreadable. "Didn't you think I could take that guy and win?" he asked softly.

She didn't need to answer him—she knew he could read her reply in her eyes. She knew how painful it was for him to walk, even with a cane. She knew his limitations. How could he have taken on a man as big as Dwayne—a man who had a knife, as well—and not been hurt? And he *had* been hurt. Badly, it looked like.

He laughed bitterly, looking away from her. "No wonder you damn near ran away from me on the beach. You don't think I'm much of a man, do you?"

Mia was shocked. "That's not true! That's not why—"

"Time to go down to X-ray," a nurse announced, pushing a wheelchair up to Frisco's bed.

Frisco didn't wait for the nurse to help him. He lifted himself off the bed and lowered himself into the chair. He jostled his knee, and it had to have hurt like hell, but he didn't say a word. When he looked up at Mia, though, she could see all of his pain in his eyes. "Just go home," he said quietly.

"They're backed up down there—this could take a while, a few hours even," the nurse informed Mia as she began pushing Frisco out of the room. "You can't come with him, so you'll just be sitting out in the waiting room. If you want to leave, he could call you when he's done."

"No, thank you," Mia said. She turned to Frisco. "Alan, you are *so* wrong about—"

"Just go home," he said again.

"No," she said. "No, I'm going to wait for you."

"Don't," he said. He glanced up at her just before the nurse pushed him out the door. "And don't call me Alan."

Frisco rode in the wheelchair back to the ER lobby with his eyes closed. His X-rays had taken a few aeons longer than forever, and he had to believe Mia had given up on him and gone home.

It was nearly eight o'clock at night. He was still supposed to meet with the doctor to talk about what his X-rays had shown. But he'd seen the film and already knew what the doctor was going to say. His knee wasn't broken. It was bruised and inflamed. There may have been ligament damage, but it was hard to tell—his injury and all of his subsequent surgeries had left things looking pretty severely scrambled.

The doctor was going to recommend shipping him over to the VA hospital for further consultation and possible treatment.

But that was going to have to wait. He had Natasha at home to take care of, and some lunatic named Dwayne to deal with.

"Where are you taking him?" It was Mia's musical voice. She was still here, waiting for him, just as she'd said. Frisco didn't know whether to feel relieved or disappointed. He kept his eyes closed, and tried not to care too much either way.

"The doctor has to take a look at the X-rays," the nurse told her. "We're overcrowded tonight. Depending on how things go, it could be another five minutes or two hours."

"May I sit with him?" Mia asked.

"Sure," the nurse said. "He can wait out here as well as anyplace else."

Frisco felt his wheelchair moved awkwardly into position, heard the nurse walk away. Then he felt Mia's cool fingers touch his forehead, pushing his hair back and off his face.

"I know you're not really asleep," she said.

Her hand felt so good in his hair. Too good. Frisco reached up and caught her wrist as he opened his eyes, pushing her away from him. "That's right," he said. "I'm just shutting everything out."

She was gazing at him with eyes that were a perfect mixture of green and brown. "Well, before you shut me out again, I want you to know—I don't judge whether or not someone is a *man* based on his ability to beat an opponent into a bloody pulp. And I wasn't running away from *you* on the beach today."

Frisco shut his eyes again. "Look, you don't have to explain why you don't want to sleep with me. If you don't, then you don't. That's all I need to know."

"I was running away from myself," she said very softly, a catch in her voice.

Frisco opened his eyes. She was looking at him with tears in her beautiful eyes and his heart lurched. "Mia, don't, really...it's all right." It wasn't, but he would have said or done anything to keep her from crying.

"No, it's not," she said. "I really want to be your friend, but I don't know if I can. I've been sitting here for the past few hours, just thinking about it, and..." She shook her head and a tear escaped down her cheek.

Frisco was lost. His chest felt so tight, he could barely breathe, and he knew the awful truth. He was glad Mia had waited for him. He was glad she'd come to the hospital. Yeah, he'd also been mortified that she'd seen him like this, but at the same time, her presence had made him feel good. For the first time in forever he didn't feel so damned alone.

But now he'd somehow made her cry. He reached for her,

cupping her face with his hand and brushing away that tear with his thumb. "It's not that big a deal," he whispered.

"No?" she said, looking up at him. She closed her eyes and pressed her cheek more fully into the palm of his hand. She turned her head slightly and brushed his fingers with her lips. When she opened her eyes again, he could see a fire burning, white-hot and molten. All sweetness, all girlish innocence was gone from her face. She was all woman, pure female desire as she gazed back at him.

His mouth went totally, instantly dry.

"You touch me, even just like this, and I feel it," she said huskily. "This chemistry—it's impossible to ignore."

She was right, and he couldn't help himself. He pushed his hand up and into the softness of her long, dark hair. She closed her eyes again at the sensation, and he felt his heart begin to pound.

"I know you feel it, too," she whispered.

Frisco nodded. Yes. He traced the soft curve of her ear, then let his hand slide down her neck. Her skin was so smooth, like satin beneath his fingers.

But then she reached for his hand, intertwining their fingers, squeezing his hand, breaking the spell. "But for me, that's not enough," she told him. "I need more than sexual chemistry. I need...love."

Silence. Big, giant silence. Frisco could hear his heart beating and the rush of his blood through his veins. He could hear the sounds of other people in the waiting room—hushed conversations, a child's quiet crying. He could hear a distant television, the clatter of an empty gurney being wheeled too quickly down the hall.

"I can't give you that," he told her.

"I know," she said softly. "And that's why I ran away." She smiled at him, so sweetly, so sadly. The seductive temptress was gone, leaving behind this nice girl who wanted more than he could give her, who knew enough not even to ask.

Or maybe she knew enough not to *want* to ask. He was no prize. He wasn't even whole.

She released his hand, and he immediately missed the warmth of her touch.

"I see they finally got you cleaned up," she said.

"I did it myself," he told her, amazed they could sit here talking like this after what she'd just revealed. "I went into the bathroom near the X-ray department and washed up."

"What happens next?" Mia asked.

What had she just revealed? Nothing, really, when it came down to it. She'd admitted that the attraction between them was powerful. She'd told him that she was looking for more than sex, that she wanted a relationship based on love. But she hadn't said that she wanted *him* to love her.

Maybe she was glossing over the truth. Maybe she'd simply omitted the part about how, even if he *was* capable of giving her what she wanted, she had no real interest in any kind of a relationship with some crippled has-been.

"The doctor will look at my X-rays and he'll tell me that nothing's broken," Frisco told her. "Nothing he can see, anyway."

How much of that fight had she seen? he wondered. Had she seen Dwayne drop him with a single well-placed blow to his knee? Had she seen him hit the sidewalk like a stone? Had she seen Dwayne kick him while he was down there, face against the concrete like some pathetic hound dog too dumb to get out of the way?

And look at him now, back in a wheelchair. He'd sworn he'd never sit in one of these damned things again, yet here he was.

"Dammit, Lieutenant, when I sent you home to rest, I meant you should *rest,* not start a new career as a street fighter." Captain Steven Horowitz was wearing his white dress uniform and he gleamed in the grimy ER waiting room. What the hell was *he* doing here?

"Dr. Wright called and said he had a former patient of mine in his emergency room, waiting to get his knee X-rayed. He said this patient's knee was swollen and damaged from a previous injury, and on top of that, it looked as if it had recently

been hit with a sledgehammer. Although apparently this patient claimed there were no sledgehammers involved in the
fight he'd been in,'' Horowitz said, arms folded across his
chest. ''The *fight* he'd been in. And I asked myself, now,
which of my former knee-injury patients would be *stupid*
enough to put himself into a threatening situation like a *fight*
that might irrevocably damage his injured knee? I came up
with Alan Francisco before Wright even mentioned your
name.''

''Nice to see you, too, Steve,'' Frisco said, wearily running
his hand through his hair, pushing it off his face. He could
feel Mia watching him, watching the Navy captain.

''What were you thinking?''

''Allow me to introduce Mia Summerton,'' Frisco said.
''Mia, I know you're going to be disappointed, but as much
as Steve looks like it, he *isn't* the White Power Ranger. He's
really only just a Navy doctor. His name's Horowitz. He answers to Captain, Doctor, Steve, and sometimes even God.''

Steven Horowitz was several years older than Frisco, but
he had an earnestness about him that made him seem quite a
bit younger. Frisco watched him do a double take as he looked
at Mia, with her long, dark hair, her beautiful face, her pretty
flowered sundress that revealed her smooth, tanned shoulders
and her slender, graceful arms. He watched Steve look back
at his own bloody T-shirt and battered face. He knew what
the doctor was thinking—what was *she* doing with him?

Nothing. She was doing nothing. She'd made that more
than clear.

Horowitz turned back to Frisco. ''I looked at the X-rays—
I think you may have been lucky, but I won't be able to know
for certain until the swelling goes down.'' He pulled a chair
over, and looked at the former SEAL's knee, probing it lightly
with gentle fingers.

Frisco felt himself start to sweat. From the corner of his
eye, he saw Mia lean forward, as if she were going to reach
for his hand. But he closed his eyes, refusing to look at her,
refusing to need her.

She took his hand anyway, holding it tightly until Steve was through. By then, Frisco was drenched with sweat again, and he knew his face must've looked gray or maybe even green. He let go of her hand abruptly, suddenly aware that he was damn near mashing her fingers.

"All right," Steve finally said with a sigh. "Here's what I want you to do. I want you to go home, and I want you to stay off your feet for the next two weeks." He took his prescription pad from his leather bag. "I'll give you something to make you sleep—"

"And I won't take it," Frisco said. "I have a...situation to deal with."

"What kind of situation?"

Frisco shook his head. "It's a family matter. My sister's in some kind of trouble. All you need to know is that I'm not taking anything that's going to make me sleep. I won't object to a local painkiller, though."

Steven Horowitz laughed in disgust. "If I give you that, your knee won't hurt. And if your knee doesn't hurt, you're going to be up running laps, doing God knows what kind of damage. No. No way."

Frisco leaned forward, lowering his voice, wishing Mia weren't listening, hating himself for having to admit his weaknesses. "Steve, you know I wouldn't ask for it if I weren't in serious pain. I *need* it, man. I can't risk taking the stuff that will knock me out."

The doctor's eyes were a flat, pale blue, but for a brief moment, Frisco saw a flare of warmth and compassion behind the customary chill. Steve shook his head. "I'm going to regret doing this. I *know* I'm going to regret doing this." He scribbled something on his pad. "I'm going to give you something to bring down the swelling, too. Go easy with it." He glared at Frisco. "In return, you have to *promise* me you won't get out of this wheelchair for two weeks."

Frisco shook his head. "I can't promise that," he said. "In fact, I'd rather die than stay in this chair for a minute longer than I have to."

Dr. Horowitz turned to Mia. "His knee has already been permanently damaged. It's something of a miracle that he can even walk at all. There's nothing he can do to make his knee any better, but he *could* make things worse. Will you please try to make him understand—"

"We're just friends," she interrupted. "I can't make him do anything."

"Crutches," Frisco said. "I'll use crutches, but no chair, all right?"

He didn't look at Mia. But he couldn't stop thinking about the way her eyes had looked filled with tears, and the way that had made him feel. She was wrong. She was dead wrong. She didn't know it, but she had the power to damn well make him do anything.

Maybe even fall in love with her.

Mia pulled the car up near the emergency room entrance. She could see Frisco through the windows of the brightly lit lobby, talking to the doctor. The doctor handed Frisco a bag, and then the two men shook hands. The doctor vanished quickly down the hallway, while Frisco moved slowly on his crutches toward the automatic door.

It slid open with a whoosh, and then he was outside, looking around.

Mia opened the car door and stood up. "Over here." She saw his surprise. This wasn't her car. This thing was about twice the size of her little subcompact—he wouldn't have any trouble fitting inside it. "I traded cars with a friend for a few days," she explained.

He didn't say a word. He just put the bag the doctor had given him into the middle of the wide bench seat and slid his crutches into the back. He climbed in carefully, lowering himself down and using both hands to lift his injured leg into the car.

She got in next to him, started the powerful engine and pulled out of the driveway. She glanced at Frisco. "How's your knee doing?"

"Fine," he said tersely.

"Do you really think Dwayne's going to come back?"

"Yep."

Mia waited for him to elucidate, but he didn't continue. He obviously wasn't in a talkative mood. Not that he ever was, of course. But somehow the fairly easygoing candidness of their previous few conversations had vanished.

She knew his knee was anything but fine. She knew it hurt him badly—and that the fact that he'd been unable to defeat his attacker hurt him even more.

She knew that his injured knee and his inability to walk without a cane made him feel like less of a man. It was idiotic. A man was made up of so much more than a pair of strong legs and an athletic body.

It was idiotic, but she understood. Suddenly she understood that the list she'd seen on Frisco's refrigerator of all the things he couldn't do wasn't simply pessimistic whining, as she'd first thought. It was a recipe. It was specific directions for a magical spell that would make Frisco a man again.

Jump, run, skydive, swim, stretch, bend, extend...

Until he could do all those things and more, he wasn't going to feel like a man.

Until he could do all those things again... But he wasn't going to. That Navy doctor had said he wasn't going to get any better. This was it. Frisco had come as far as he could—and the fact that he could walk at all was something of a miracle at that.

Mia pulled the car into the condominium parking lot and parked. Frisco didn't wait for her to help him out of the car. Of course not. Real men didn't need help.

Her heart ached for him as she watched him pull out his crutches from the back seat. He grimly positioned them under his arms, and carrying the bag that the doctor had given him, swung toward the courtyard.

She followed more slowly.

Jump, run, skydive, swim, stretch, bend, extend...

It wasn't going to happen. Dr. Horowitz knew it. Mia knew it. And she suspected that deep inside, Frisco knew it, too.

She followed him into the courtyard and could barely stand to watch as he pulled himself painfully up the stairs.

He was wrong. He was wrong about it all. Moving onto the ground floor wouldn't make him less of a man. Admitting that he had physical limitations—that there were things he could no longer do—that wouldn't make him less of a man, either.

But relentlessly questing after the impossible, making goals that were unattainable, setting himself up only for failure— that would wear him down and burn him out. It would take away the last of his warmth and spark, leaving him bitter and angry and cold and incomplete. Leaving him less of a man.

10

Frisco sat in the living room, cleaning his handgun.

When Sharon's charming ex-boyfriend Dwayne had pulled out his knife this afternoon, Frisco had felt, for the first time in a while, the noticeable lack of a sidearm.

Of course, carrying a weapon meant concealing that weapon. Although he was fully licensed to carry whatever he damn well pleased, he couldn't exactly wear a weapon in a belt holster, like a cop or an old West gunslinger. And wearing a shoulder holster meant he'd have to wear a jacket over it, at least out in public. And—it was a chain reaction—if he wore a jacket, he'd have to wear long pants. Even *he* couldn't wear a jacket with shorts.

Of course, he could always do what Blue McCoy did. Blue was the Alpha Squad's XO—Executive Officer and second in command of the SEAL unit. Blue rarely wore anything other than cutoffs and an old worn-out, loose olive-drab fatigue shirt with the sleeves removed. And he always wore one of the weapons he carried in a shoulder holster underneath his shirt, the smooth leather directly against his skin.

Frisco's knee twinged, and he glanced at the clock. It was nearly 0300. Three o'clock in the morning.

Steve Horowitz had given him a number of little vials filled with a potent local pain reliever similar to novocaine. It wasn't yet time for another injection, but it was getting close. Frisco had given himself an injection at close to nine o'clock, after Mia had driven him home from the hospital.

Mia...

Frisco shook his head, determined to think about anything but Mia, separated from him by only a few thin walls, her hair spread across her pillow, wearing only a tantalizingly thin cotton nightgown. Her beautiful soft lips parted slightly in sleep....

Yeah, he was a master at self-torture. He'd been sitting here, awake for hours, spending most of his time remembering—hell, *reliving*—the way Mia had kissed him at the beach. Dear, sweet God, what a kiss that had been.

It wasn't likely he was going to get a chance to kiss her like that again. She'd made it clear that she wouldn't welcome a repeat performance. If he knew what was best, he'd stay far, far away from Mia Summerton. That wasn't going to be hard to do. From now on, she was going to be avoiding him, too.

A loud thump from the bedroom made him sit up. What the hell was that?

Frisco grabbed his crutches and his handgun and moved as quickly as he could down the hall to Tasha's room.

He'd bought a cheap portable TV. It was quite possibly the most expensive night-light and white noise machine in the world. Its bluish light flickered, illuminating the small room.

Natasha was sitting on the floor, next to her bed, sleepily rubbing her eyes and her head. She was whimpering, but only very softly. Her voice almost didn't carry above the soft murmurings of the television.

"Poor Tash, did you fall out of bed?" Frisco asked her, moving awkwardly through the narrow doorway and into the room. He slipped the safety onto his weapon and slid it into the pocket of his shorts. "Come on, climb back up. I'll tuck you in again."

But when Tasha stood up, she staggered, almost as if she'd had too much to drink, and sat back down on her rear end. As Frisco watched, she crumpled, pressing her forehead against the wall-to-wall carpeting.

Frisco leaned his crutches against the bed and bent down

to pick her up. "Tash, it's three in the morning. Don't play silly games."

Lord, the kid was on fire. Frisco felt her forehead, her cheek, her neck, double-checking, praying that he was wrong, praying that she was simply sweaty from a nightmare. But with each touch, he knew. Natasha had a raging fever.

He lifted her and put her in her bed.

How could this have happened? She'd been fine all day today. She'd had her swimming lesson with her usual enthusiasm. She'd gone back into the water over and over again with her usual energy. True, she'd been asleep when he'd returned from the hospital, but he'd chalked that up to exhaustion after the excitement of the day—watching Uncle Frisco get the living daylights kicked out of him by old, ugly Dwayne had surely been tiring for the kid.

Her eyes were half-closed and she pressed her head against her pillow as if it hurt, still making that odd, whimpering sound.

Frisco was scared to death. He tried to judge how high her fever was by the touch of his hand, and she seemed impossibly, dangerously hot.

"Tasha, talk to me," he said, sitting next to her on the bed. "Tell me what's wrong. Tell me your symptoms."

Cripes, listen to him. *Tell me your symptoms.* She was five years old, she didn't know what the hell a symptom was. And from the looks of things, she didn't even know she was here, couldn't hear him, couldn't see him.

He had medical training, but most of it was first-aid. He could handle gunshot wounds, knife wounds, burns and lacerations. But sick kids with sky-high fevers...

He had to get Natasha to the hospital.

He could call a cab, but man, he wouldn't be able to get Tasha down the stairs. He could barely make it himself with his crutches. He certainly couldn't do it carrying the girl, could he? It would be far too dangerous to try. What if he dropped her?

"I'll be right back, Tash," he told her, grabbing his

crutches and heading out toward the kitchen telephone, where he kept his phone book.

He flipped the book open, searching for the phone number for the local cab company. He quickly dialed. It rang at least ten times before someone picked up.

"Yellow Cab."

"Yeah," Frisco said. "I need a cab right away. 1210 Midfield Street, unit 2C. It's the condo complex on the corner of Midfield and Harris?"

"Destination?"

"City Hospital. Look I need the driver to come to the door. I got a little girl with a fever, and I'll need help carrying her down—"

"Sorry, sir. Our drivers do not leave their vehicles. He'll wait for you in the parking lot."

"Didn't you hear what I just said? This is an emergency. I have to get this kid to the hospital." Frisco ran his hand through his hair, trying to curb his anger and frustration. "I can't get her down the stairs by myself. I'm..." He nearly choked on the words. "I'm physically disabled."

"I'm sorry, sir. The rule is for our drivers' safety. However, the cab you requested will arrive in approximately ninety minutes."

"Ninety minutes? I can't wait *ninety* minutes!"

"Shall I cancel your request for a cab?"

"Yes." Cursing loudly, Frisco slammed down the phone.

He picked it up again and quickly dialed 911. It seemed to take forever before the line was picked up.

"What is the nature of your emergency?"

"I have a five-year-old with a very high fever."

"Is the child breathing?"

"Yes—"

"Is the child bleeding?"

"No, I said she's got a fever—"

"I'm sorry, sir. We have quite a number of priority calls and a limited number of ambulances. You'll get her to the hospital faster if you drive her yourself."

We'd like to send you two free books to introduce you to "The Best of the Best™." Your two books have a combined cover price of $11.98 or more in the U.S. and $13.98 or more in Canada, but they are yours free! We'll even send you a wonderful mystery gift. You can't lose!

#1 *New York Times* Bestselling author
SHARON SALA
Dark Water

New York Times Bestselling Author
JOAN JOHNSTON
SISTERS FOUND

Lifetime Surpassing A...ness
JASMINE CRESSWELL
Till death us do part
THE THIRD WIFE

MEG O'BRIEN
The bestselling author of *Gathering Lies*

Girls Night
"Indulge yourself—*Girls Night* is daring and irresistible."
—Joan Johnston, author of *Sisters Found*
STEF ANN HOLM

ROSEMARY ROGERS
NEW YORK TIMES BESTSELLING AUTHOR
AN HONORABLE MAN
In a sweeping new romance, one woman finds an ally in the man she loves to hate...and hates to love.

CRIMSON RAIN
Someone has unleashed a vengeful fury

FREE BONUS GIFT!

The **TWO FREE** books we send you will be selected from a variety of the **best** fiction - from romances to thrillers to family sagas - written by some of today's most popular authors!

We'll send you a wonderful surprise gift, absolutely FREE, just for giving "The Best of the Best" a try! Don't miss out — mail the reply card today!

2 Get FREE BOOKS!

Hurry!

Return this card promptly to GET 2 FREE BOOKS & A FREE GIFT!

The Best of the Best ™

YES! Please send me the 2 FREE "The Best of the Best" books and FREE gift for which I qualify. I understand that I am under no obligation to purchase anything further, as explained on the back and on the opposite page.

> Affix peel-off MIRA sticker here

385 MDL DRSU   185 MDL DRSQ

FIRST NAME	LAST NAME

ADDRESS

APT.#	CITY

STATE/PROV.	ZIP/POSTAL CODE

The Best of the Best™ — Here's How it Works:

Accepting your 2 free books and gift places you under no obligation to buy anything. You may keep the books and gift and return the shipping statement marked "cancel." If you do not cancel, about a month later we will send you 4 additional books and bill you just $4.74 each in the U.S., or $5.24 each in Canada, plus 25¢ shipping & handling per book and applicable taxes if any.* That's the complete price and — compared to cover prices starting from $5.99 each in the U.S. and $6.99 each in Canada — it's quite a bargain! You may cancel at any time, but if you choose to continue, every month we'll send you 4 more books, which you may either purchase at the discount price or return to us and cancel your subscription.

*Terms and prices subject to change without notice. Sales tax applicable in N.Y. Canadian residents will be charged applicable provincial taxes and GST. Credit or Debit balances in a customer's account(s) may be offset by any other outstanding balance owed by or to the customer.

If offer card is missing write to: The Best of the Best, 3010 Walden Ave., P.O. Box 1867, Buffalo, NY 14240-1867

BUSINESS REPLY MAIL
FIRST-CLASS MAIL   PERMIT NO. 717-003   BUFFALO NY

POSTAGE WILL BE PAID BY ADDRESSEE

THE BEST OF THE BEST
3010 WALDEN AVE
PO BOX 1867
BUFFALO NY 14240-9952

NO POSTAGE
NECESSARY
IF MAILED
IN THE
UNITED STATES

Frisco fought the urge to curse. "I don't have a car."

"Well, I can put you on the list, but since your situation isn't life or death per se, you risk being continuously bumped down as new calls come in," the woman told him. "Things usually slow down by dawn."

Dawn. "Forget it," Frisco said, hanging up none too gently.

Now what?

Mia. He was going to have to ask Mia for help.

He moved as quickly as he could back down the hall to Tasha's room. Her eyes were closed, but she was moving fitfully. She was still as hot to the touch. Maybe even hotter.

"Hang on, kid," Frisco said. "Hang on, princess. I'll be back in a sec."

He was starting to be able to move pretty nimbly with the crutches. He made it into the living room and out of the front door before he'd even had time to think.

But as he rang Mia's bell again and again, as he opened up the screen and hammered on the heavy wooden door, as he waited for her to respond, he couldn't help but wonder.

What the hell was he doing? He'd just spent the past six hours resolving to stay away from this woman. She didn't want him—she'd made that more than clear. So here he was, pounding on her door in the middle of the night, ready to humiliate himself even further by having to ask for help carrying a featherweight forty-pound little girl down the stairs.

The light went on inside Mia's apartment. She opened the door before she'd even finished putting on her bathrobe.

"Alan, what's wrong?"

"I need your help." She would never know how much it cost him to utter those words. It was only for Natasha that he would ask for help. If it had been himself in there, burning up with fever, he wouldn't've asked. He would have rather died. "Tasha's sick. She's got a really high fever—I want to take her over to the hospital."

"All right," Mia said without hesitation. "Let me throw

on a pair of shorts and some sneakers and I'll pull the ca
around to the outside stairs.''

She moved to go back toward her bedroom and her clothes
but he stopped her.

"Wait."

Mia turned back to the door. Frisco was standing on the
other side of the screen, crutches under his arms. He was
staring away from her, down at the carpeting. When he looked
up, all of his customary crystal anger was gone from his eyes
leaving only a deeply burning shame. He could barely hold
her gaze. He looked away, but then he forced himself to look
up again, this time steadily meeting her eyes.

"I can't carry her down the stairs."

Mia's heart was in her throat. She knew what it had taken
for him to say those words, and she so desperately didn't wan
to say the wrong thing in response. She didn't want to make
light of it, but at the same time, she didn't want to embarrass
him further by giving it too much weight.

"Of course not," she said quietly. "That would be dan
gerous to try on crutches. I'll get the car, then I'll come back
up for Natasha."

He nodded once and disappeared.

She'd said the right thing, but there was no time to sag with
relief. Mia dashed into her bedroom to change her clothes.

"An *ear* infection?" Frisco repeated, staring at the emer
gency room doctor.

This doctor was an intern, still in his twenties, but he had
a bedside manner reminiscent of an old-fashioned, elderly
country doctor, complete with twinkling blue eyes and a warm
smile.

"I already started her on an antibiotic, and I gave her some
thing to bring down that fever," he said, looking from Frisco
to Mia, "along with a decongestant. That'll keep her knocked
out for a while. Don't be surprised if she sleeps later than
usual in the morning."

"That's it?" Frisco asked. "It's just an ear infection?" He

looked down at Tasha, who was sound asleep, curled up in the hospital bed. She looked impossibly small and incredibly fragile, her hair golden red against the white sheets.

"She may continue to experience the dizziness you described for a day or two," the doctor told them. "Keep her in bed if you can, and make sure she finishes the *entire* bottle of antibiotic. Oh, and ear plugs next time she goes swimming, all right?"

Frisco nodded. "You sure you don't want to keep her here for a while?"

"I think she'll be more comfortable at home," the young doctor said. "Besides, her fever's already gone down. Call me if she doesn't continue to improve."

An ear infection. Not encephalitis. Not appendicitis. Not scarlet fever or pneumonia. It still hadn't fully sunk in. Tash was going to be all right. An ear infection wasn't life threatening. The kid wasn't going to die. Frisco still couldn't quite believe it. He couldn't quite shake the tight feeling in his chest—the incredible fear, the sense of total and complete helplessness.

He felt Mia touch his arm. "Let's get her home," she said quietly.

"Yeah," he said, looking around, trying to collect himself, wondering when the relief was going to set in and push away this odd sensation of tightness and fear. "I've had enough of this place for one day."

The ride home was shorter than he remembered. He watched as Mia carried Tash back up the stairs and into his condo. She gently placed the still sleeping child into bed, and covered her with a sheet and a light blanket. He watched, trying not to think about the fact that she was taking care of Tasha because he couldn't.

"You ought to try to get some sleep, too," Mia told him, whispering as they went back down the hallway to the living room. "It's nearly dawn."

Frisco nodded.

Mia's face was in the shadows as she stood at the doorway, looking back at him. "Are you all right?"

No. He wasn't all right. He nodded. "Yeah."

"Good night, then." She opened the screen door.

"Mia…"

She stopped, turning back to face him. She didn't say a word, she just waited for him to speak.

"Thank you." His voice was husky, and to his horror he suddenly had tears in his eyes. But it was dark in the predawn, and there was no way she could have noticed.

"You're welcome," she said quietly and closed the door behind her.

She disappeared, but the tears that flooded his eyes didn't do the same. Frisco couldn't stop them from overflowing and running down his face. A sob escaped him, shaking him, and like ice breaking up on a river, another followed, faster and harder until, God, he was crying like a baby.

He'd honestly thought Tasha was going to die.

He had been totally terrified. Him, Frisco, terrified. He'd gone on rescue missions and information-gathering expeditions deep into hostile territory where he could've been killed simply for being American. He'd sat in cafés and had lunch, surrounded by the very people who wouldn't have hesitated to slit his throat had they known his true identity. He'd infiltrated a terrorist fortress and snatched back a cache of stolen nuclear weapons. He'd looked death—his own death—in the eye on more than one occasion. He'd been plenty scared all those times; only a fool wouldn't have been. That fear had been sharp edged, keeping him alert and in control. But it was nothing compared to the sheer, helpless terror he'd felt tonight.

Frisco stumbled back into the sanctuary of his bedroom, unable to stanch the flow of his tears. He didn't want to cry, dammit. Tasha was safe. She was okay. He should have enough control over his emotions to keep the intensity of his relief from wiping him out this way.

He clenched his teeth and fought it. And lost.

Yeah, Tasha was safe. For now. But what if he hadn't been able to get her to the hospital? It had been good that he'd brought her in when he did, the doctor had said. Her fever had been on the verge of becoming dangerously high.

What if Mia hadn't been home? What if he hadn't been able to get Tash down the stairs? Or what if during the time he spent figuring out how to get Tash to the hospital, her fever *had* risen dangerously high? What if his inability to do something so simple as carry a child down a set of stairs had jeopardized her life? What if she had died, because he lived on the second floor? What if she had died, because he was too damn proud to admit the truth—that he was physically disabled.

He'd said the words tonight when he spoke to the cab dispatcher. *I'm physically disabled.* He wasn't a SEAL anymore. He was a crippled man with a cane—crutches now—who might've let a kid die because of his damned pride.

Frisco sat down on his bed and let himself cry.

Mia set her purse down on her kitchen table with an odd-sounding thunk. She lifted it up and set it down again. Thunk.

What was in there?

She remembered even before she opened the zipper.

Natasha's medicine. Frisco had picked up Tasha's antibiotic directly from the hospital's twenty-four-hour pharmacy.

Mia took it out of her purse and stared at it. Tash wasn't due for another dose of the liquid until a little before noon, unless she woke up earlier.

She'd better take it over now, rather than wait.

She left her apartment and went over to Frisco's. All of his windows were dark. Damn. She opened the screen door, wincing as it screeched, and tried the door knob.

It was unlocked.

Slowly, stealthily, she let herself in. She'd tiptoe into the kitchen, put the medicine in the fridge and...

What was that...? Mia froze.

It was a strange sound, a soft sound, and Mia stood very, very still, hardly daring to breathe as she listened for it again.

There it was. It was the sound of ragged breathing, of nearly silent crying. Had Tasha awoken? Was Frisco already so soundly asleep that he didn't hear her?

Quietly Mia crept down the hall toward Tasha's bedroom and peeked in.

The little girl was fast asleep, breathing slowly and evenly.

Mia heard the sound again, and she turned and saw Frisco in the dim light that filtered in through his bedroom blinds.

He was sitting on his bed, doubled over as if in pain, his elbows resting on his legs, one hand covering his face; a picture of despair.

The noise she had heard—it was Frisco. Alan Francisco was weeping.

Mia was shocked. Never, *ever* in a million years had she expected him to cry. She would have thought him incapable, unable to release his emotions in such a visible, expressive way. She would have expected him to internalize everything, or deny his feelings.

But he was crying.

Her heart broke for him, and silently she backed away, instinctively knowing that he would feel ashamed and humiliated if he knew she had witnessed his emotional breakdown. She crept all the way back into his living room and out of his apartment, holding her breath as she shut the door tightly behind her.

Now what?

She couldn't just go back into her own condominium, knowing that he was alone with all of his pain and fears. Besides, she was still holding Tasha's medicine.

Taking a deep breath, knowing full well that even if Frisco *did* come to the door, he might very well simply take the medicine and shut her out, she rang the bell.

She knew he heard it, but no lights went on, nothing stirred. She opened the screen and knocked on the door, pushing it open a few inches. "Alan?"

"Yeah," his voice said raspily. "I'm in the bathroom. Hang on, I'll be right out."

Mia came inside again, and closed the door behind her. She stood there, leaning against it, wondering if she should turn on the lights.

She heard the water running in the bathroom sink and could picture Frisco splashing his face with icy water, praying that she wouldn't be able to tell that he'd been crying. She left the lights off.

And he made no move to turn them on when he finally appeared at the end of the darkened hallway. He didn't say anything; he just stood there.

"I, um...I had Tasha's medicine in my purse," Mia said. "I thought it would be smart to bring it over now instead of...in the morning...."

"You want a cup of tea?"

His quiet question took her entirely by surprise. Of all the things she'd imagined he'd say to her, inviting her to stay for a cup of tea was not one of them. "Yes," she said. "I would."

His crutches creaked as he went into the kitchen. Mia followed more hesitantly.

He didn't turn on the overhead lamp. He didn't need to. Light streamed in through the kitchen window from the brightly lit parking lot. It was silvery and it made shadows on the walls, but it was enough to see by.

As Frisco filled a kettle with water from the faucet, Mia opened the refrigerator door and put Tasha's medicine inside. As she closed the door, she saw that list that he kept there on the fridge, the list of all the things he could no longer do— the list of things that kept him, in his eyes, from being a man.

"I know it was hard for you to come and ask me for help tonight," she said softly.

Using only his right crutch for support, he carried the kettle to the stove and set it down. He didn't say a word until after he'd turned the burner on. Then he turned to face her. "Yeah," he said. "It was."

"I'm glad you did, though. I'm glad I could help."

"I actually..." He cleared his throat and started again. "I actually thought she was going to die. I was scared to death."

Mia was startled by his candidness. *I was scared to death.* Another surprise. She never would have expected him to admit that. Ever. But then again, this man had been surprising her right from the start.

"I don't know how parents handle it," he said, pushing down on top of the kettle as if that would make the water heat faster. "I mean, here's this kid that you love more than life itself, right? And suddenly she's so sick she can't even stand up." His voice tightened.

"The thing that kills me is that if I had been the only one left in the world, if it had been up to me and me alone, we wouldn't've made it to that hospital. I'd still be here, trying to figure out a way to get her down those stairs." He turned suddenly, slamming his hand down on top of the counter in frustration and anger. "I *hate* feeling so damned helpless!"

His shoulders looked so tight, his face so grim. Mia wrapped her arms around herself to keep from reaching for him. "But you're not the only one left in the world. You're *not* alone."

"But I *am* helpless."

"No, you're not," she told him. "Not anymore. You're only helpless if you refuse to ask for help."

He laughed, an exhale of bitter air. "Yeah, right—"

"Yeah," she said earnestly. "*Right.* Think about it, Alan. There are things that we all don't do, things that we probably couldn't do—look at your shirt," she commanded him, stepping closer. She reached out and touched the soft cotton of his T-shirt. She lifted it, turning it over and bringing the factory-machine-sewn hem into the light from the kitchen window. "You didn't sew this shirt, did you? Or weave the cotton to make the fabric? Cotton grows in fields—you knew that, right? Somehow a whole bunch of people did something to that little fluffy plant to make it turn into this T-shirt. Does it mean that you're helpless just because you didn't do it your-self?''

Mia was standing too close to him. She could smell his musky, masculine scent along with some kind of decadently delicious after-shave or deodorant. He was watching her, the light from the window casting shadows across his face, making his features craggy and harsh. His eyes gleamed color-lessly, but the heat within them didn't need a color to be seen. She released her hold on his T-shirt but she didn't back away. She didn't want to back away, even if it meant spontaneous combustion from the heat in his eyes.

''So what if you can't make your own clothes?'' she con-tinued. ''The good people at Fruit of the Loom and Levi's will make them for you. So what if you can't carry Tasha down the stairs. *I'll* carry her for you.''

Frisco shook his head. ''It's not the same.''

''It's *exactly* the same.''

''What if you're not home? What then?''

''Then you call Thomas. Or your friend, what's-his-name...Lucky. And if they're not home, you call someone else. Instead of this,'' she said, gesturing toward the list on his refrigerator, ''you should have a two-page list of friends you can call for help. Because you're only helpless if you have no one to call.''

''Will they run on the beach for me?'' Frisco asked, his voice tight. He stepped closer to her, dangerously closer. His body was a whisper away from hers, and she could feel his breath, hot and sweet, moving her hair. ''Will they get back in shape for me, get reinstated as an active-duty SEAL for me? And then will they come along on my missions with me, and run when I need to run, and swim against a two-knot current when I need to swim? Will they make a high-altitude, low-opening jump out of an airplane for me? Will they fight when I need to fight, and move without making a noise when I need to be silent? Will they do all those things that I'd need to do to keep myself and the men in my unit alive?''

Mia was silent.

"I know you don't understand," he said. The teakettle started to hiss and whistle, a lonely, high-pitched keening sound. He turned away from her, moving toward the stove. He hadn't touched her, but his presence and nearness had been nearly palpable. She sagged slightly as if he had been holding her up, and backing away, she lowered herself into one of his kitchen chairs. As she watched, he removed the kettle from the heat and took two mugs down from the cabinet. "I wish I could make you understand."

"Try."

He was silent as he opened the cabinet again and removed two tea bags. He put one into each mug, then poured in the steaming water from the kettle. He set the kettle back onto the stove and was seemingly intent on steeping the tea bags as he began, haltingly, to speak.

"You know that I grew up here in San Felipe," he said. "I also told you that my childhood wasn't a barrel of laughs. That was sort of an understatement. Truth was, it sucked. My old man worked on a fishing boat—when he wasn't too hung over to get out of bed. It wasn't exactly like living an episode of 'Leave it to Beaver,' or 'Father Knows Best.'" He looked at her, the muscle in his jaw tight. "I'm going to have to ask you to carry the mugs of tea into the living room for me."

"Of course." Mia glanced at him from the corner of her eyes. "That wasn't really so hard, was it?"

"Yes, it was." With both crutches securely under his arms, Frisco led the way into the living room. He switched on only one lamp and it gave the room a soft, almost golden glow. "Excuse me for a minute," he said, then vanished down the hallway to his bedroom.

Mia put both mugs down on the coffee table in front of the plaid couch and sat down.

"I wanted to check on Tash," he said, coming back into the living room, "and I wanted to get *this*." He was holding a paper bag—the bag the doctor had given him at the hospital. He winced as he sat down on the other side of the long couch and lifted his injured leg onto the coffee table. As Mia watched, he opened the bag and took out a syringe and a small vial. "I need to have my leg up. I hope you don't mind if I do this out here."

"What exactly is it that you're doing?"

"This is a local painkiller, kind of like novocaine," he explained, filling the syringe with the clear liquid. "I'm going to inject it into my knee."

"*You're* going to *inject* it into... You're kidding."

"As a SEAL, I've had training as a medic," he said. "Steve gave me a shot of cortisone in the hospital, but that won't kick in for a while yet. This works almost right away, but the down side is that it wears off after a few hours, and I have to remedicate. Still, it takes the edge off the pain without affecting my central nervous system."

Mia turned away, unable to watch as he stuck the needle into his leg.

"I'm sorry," he murmured. "But it was crossing the border into hellishly painful again."

"I don't think I could ever give myself a shot," Mia admitted.

He glanced over at her, his mouth twisted up into a near smile. "Well, it's not my favorite thing in the world to do, either, but can you imagine what would have happened tonight if I'd taken the painkiller Steve wanted to prescribe for me? I would never have heard Tasha fall out of bed. She'd still be in there, on the floor, and I'd be stupid, drooling and unconscious in my bed. This way, my knee gets numb, not my brain."

"Interesting philosophy from a man who drank himself to sleep two nights in a row."

Frisco could feel the blessed numbing start in his knee. He rolled his head to make his shoulders and neck relax. "Jeez, you don't pull your punches, do you?"

"Four-thirty in the morning is hardly the time for polite conversation," she countered, tucking her legs up underneath her on the couch and taking a sip of her tea. "If you can't be baldly honest at four-thirty in the morning, when can you be?"

Frisco reached up with one hand to rub his neck. "Here's a baldly honest truth for you, then—and it's true whether it's 0430 or high noon. Like I said before, I'm not drinking anymore."

She was watching him, her hazel eyes studying him, looking for what, he didn't know. He had the urge to turn away or to cover his face, afraid that somehow she'd be able to see the telltale signs of his recent tears. But instead, he forced himself to hold her gaze.

"I can't believe you can just quit," she finally said. "Just like that. I mean, I look at you, and I can tell that you're sober, but..."

"The night we met, you didn't exactly catch me at my best. I was...celebrating my discharge from the Navy—toasting their lack of faith in me." He reached forward, picked up his mug of tea and took a sip. It was too hot and it burned all the way down. "I told you—I don't make a habit out of drinking too much. I'm not like Sharon. Or my father. Man, he was a bastard. He had two moods—drunk and angry, and hung over and angry. Either way, my brothers and Sharon and I learned to stay out of his way. Sometimes one of us would end up in the wrong place at the wrong time, and then we'd get hit. We used to sit around for hours thinking up excuses to tell our friends about where we got all our black eyes and bruises." He snorted. "As if any of our friends didn't know exactly what was going on. Most of them were living the same bad dream.

"You know, I used to pretend he wasn't really my father. I came up with this story about how I was some kind of mercreature that had gotten tangled in his nets one day when he was out in the fishing boat."

Mia smiled. "Like Tasha pretending she's a Russian princess."

Her smile was hypnotizing. Frisco could think of little but the way her lips had felt against his, and how much he wanted to feel that sweet sensation again. He resisted the urge to reach out and touch the side of her beautiful face. She looked away from him, her smile fading, suddenly shy, as if she knew what he was thinking.

"So there I was," Frisco continued with his story, "ten years old and living with this nightmare of a home life. It was that year—the year I was in fourth grade—that I started riding my bike for hours on end just to get out of the house."

She was listening to him, staring intently into her mug as if it held the answers to all of her questions. She'd kicked off her sneakers and they lay on their side on the floor in front of her. Her slender legs were tucked up beneath her on the couch, tantalizingly smooth and golden tan. She was wearing a gray hooded sweatshirt over her cutoffs. She'd had it zipped up at the hospital, but at some point since they'd returned home, she'd unzipped it. The shirt she wore underneath was white and loose, with a small ruffle at the top.

It was her nightgown, Frisco realized. She'd simply thrown her clothes on over her nightgown, tucking it into her shorts and covering it with her sweatshirt.

She glanced up at him, waiting for him to continue.

Frisco cleared the sudden lump of desire from his throat and went on. "One day I rode my bike a few miles down the coast, to one of the beaches where the SEALs do a lot of their training exercises. It was just amazing to watch these guys." He smiled, remembering how he'd thought the SEALs were crazy that first time he'd seen them on the beach. "They were always wet. Whatever they were doing, whatever the weather, the instructors always ran 'em into the surf first and got 'em soaked. Then they'd crawl across the beach on their bellies and get coated with sand—it'd get all over their faces, in their hair, everywhere. And *then* they'd run ten miles up and down the beach. They looked amazing—to a ten-year-old it was pretty funny. But even though I was just a kid, I could see past the slapstick. I knew that whatever they were going to get by doing all these endless, excruciating endurance tests, it had to be pretty damn good."

Mia had turned slightly to face him on the couch. Maybe it was because he knew she was wearing her nightgown under her clothes, or maybe it was the dark, dangerous hour of the night, but she looked like some kind of incredible fantasy sitting there like that. Taking her into his arms and making love to her would be a blissful, temporary escape from all of his pain and frustration.

He knew without a shadow of a doubt that one kiss would melt away all of her caution and reserve. Yes, she was a nice girl. Yes, she wanted more than sex. She wanted love. But even nice girls felt the pull of hot, sweet desire. He could show her—and convince her with one single kiss—that sometimes pure sex for the sake of pleasure and passion was enough.

But oddly enough, he wanted more from this woman than the hot satisfaction of a sexual release. Oddly enough, he wanted her to understand how he felt—his frustration, his anger, his darkest fear.

Try, she'd said. Try to make her understand.

He was trying.

"I started riding to the naval base all the time," he continued, forcing himself to focus on her wide green eyes rather than the soft smoothness of her thighs. "I started hanging out down there. I snuck into this local dive where a lot of the off-duty sailors went, just so I could listen to their stories. The SEALs didn't come in too often, but when they did, man, they got a hell of a lot of respect. A *hell* of a lot of respect—from both the enlisted men *and* the officers. They had this aura of greatness about them, and I was convinced, along with the rest of the Navy, that these guys were gods.

"I watched 'em every chance I could get, and I noticed that even though most of the SEALs didn't dress in uniform, they all had this pin they wore. They called it a Budweiser—it was an eagle with a submachine gun in one claw and a trident in the other. I found out they got that pin after they went through a grueling basic training session called BUD/S. Most guys didn't make it through BUD/S, and some classes even had a ninety-percent drop-out rate. The program was weeks and weeks of organized torture, and only the men who stayed in to the end got that pin and became SEALs.''

Mia was still watching him as if he were telling her the most fascinating story in all of the world, so he continued.

"So one day," Frisco told her, "a few days before my twelfth birthday, I saw these SEALs-in-training bring their IBSs—their little inflatable boats—in for a landing on the rocks over by the Coronado Hotel. It was toward the end of the first phase of BUD/S. That week's called Hell Week, because it *is* truly hell. They were exhausted, I could see it in their faces and in the way they were sitting in those boats. I was sure they were all going to die. Have you seen the rocks over there?"

She shook her head, no.

"They're deadly. Jagged. And the surf is always rough— not a good combination. But I saw these guys put their heads down and do it. They could've died—men *have* died doing that training exercise.

"All around me, I could hear the tourists and the civilian onlookers making all this noise, wondering aloud why these men were risking their lives like that when they could be regular sailors, in the regular Navy, and not have to put themselves in that kind of danger."

Frisco leaned closer to Mia, willing her to understand. "And I stood there—I was just a kid—but I *knew*. I knew why. If these guys made it through, they were going to be SEALs. They were going to get that pin, and they were going to be able to walk into any military base in the world and get automatic respect. And even better than that, they would have self-respect. You know that old saying, 'Wherever you go, there you are'? Well, I knew that wherever they went, at least one man would respect them, and that man's respect was the most important of all."

Mia gazed back at Frisco, unable to look away. She could picture him as that little boy, cheeks smooth, slight of frame and wire thin, but with these same intense blue eyes, impossibly wise beyond his tender years. She could picture him escaping from an awful childhood and an abusive father, searching for a place to belong, a place to feel safe, a place where he could learn to like himself, a place where he'd be respected—by others and himself.

He'd found his place with the SEALs.

"That was when I knew I was going to be a SEAL," he told her quietly but no less intensely. "And from that day on, I respected myself even though no one else did. I stuck it out at home another six years. I made it all the way through high school because I knew I needed that diploma. But the day I graduated, I enlisted in the Navy. And I made it. I did it. I got through BUD/S, and I landed my IBS on those rocks in Coronado.

"And I got that pin."

He looked away from her, staring sightlessly down at his injured knee, at the bruises and the swelling and the countless crisscrossing of scars. Mia's heart was in her throat as she watched him. He'd told her all this to make her understand, and she *did* understand. She knew what he was going to say next, and even as yet unspoken, his words made her ache.

"I always thought that by becoming a SEAL, I escaped from my life—you know, the way my life *should* have turned out. I should've been killed in a car accident like my brother Rob was. He was DUI, and he hit a pole. Or else I should've got my high school girlfriend pregnant like Danny did. I should have been married with a wife and child to support at age seventeen, working for the same fishing fleet that my father worked for, following in the old bastard's footsteps. I always sort of thought by joining the Navy and becoming a SEAL, I cheated destiny.

"But now look at me. I'm back in San Felipe. And for a couple nights there, I was doing a damned good imitation of my old man. Drink 'til you drop, 'til you feel no pain."

Mia had tears in her eyes, and when Frisco glanced at her, she saw that his jaw was tight, and his eyes were damp, too. He turned his head away. It was a few moments before he spoke again, and when he finally did, his voice was steady but impossibly sad.

"Ever since I was injured," he said softly, "I feel like I've slipped back into that nightmare that used to be my life. I'm not a SEAL anymore. I lost that, it's gone. I don't know who I am, Mia—I'm some guy who's less than whole, who's just kind of floating around." He shook his head. "All I know for sure is that my self-respect is gone, too."

He turned to her, no longer caring if she saw that his eyes were filled with tears. "That's why I've got to get it all back. That's why I've got to be able to run and jump and dive and do all those things on that list." He wiped roughly at his eyes with the back of one hand, refusing to give in to the emotion that threatened to overpower him. "I want it back. I want to be whole again."

11

Mia couldn't help herself. She reached for Frisco.

How could she keep her distance while her heart was aching for this man?

But he caught her hand before she could touch the side of his face. "You don't want this," he said quietly, his eyes searching as he gazed at her. "Remember?"

"Maybe we both need each other a little bit more than I thought," she whispered.

He forced his mouth up into one of his heartbreakingly poignant half smiles. "Mia, you don't need me."

"Yes, I do," Mia said, and almost to her surprise, her words were true. She did need him. Desperately. She had tried. She had honestly tried not to care for this man, this *soldier*. She'd tried to remain distant, aloof, unfeeling, but somehow over the past few days, he had penetrated all of her defenses and gained possession of her heart.

His eyes looked so sad, so soft and gentle. All of his anger was gone, and Mia knew that once again she was seeing the man that he had been—the man all of his pain and bitterness had made him forget how to be.

He could be that man again. He was *still* that man. He simply needed to stop basing his entire future happiness on attaining the unattainable. She couldn't do that for him. He'd have to do it for himself. But she *could* be with him now, tonight, and help him remember that he *wasn't* alone.

"I can't give you what you want," he said huskily. "I know it matters to you."

Love. He was talking about love.

"That makes us even." Mia gently freed her hand from his, and touched the side of his face. He hadn't shaved in at least a day, and his cheeks and chin were rough, but she didn't care. She didn't care if he loved her, either. "Because I can't give you what *you* want."

She couldn't give him the power to become a SEAL again. But if she could have, she would.

She leaned forward and kissed him. It was a light kiss, just a gentle brushing of her lips against his.

Frisco didn't move. He didn't respond. She leaned forward to kiss him again, and he stopped her with one hand against her shoulder.

She was kneeling next to him on the couch, and he looked down at her legs, at the soft cotton of her nightgown revealed by her unzipped sweatshirt and finally into her eyes. "You're playing with fire," he said quietly. "There may be an awful lot of things that I can't do anymore, but making love to a beautiful woman isn't one of them."

"Maybe we should start a new list. Things you *can* still do. You could put 'making love' right on the top."

"Mia, you better go—"

She kissed him again, and again he pulled back.

"Dammit, you *told* me—"

She kissed him harder this time, slipping her arms up around his neck and parting his lips with her tongue. He froze, and she knew that he hadn't expected her to be so bold—not in a million years.

His hesitation lasted only the briefest of moments before he pulled her close, before he wrapped her in his arms and nearly crushed her against the hard muscles of his chest.

And then he was kissing her, too.

Wildly, fiercely, he was kissing her, his hot mouth gaining possession of hers, his tongue claiming hers with a breathtaking urgency.

It didn't seem possible. She had only kissed him once before, on the beach, yet his mouth tasted sweetly familiar and kissing him was like coming home.

Mia felt his hands on her back, sweeping up underneath her sweatshirt and down to the curve of her bottom, pulling her closer, seeking the smooth bareness of her legs. He shifted her weight toward him, pulling her over and on top of him so that she was straddling his lap as still they kissed.

Her fingers were deep in his hair. It was incredibly, decadently soft. She would have liked to spend the entire rest of her life right there, kissing Alan Francisco and running her hands through his beautiful golden hair. It was all she needed, all she would ever need.

And then he shifted his hips and she felt the hardness of his arousal pressing up against her and she knew she was wrong. She both needed and wanted more.

He pulled at her sweatshirt, pushing it off her shoulder and down her arms. He tugged her nightgown free from the top of her shorts, and she heard herself moan as his work-roughened hands glided up and across the bare skin of her back. And then he pulled away from her, breathing hard.

"Mia." His lean, handsome face was taut with frustration. "I want to pick you up and take you to my bed." But he couldn't. He couldn't carry her. Not on crutches, not even with a cane.

This was not the time for him to be thinking about things he couldn't do. Mia climbed off of him, slipping out of his grasp. "Why don't we synchronize watches and plan to rendezvous there in, say…" She pretended to look at an imaginary watch on her wrist. "Oh two minutes?"

His face relaxed into a smile, but the tension didn't leave his eyes. "You don't need to say 'oh.' You could say 0430, but two minutes is just two minutes."

"I know that," Mia said. "I just wanted to make you smile. If that hadn't worked, I would have tried this…." She slowly pulled her nightgown up and over her head, dropping it down into his lap.

But Frisco's smile disappeared. He looked up at her, his gaze devouring her bare breasts, heat and hunger in his eyes.

Mia was amazed. She was standing half-naked in front of this man that she had only known for a handful of days. He was a soldier, a fighter who had been trained to make war in more ways than she could probably imagine. He was the toughest, hardest man she'd ever met, yet in many ways he was also the most vulnerable. He'd trusted her enough to share some of his secrets with her, to let her see into his soul. In comparison, revealing her body to him seemed almost insignificant.

And she could stand here like this, she realized, without a blush and with such certainty, because she was absolutely convinced that loving this man was the right thing to do. She'd never made love to a man before without a sense of unease, without being troubled by doubts. But she'd never met a man like Alan Francisco—a man who seemed so different from her, yet who could look into her eyes, and with just a word or a touch, make her feel so totally connected to him, so instantly in tune.

Mia had never considered herself an exhibitionist before, but then again, no one had ever looked at her the way Frisco did. She felt her body tighten with anticipation under the scalding heat of his gaze. It was seductive, the way he looked at her—and nearly as pleasurable as a caress.

She reached up, slowly and deliberately, taking her time as she unfastened her ponytail, letting him watch her as she loosened her long hair around her shoulders, enjoying the sensation of his eyes on her body.

"You're not smiling," she whispered.

"Believe me, I'm smiling inside."

And then he did smile. It was half crooked and half sad. It was filled with doubt and disbelief, laced with wonder and anticipation. As she gazed into his eyes, Mia could see the first glimmer of hope. And she felt herself falling. She knew in that single instant that she was falling hopelessly and totally in love with this man.

Afraid he'd see her feelings in her eyes, she picked up her sweatshirt from the floor and turned, moving quickly down the hall to his bedroom. To his bed.

Frisco wasn't far behind, but she heard him stop at Natasha's room and go inside to check on the little girl.

"Is she all right?" she asked, as he came in a few moments later. He closed the door behind him. And locked it.

He stood there, a dark shape at the far end of the room. "She's much cooler now," he said.

Mia crossed to the window and adjusted the blinds slightly, allowing them both privacy and some light. The dim light from the landing streamed up in a striped pattern across the ceiling, giving the ordinary room an exotic glow. She turned back to find Frisco watching her.

"Do you have protection?" she asked.

"Yes. It's been a while," he admitted, "but…yes."

"It's been a while for me, too," she said softly.

"It's not too late to change your mind." He moved away from the door, allowing her clear access to make an escape. He looked away, as if he knew that his gaze had the power to imprison her.

"Why would I want to do that?"

He gave her another of his sad smiles. "A sudden burst of sanity?" he suggested.

"I want to make love to you," she said. "Is that really so insane?"

He looked up at her. "You could have your choice of anyone. Anyone you want." There was no self-pity in his voice or on his face. He was merely stating a fact that he believed was true.

"Good," she said. "Then I'll choose you."

Frisco heard her soft words, but it wasn't until she smiled and moved toward him that they fully sank in.

Mia wanted him. She wanted *him*.

The light from the outside walkway gleamed on her bare skin. Her body was even more beautiful than he'd imagined. Her breasts were full and round—not too big, but not too small, either. He ached to touch her with his hands, with his mouth, and he smiled, knowing he was going to do just that, and soon.

But she stopped just out of his reach.

Holding his gaze, she unfastened her shorts and let them glide down her legs.

He'd seen her in her bathing suit just that afternoon—he was well aware that her trim, athletic body was the closest thing to his idea of perfection he'd ever seen. She wasn't voluptuous by any definition of the word—in fact, some men might've found her too skinny. Her hips were slender, curving in to the softness of her waist. She was willowy and gracefully shaped, a wonderful combination of smooth muscles and soft, flowing lines.

Frisco sat down on the edge of the bed and she turned toward him. He reached for her and she went willingly into his arms, once again straddling his lap.

"I think this is where we were," she murmured and kissed him.

Frisco spun, caught in a vortex of pleasure so intense, he couldn't keep from groaning aloud. Her skin was so smooth, so soft beneath his hands, and her kisses were near spiritual experiences, each one deeper and longer than the last, infusing him with her joyful vitality and sweet, limitless passion.

She tugged at his T-shirt, and he broke free from their embrace to yank it up and over his head. And then she was kissing him again, and the sensation of her bare skin against his took his breath away.

He tumbled her back with him onto the bed, pulling her down on top of him, slipping his hand between them to touch the sweet fullness of her breasts. Her nipples were taut and erect with desire and he pulled her to his mouth, laving her with his tongue, suckling first gently then harder as she gasped her pleasure, as she arched her back.

"I like that," she breathed. "That feels so good...."

Her whispered words sent a searing flame of need through him and he pulled her even closer.

His movement pressed her intimately, perfectly against his arousal and she held him there tightly for a moment. He could feel her heat, even through her panties and his shorts. He wanted to touch her, to taste her, to fill her completely. He wanted her all. He wanted her now. He wanted her forever, for all time.

Her hair surrounded them like a sensuous, sheer, black curtain as he kissed her again, as she began to move on top of him, slowly sliding against the hard length of him. Oh, man, if she kept this up, he was going to lose it before he even got inside of her.

"Mia—" he groaned, his hands on her hips, stilling her movement.

She pulled back to look down at him, her eyes heavy-lidded with pleasure and desire, a heart-stoppingly sexy smile curving her lips. Flipping her long hair back over one shoulder, she reached for the button at the waistband of his shorts. She undid it quickly, deftly, then slid back, kneeling over his thighs to unfasten the zipper.

His arousal pressed up, released from his shorts, and she covered him with her delicate hands, gazing down into his eyes, touching him through his briefs.

She looked like some kind of extremely erotic fantasy, kneeling above him, wearing those barely-there panties, the white silk contrasting perfectly with the gleaming golden color of her smooth skin. Her long, thick hair fell around her shoulders, several strands curving around her beautiful breasts.

Frisco reached for her, wanting to touch all of her, running his hands down her arms, caressing her breasts.

She pulled his shorts and his briefs down, watching his eyes and smiling at the pleasure on his face as her hands finally closed around him, closing her eyes in her own ecstasy as his hand tightened on her breast.

She leaned forward and met his lips in a hard, wild kiss, then pulled away, leaving a trail of kisses from his mouth down his neck, to his chest, as with one hand she still held him possessively.

Her hair swept across him in the lightest of caresses and Frisco bit back a cry as her mouth moved even lower, as he nearly suffocated in a wave of exquisite, mind-numbing pleasure.

This was incredible. This was beyond incredible, but it wasn't what he wanted. He reached for her, roughly pulling her up and into his arms.

"Didn't you like that?" She was laughing—she knew damn well that he'd liked it. She knew damn well that she'd come much too close to pushing him over the edge.

He tried to speak, but his voice came out as only a growl. She laughed again, her voice musical, her amusement contagious. He covered her mouth in the fiercest of kisses, and he could feel laughter and sheer joy bubbling up from inside of her and seeping into him, flowing through his veins, filling him with happiness.

Happiness. Dear God, when was the last time he'd felt happy? It was odd, it was weird, it was *beyond* weird, because even remembering back to when he had been happy, before his injury, he had never associated that particular emotion with making love. He'd felt desire, he'd felt sexual satisfaction, he'd felt interested, amused, in control or even out of control. He'd felt confident, self-assured and powerful.

But he'd never felt so unconditionally, so inarguably *happy*. He had never felt anything remotely like this.

He'd also never made love to a woman who was, without a doubt, his perfect sexual match.

Mia was openly, unabashedly sexy and unembarrassed by her powerful sensuality. She was unafraid to take the lead in their lovemaking. She was confident and daringly fearless and bold.

If it hadn't been for that glimpse she'd given him in the hospital lobby of her sensual side, he never would have expected it. She was so sweet natured, so gentle and kind. She was *nice*. She was the kind of woman a man would marry, content to spend the rest of his life surrounded by her quiet warmth.

But Mia didn't carry her quietness with her into the bedroom. And she wasn't warm—she was incredibly, scaldingly, moltenly hot.

His hands swept down the smooth expanse of her stomach, down underneath the slip of silk that covered her. She was hot and sleek and ready for him, just as he'd known she would be. She arched up against his fingers, pushing him deeply inside of her, pulling his head toward her and guiding his mouth to her breast.

"I want to get on top of you," she gasped. "Please—"

It was an incredible turn-on—knowing this fiercely passionate woman wanted him so completely.

He released her, rolling onto his side to reach into the top drawer of his bedside table. He rifled through the clutter, and miraculously his hand closed on a small foil packet. He tore it open and covered himself as Mia pushed down her panties and kicked her legs free. And then she *was* on top of him.

She came down, and he thrust up, and in one smooth, perfect, white-hot movement, he was inside of her.

The look on her face was one he knew he'd remember and carry with him to his grave. Her eyes were closed, her lips slightly parted, her head thrown back in sheer, beautiful rapture.

He was making her feel this way.

She opened her eyes and gazed down at him, searching his face for God knew what. Whatever she was looking for, she seemed to have found it, because she smiled at him so sweetly. Frisco felt as if his heart were suddenly too large to fit inside of his chest.

She began to move on top of him, slowly at first. Her smile faded, but still she looked into his eyes, holding his gaze.

"Alan...?"

He wasn't sure he could speak, but he moistened his lips and gave it a try. "Yeah...?"

"This is really good."

"Oh, yeah." He had to laugh. It came bubbling up from somewhere inside of him, and he recognized his laughter as belonging to her.

She was moving faster now and he tried to slow her down. He wanted this to last forever, but at the rate they were going... But she didn't want to slow down, and he could refuse her nothing.

He pulled her down on top of him and kissed her frantically, fighting for his tenuous control. But he was clinging to the side of a cliff, and his fingerhold was slipping fast.

"Alan..." She gasped his name as she clutched him tightly, and he felt the first waves of her tumultuous release.

Frisco went over the edge. But instead of falling, he sailed upward, soaring impossibly high, higher than he'd ever gone before. Pleasure rocketed through him, burning him, scorching him, leaving him weak and stunned, shattered and depleted—yet still filled, completely and thoroughly, with happiness.

Mia's long, soft hair was in his face and he closed his eyes, just breathing in the sweet scent of her shampoo as he slowly floated back to earth.

After a moment, she sighed and smiled—he could feel her lips move against his neck. He wondered if she could feel his own smile.

Mia lifted her head, pulling her hair from his face. "Are you still alive?"

He felt his smile get broader as he met her eyes. Hazel was his new favorite color. "Definitely."

"I think we can safely add 'making love' to the list of things that you can still do," she said with a smile.

His knee. Man, he hadn't thought about his knee since he'd locked his door behind them. He *still* didn't want to think about it, and he fought to hold on to the peacefulness of this moment.

"I don't know," he said. "Maybe we should make sure that it wasn't some kind of fluke. Maybe we better try it again."

Mia's smile turned dangerous. "I'm ready when you are."

Frisco felt a surge of desire course through him, hot and sweet. "Give me a few minutes...."

He kissed her, a slow, deep kiss that promised her unlimited pleasure.

Mia sighed, pulling back to look at him again. "I'd love to stay, but..."

"But...?"

She smiled, running her fingers through his hair. "It's after six in the morning, Alan. I don't think it's smart for me to be here when Natasha wakes up. She's had enough turbulence recently in her life, without her having to worry about whether she's got to compete with me for your time and affection."

Frisco nodded. Mia was probably right. He was disappointed to see her leave so soon, but he had to consider the kid.

Mia slipped out of his arms and out of his bed. He turned onto his side to watch her gather her clothes from his floor.

"You called me Alan again," he said.

She looked up at him in surprise as she slipped on her shorts. "Did I? I'm sorry."

"You think of me as Alan, don't you?" he asked. "Not Frisco."

She zipped up her sweatshirt and then came and sat down next to him on the bed. "I like your name," she admitted. "I'm sorry if it keeps slipping out."

He propped himself up on one elbow. "It slipped out a lot while we were making love."

"God, I hope that didn't ruin it for you." She was half-serious.

Frisco laughed. "If you had called me Bob, that might've ruined it, but..." He touched the side of her face. "That was the first time in a long time that I've actually enjoyed being called Alan. And I *did* enjoy it."

She closed her eyes briefly, pressing her cheek against the palm of his hand. "Well, I certainly enjoyed calling you Alan, that's for sure."

"Who knows," he murmured, tracing her lips with his thumb. "If we keep this up, I might even get used to it."

Mia opened her eyes and gazed at him. "Do you...want to keep this up?" she asked. All teasing was gone from her voice, and for the first time all night, she sounded less than certain.

Frisco couldn't respond. It wasn't her question that shocked him—it was his own immediate and very certain answer. Yes. God, yes.

This was dangerous. This was extremely dangerous. He didn't want to feel anything but pleasure and satisfaction when he thought about this woman. He didn't want anything more than neighborly, casual, no-strings sex.

Yet there was no way he could let her walk out of here thinking that one night had been enough. Because it hadn't. Because the thought of her leaving simply to go home was hard enough to tolerate. He didn't want to think about how he would feel if she ever left for good. He *couldn't* think about that.

"Yes," he finally answered, "but I have to be honest, I'm not in any kind of place right now where I can—"

She silenced him with a kiss. "I want to, too," she told him. "That's all we both need to know right now. It doesn't have to be any more complicated than that."

But it *was* more complicated than that. Frisco knew just from looking at her. She cared for him. He could see it in her eyes. He felt a hot flash of elation that instantly turned to cold despair. He didn't want her to care for him. He didn't want her to be hurt, and if she cared too much, she would be.

"I just want to make sure you don't go turning this into some kind of fairy tale," he said quietly, unable to resist touching the soft silk of her hair, praying that his words weren't going to sting too badly. Still, a small sting now was better than a mortal wound in the long run. "I know what we've got going here looks an awful lot like *Beauty and the Beast*, but I need more than a pretty girl to turn me back into a prince—to make me whole again. I need a whole hell of a lot more to do that. And I've got to be honest with you, I…''

He couldn't say it. His throat closed on the words, but he had to make sure she understood.

''I'm scared that the doctors are right,'' he admitted. ''I'm scared that my knee is as good as it's going to get.''

Mia's beautiful eyes were filled with compassion and brimming with emotion. ''Maybe it would be a good thing if you could admit that—if you could accept your limitations.''

''A *good* thing…?'' He shook his head, exhaling his disbelief. ''If I give up trying, I'm condemning myself to a lifetime of this limbo. I'm not dead, but I'm not really alive, either.''

Mia looked away from him, and he knew what she was thinking. He'd certainly seemed full of life when they'd made love, just a short time ago. But this wasn't about sex. This wasn't about her. ''I need to know who I am again,'' he tried to explain.

Her head came up and she nearly burned him with the intensity of her gaze. ''You're Lieutenant Francisco, from San Felipe, California. You're a man who walks with a cane and a hell of a lot of pain because of that. You're a Navy SEAL—you'll always be a SEAL. You were when you were eleven years old. You will be when you die.''

She cupped his face with her hands and kissed him—a sweet, hot kiss that made him almost believe her.

''I haven't really known you that long,'' she continued, ''but I think I know you well enough to be certain that you're going to win. You're not going to settle for any kind of limbo. I know you're going to do whatever it takes to feel whole again. I know you'll make the right choices. You *are* going to live happily ever after. Just don't give up.'' She kissed him again and stood up. ''I'll see you later, okay?''

''Mia—''

But she was already closing his door quietly behind her.

Frisco lay back in his bed and gazed up at the ceiling. She had such faith in him. *Just don't give up.* She seemed convinced he would do whatever it took to get back into active duty.

He used to have that kind of faith, but it was worn mighty thin from time and countless failure, and now all of his doubts were showing through. And over the past several days, those doubts had grown pretty damn strong. It was becoming as clear as the daylight that was streaming in through his blinds that his recovery was not something that was in his control. He could bully himself, push himself to the edge, work himself until he dropped, but if his knee couldn't support his weight, if the joint was unable to move in certain ways, he would be doing little more than slamming his head against a stone wall.

But now he had Mia believing in him, believing he had what it would take to overcome his injury, to win, to be an active-duty SEAL again.

She cared more about him than she was letting on. Frisco knew without a doubt that she wouldn't have made love to him without feeling *some*thing for him. Was she falling in love with him? It was entirely likely—she was softhearted and kind. He wouldn't be the first down-on-his-luck stray she took into her heart.

Somehow he'd fooled her into thinking he was worth her time and emotion. Somehow he'd tricked her into believing his pipe dream. Somehow she'd bought into his talk of happily ever after.

He closed his eyes. He wanted that happily ever after. He wanted to stand up from this bed and walk into the bathroom without having to use his cane. He wanted to lace up his running shoes and clock himself five miles before breakfast. He wanted to head over to the naval base and join the team for some of their endless training. He wanted to be back in the game, to be ready for anything and everything, ready to be sent out at a moment's notice should the Alpha Squad be needed.

And he wanted to come home after a tough assignment to

the sweetness of Mia's arms, the heaven of her kisses and the warm light of love in her eyes.

God, he wanted that.

But would Mia want him if he failed? Would she want to spend her time always waiting for him to catch up? Would she want to be around a man trapped forever in the limbo between what he once was and what he hoped never again to be?

You're not going to settle for any kind of limbo, she'd told him. *I know you're going to do whatever it takes to feel whole again.*

You're going to win.

But what if he didn't win? What if his knee didn't allow him to rejoin the SEALs? And in his mind, rejoining the SEALs was the only way to win. Anything short of that, and he'd be a loser.

But Mia had faith in him.

He, however, no longer had her confidence. He knew how easy it was to lose when things were out of his control. And as much as he wanted it to be, his recovery was *not* in his control.

Frisco's knee began to throb, and he reached for his painkiller.

He wished he had something that would work as quickly and effectively to ease the ache in his heart.

12

The man called Dwayne was walking across the condo parking lot.

Mia was in her kitchen, standing at the sink, and she just happened to look up and see him.

Not that he was easy to miss. His size called immediate attention to himself. He was wearing another well-tailored suit and a pair of dark sunglasses that didn't succeed in hiding the bandage across the bridge of his nose or the bruises on his face.

Mia went into her living room, where Natasha was sitting on the floor, working with painstaking care on a drawing. Crayons and paper were spread out in front of her on the wicker coffee table.

Trying to look casual, Mia locked and bolted her door, and then closed the living room curtains.

Dwayne's presence here was no coincidence. He was looking for Frisco. Or Natasha. But he wasn't going to find either of them.

Tasha didn't do more than glance up at Mia as she turned on the lamp to replace the sunlight that was now blocked by the curtains.

"Need more juice?" Mia asked the little girl. "You know, you'll get better faster if you have more juice."

Tasha obediently picked up her juice box and took a sip.

Frisco had knocked on Mia's door at a little after eleven. She almost hadn't recognized him at first.

He was wearing his dress uniform. It fit him like a glove—

white and starched and gleaming in the midmorning sun. The rows and rows and rows of colored bars on his chest also reflected the light. The effect was blinding. Even his shoes seemed to glow.

His hair was damp from a shower and neatly combed. His face was smooth shaven. He looked stern and unforgiving and dangerously professional. He looked like some kind of incredibly, breathtakingly handsome stranger.

And then he smiled. "You should see the look on your face."

"Oh, really? Am I drooling?"

Heat flared in his eyes, but then he turned and looked down, and Mia saw that Tasha was standing next to him.

"May we come in?" he asked.

Mia pushed open the screen. Tasha was already feeling much better. The little girl was quick to show Mia the second medal she'd had pinned to her T-shirt, awarded for following Frisco's rules all morning long. Of course, she'd been asleep nearly all morning long, but no one mentioned that.

She'd recovered from her high fever with the remarkable resilience of a small child. The antibiotic was working, and Tasha was back in action, alert and energetic.

Frisco touched Mia gently and lightly as he came inside— just a quick sweep of his fingers down her bare arm. It was enough to take her breath away, enough to remind her of the love they'd made just a few short hours ago. Enough to let her know he remembered, too.

He was wondering if she would mind watching Tasha for a few hours, while he went to the detox hospital and tried to see his sister. That was why he was all dressed up. He figured he had a better shot at getting past the "no visitors" rule if he looked like some kind of hero. One way or another, he was hell-bent on finding out exactly why Dwayne was after Sharon.

Mia volunteered to watch Natasha in Frisco's condo, but he'd told her he'd rather Tasha stay here at her place—he'd feel less as if he were bothering her. And despite Mia's re-assurances otherwise, her condo was where they'd ended up.

Now she had to wonder—had Frisco expected Dwayne to come looking for him again? Was that why he'd insisted she and Tash stay at her place instead of his?

Resisting the urge to peer out from behind her closed curtains to see if Dwayne was climbing up the stairs, Mia sat down next to Tasha. "What are you drawing?" she asked.

Her heart was drumming in her chest. Dwayne was going to ring Frisco's doorbell, and realize that no one was home. What then? Would he try the neighbors' doors in an attempt to find out where the man had gone? What if he rang her bell? What was she going to tell Tasha? How was she going to explain why she wasn't going to answer her door?

And, dear God—what if Frisco came home while Dwayne was still there?

Natasha carefully selected a red crayon from the brand-new box Frisco had bought her. "I'm making a medal," she told Mia, carefully staying within the lines she had drawn. "For Frisco. He needs a medal today, too. We were in the kitchen, and he dropped the milk and it spilled on the floor. He didn't say any bad words." She put the crayon back and took another. "He wanted to—I could tell—but he didn't."

"He's going to like that medal a lot," Mia said.

"And then," Natasha continued, "even though he was mad, he started to laugh." She chose another crayon. "I asked him if milk felt all funny and squishy between his toes, but he said he was laughing because there was something funny on the refrigerator. I looked, but I didn't see anything funny. Just a piece of paper with some writing on it. But I can't read, you know."

"I know." Mia had to smile, despite her racing heart. "He laughed, huh?" Before she'd left Frisco's condo early this morning, she'd started a new list and stuck it onto his refrigerator, next to his other list. Her new list included some of the things he *could* still do, even with his injured leg. She'd listed things like sing, hug Tasha, laugh, read, watch old movies, lie on the beach, do crossword puzzles, breathe and eat pizza. She'd begun and ended the list, of course, with "make love." And she'd peppered it thoroughly with spicy and sometimes extremely explicit suggestions—all of which she was quite sure he was capable of doing.

She was glad he'd laughed. She liked it when he laughed.

She liked it when he talked to her, too. He'd revealed quite a bit of himself last night. He had admitted he was afraid his knee wasn't going to get any better. Mia was almost certain he had been voicing his fears aloud for the very first time.

Frisco's friend Lucky had told her there was an instructor position waiting for Frisco at the base. Sure, it wasn't the future he'd expected or intended, but it *was* a future. It would take him out of this limbo that he feared. It would keep him close to the men he admired and respected. It would make him a SEAL again.

Mia went to the window. She moved the curtain a fraction of an inch then quickly dropped it back into place as she saw Dwayne pulling his large girth up the stairs.

She stood by her front door, listening intently, heart hammering. She could hear the faint sound of Frisco's doorbell through the thin wall that separated their two condos. It rang once, twice, three times, four.

Then there was silence.

Mia waited, wondering if the man had gone away, or if he was out in the courtyard—or standing in front of her own door.

And then she heard the sound of breaking glass. There was another sound, a crash, and then several more thumps—all coming from inside Frisco's condominium.

Dwayne had gone inside. He'd broken in, and from the sound of things, the son of a bitch was destroying Frisco's home.

Mia leapt for her telephone and dialed 911.

Police cars—three of them—were parked haphazardly in the condominium lot.

Frisco threw a ten-dollar bill at the taxi driver and pulled himself and his crutches as quickly as he could out of the cab.

His heart was in his throat as he raced into the courtyard. People were outside of their units, standing around, watching the police officers, several of whom were outside of both his and Mia's condos.

Both doors were open wide and one of the uniformed officers went into Mia's place.

Still on his crutches, Frisco took the stairs dangerously fast. If he lost his balance, he'd seriously hurt himself, but he wasn't going to lose his balance, dammit. He needed to get up those stairs.

"Mia," he called. "Tash?"

Thomas King stepped out of Mia's condo. "It's okay, Navy," he said. "No one was hurt."

But Frisco didn't slow down. "Where are they?"

"Inside."

He went in, squinting to adjust his eyes to the sudden dimness. Despite Thomas's reassurance, he had to see with his own eyes that they were okay. Mia was standing near the kitchen, talking to one of the policewomen. She looked all right. She was still wearing the shorts and sleeveless top she'd had on earlier. Her hair was still back in a single braid. She looked calm and composed.

"Where's Tasha?"

She looked up at him and a flurry of emotions crossed her face and he knew she wasn't quite as composed as she looked. "Alan. Thank God. Tasha's in my office, playing computer games. She's fine." She took a step toward him as if she wanted to reach for him, but stopped, glancing back at the police officer, as if she were embarrassed or uncertain as to his reception.

Frisco didn't give a damn who was watching. He wanted her in his arms, and he wanted her *now*. He dropped his crutches and pulled her close, closing his eyes and breathing in her sweet perfume. "When I saw those police cars..." He couldn't continue. He just held her.

"Excuse me," the policewoman murmured, slipping past them and disappearing out of the open condo door.

"Dwayne came looking for you," Mia told him, tightening her arms around his waist.

Dwayne. He held her tighter, too. "Dammit, I shouldn't have left you alone. Are you sure he didn't hurt you?"

"I saw him coming and we stayed inside," she said, pulling back to look up at him. "Alan, he totally trashed your living room and kitchen. The rest of the apartment's okay—I called the police and they came before he went into the bedrooms, but—"

"He didn't talk to you, didn't threaten you or Tash in any way?"

She shook her head. "He ran away when he heard the police sirens. He never even knew we were next door."

Frisco felt a rush of relief. "Good."

Her eyes were wide. "Good? But your living room is wrecked."

"To hell with my living room. I don't care about my living room."

He gazed down into her eyes, and at her beautiful lips parted softly in surprise, and he kissed her.

It was a strange kiss, having nothing to do with attraction and desire. He wasn't kissing her because he wanted her. He kissed her because he wanted to vanquish the last of his fears. He wanted to convince himself without a doubt that she truly was all right. It had nothing to do with sex and everything to do with the flood of emotions he'd felt while running up those stairs.

Her lips were warm and sweet and pliant under his own. She kissed him eagerly, both giving and taking comfort in return.

When they finally pulled apart, Mia had tears in her eyes. She wiped at them, forcing an apologetic smile. "I was scared out of my mind that Dwayne was going to somehow find you before you got home—"

"I can handle Dwayne."

She looked away, but not before he caught a glimpse of the skepticism in her eyes. He felt himself tense with frustration, but stopped himself from reacting. Why shouldn't she doubt his ability to protect himself? Just yesterday, she'd watched Dwayne beat the crap out of him.

He pulled her hand up, positioning it on the outside of his jacket, just underneath his left arm. There was surprise on her face as she felt the unmistakable bulge of his shoulder holster and sidearm.

"I can handle Dwayne," he said again.

"Excuse me, Lieutenant Francisco...?"

Frisco released Mia and turned to see one of the cops standing just inside the door. He was an older man, balding and gray with a leathery face and a permanent squint to his eyes from the bright California sun. He was obviously the officer in charge of the investigation.

"I'm wondering if we might be able to ask you some questions, sir?"

Mia bent down and picked up Frisco's crutches, her head spinning.

A gun. Her lover was carrying a *gun*. Of course, it made sense that he would have one. He was a professional soldier, for crying out loud. He probably had an entire collection of firearms. She simply hadn't thought about it before this. Or maybe she hadn't *wanted* to think about it. It was ludicrous, actually. She, who was so opposed to violence and weapons of any kind, had fallen in love with a man who not only wore a gun, but obviously knew how to use it.

"Thanks," he murmured to her, positioning his crutches under his arms. He started toward the policeman. "I'm not sure I can give you any answers," he said to the man. "I haven't even seen the damage yet."

Mia followed him out the door. Thomas was still standing outside. "Will you stay with Tasha for a minute?" she asked him.

He nodded and went inside.

She caught up with Frisco as he was stepping into his

condo. His face was expressionless as he gazed at what used to be his living room.

The glass-topped coffee table was shattered. The entertainment center that had held his TV and a cheap stereo system had been toppled forward, away from the wall. The heavy wood of the shelves was intact, but the television was smashed. All of his lamps were broken, and the ugly plaid couch had been slashed and shredded, and wads of white stuffing and springs were exposed.

His dining area and kitchen contained more of the same. His table and chairs had been knocked over and the kitchen floor was littered with broken glasses and plates swept down from the cabinets. The refrigerator was open and tipped forward, its contents smashed and broken on the floor, oozing together in an awful mess.

Frisco looked, but didn't say a word. The muscle in his jaw moved, though, as he clenched his teeth.

"Your...friend ID'd the man who broke in as someone named Dwayne...?" the policeman said.

His *friend*. As Mia watched, Frisco's eyes flickered in her direction at the officer's tactful hesitation. The man could have called her his neighbor, but it was obvious to everyone that she was more than that. Mia tried not to blush, remembering the bright-colored condom wrapper that surely still lay on Frisco's bedroom floor. These police officers had been crawling all over this place for the past twenty-five minutes. They surely hadn't missed seeing that wrapper—or the way Frisco had pulled her possessively into his arms when he'd arrived. These were seasoned cops. They were especially good at deductive reasoning.

"I don't know anyone named Dwayne," Frisco told the policeman. He unbuttoned his jacket, and carefully began maneuvering his way through the mess toward his bedroom. "Mia must've been mistaken."

"Alan, I saw—"

He glanced at her, shaking his head, just once, in warning. "Trust me," he murmured. Mia closed her mouth. What was he doing? He knew damn well who Dwayne was, and she *wasn't* mistaken.

"I appreciate your coming all the way down here, Officer," he said, "but I won't be pressing charges."

The policeman was respectful of Frisco's uniform and his rows of medals. Mia could hear it in the man's voice. But he was also obviously not happy with Frisco's decision. "Lieutenant, we have four different witnesses who saw this man either entering or leaving your home." He spread his hands, gesturing to the destruction around them. "This is no small amount of damage that was done here this afternoon."

"No one was hurt," Frisco said quietly.

Mia couldn't keep quiet. "No one was hurt?" she said in disbelief. "Yesterday someone was hurt...." She bit her lip to keep from saying more. Yesterday that man had sent Frisco to the hospital. His name had been Dwayne then, and it was still Dwayne today. And if Frisco had been home this afternoon...

But *trust me,* he'd whispered. And she did. She trusted him. So she had swallowed her words.

But her outburst had been enough, and for the first time since he'd stepped inside his condo, Frisco's face flashed with emotion. "This is not something that's going to go away by arresting this bastard on charges of breaking and entering and vandalism," he told her. "In fact, it'll only make things worse." He looked from Mia to the cop, as if aware he'd nearly said too much. With effort, he erased all signs of his anger from his face and when he spoke again, his voice was matter of fact. "Like I said, I don't want to press charges."

He started to turn away, but the policeman wouldn't let him go. "Lieutenant Francisco, it sounds like you have some kind of problem here. Maybe if you talked to one of the detectives in the squad...?"

Frisco remained expressionless. "Thank you, but no. Now, if you don't mind, I want to change my clothes and start cleaning up this mess."

"I don't know what's going on here," the cop warned him,

"but if you end up taking the law into your own hands, my friend, you're only going to have a bigger problem."

"Excuse me." Frisco disappeared into his bedroom, and after a moment, the policeman went out the door, shaking his head in exasperation.

Mia followed Frisco. "Alan, it *was* Dwayne."

He was waiting for her at his bedroom door. "I know it was. Hey, don't look at me that way." He pulled her inside and closed the door behind her, drawing her into his arms and kissing her hard on the mouth, as if trying to wipe the expression of confusion and apprehension off her face. "I'm sorry if I made you feel foolish in front of the police—claiming you were mistaken that way. But I didn't know what else to say."

"I don't understand why you won't press charges."

She looked searchingly up at him and he met her gaze steadily. "I know. Thanks for trusting me despite that." His face softened into his familiar half smile and he kissed her again, more gently this time.

Mia felt herself melt. His clean-shaven cheeks felt sensuously smooth against her face as she deepened their kiss, and she felt a hot surge of desire. His arms tightened around her, and she knew he felt it, too.

But he gently pushed her away, laughing softly. "Damn, you're dangerous. I've got a serious jones for you."

"A...jones?"

"Addiction," he explained. "Some guys get a traveling jones—they can't stay in one place for very long. I've had friends with a skydiving jones, can't go for more than a few days without making a jump." He crossed to his closet and leaned his crutches against the wall, turning back to smile at her again. "Looks like I've got myself a pretty severe Mia Summerton jones." His voice turned even softer and velvet smooth. "I can't go for more than an hour or two without wanting to make love to you."

The heat coursing through her got thicker, hotter. *I've got a serious jones for you*—the words weren't very romantic,

Yet, when Frisco said it, with his husky voice and his liquid-fire eyes, and that incredibly sexy half smile…it was. It was pure romance.

He turned away from her, somehow knowing that if he looked at her that way another moment longer, she'd end up in his arms, and they'd wind up in his bed again.

And there was no time for that now, as nice as it would have been. Thomas was back at her condo, watching Natasha. And Mia was still waiting for Frisco's explanation.

"Why won't you press charges?" she asked again.

She sat down on his bed, watching as he took off his jacket and hung it carefully in the closet.

"I saw Sharon," he told her, glancing back at her, his eyes grim and his smile gone. He was wearing a white shirt, and the dark nylon straps of his shoulder holster stood out conspicuously. He unfastened the holster and tossed it, gun included, next to her onto his bed.

Mia couldn't help but stare at that gun lying there like that, several feet away from her. He'd treated it so casually, as if it weren't a deadly weapon, capable of enabling him to take a human life with the slightest effort.

"It turns out that she *does* owe Dwayne some money. She says she 'borrowed' about five grand when she moved out of his place a few months ago." He hopped on one leg over to the bed and sat down next to her. Bending down, he pulled off his shoes and socks. His shirt was unbuttoned, revealing tantalizing glimpses of his tanned, muscular chest. But even that wasn't enough to pull Mia's attention away from the gun he'd thrown onto the bed.

"Please—I'd like it if you would move this," she interrupted him.

He glanced at her, and then down at his holstered gun. "Sorry." He picked it up and set it down, away from her, on the floor. "I should've known you wouldn't like firearms."

"I don't dislike them. I *hate* them."

"I'm a sharpshooter—*was* a sharpshooter, I'm a little rusty these days—and I know firearms so well, I'd be lying if I told you I hated them. I'd also be lying if I told you I didn't feel more secure when I'm carrying. What I do hate is when weapons get into the wrong hands."

"In my opinion, *any* hands are the wrong hands. Guns should be banned from the surface of the earth."

"But they exist," Frisco pointed out. "It's too late to simply wish them away."

"It's not too late to set restrictions about who can have them," she said hotly.

"Legally," he added, heat slipping into his voice, too. "Who can have them *legally.* The people who shouldn't have them—the bad guys, the criminals and the terrorists—they're going to figure out some way to get their hands on them no matter *what* laws are made. And as long as *they* can get their hands on firearms, I'm going to make damn sure that I have one, too."

His jaw was set, his eyes hard, glittering with an intense blue fire. They were on opposite sides of the fence here, and Mia knew with certainty that he was no more likely to be swayed to her opinion than she was to his.

She shook her head in sudden disbelief. "I can't believe I'm..." She looked away from him, shocked at the words she almost said aloud. *I can't believe I'm in love with a man who carries a gun.*

He touched her, gently lifting her hand and intertwining their fingers, correctly guessing at half of what she nearly said. "We're pretty different from each other, huh?"

She nodded, afraid to look into his eyes, afraid he'd guess the other half of her thoughts, too.

He smiled wryly. "Where do you stand on abortion? Or the death penalty?"

Mia smiled despite herself. "Don't ask." No doubt their points of view were one hundred and eighty degrees apart on those issues, too.

"I like it this way," he said quietly. "I like it that you don't agree with everything that I think."

She *did* look up at him then. "We probably belong to opposite political parties."

"Is that so bad?"

"Our votes will cancel each other out."

"Democracy in action."

His eyes were softer now, liquid instead of steel. Mia felt herself start to drown in their blueness. Frisco wasn't the only one who had a jones, an addiction. She leaned forward and he met her in a kiss. Her hands went up underneath his open shirt, skimming against his bare skin, and the sensation made them both groan.

But when Mia would've given in, when she would have fallen back with him onto his bed, Frisco made himself pull away. He was breathing hard and the fire in his eyes was unmistakable. He wanted her as much as she wanted him. He may have been addicted, but he had a hell of a lot of willpower.

"We have to get out of here," he explained. "Dwayne's going to come back, and I don't want you and Tasha to be here when he does."

"I still don't understand why you won't press charges," Mia said. "Just because your sister owes this guy some money, that doesn't give him the right to destroy your condo."

Frisco stood up, shrugging out of his shirt. He wadded it into a ball and tossed it into the corner of his room, on top of his mountain of dirty laundry. "His name is Dwayne Bell," he told her. "And he's a professional scumbag—drugs, stolen goods, black-market weapons—you name it, he's involved. And he doesn't earn six figures a year by being nice about unpaid loans."

He glanced at her as he unfastened and stepped out of his pants. Mia knew she shouldn't be staring. It was hardly polite to stare at a man dressed only in utilitarian white briefs, but she couldn't look away.

"Sharon lived with him for about four months," he told her, hopping toward his duffel bags and searching through them. "During that time, she worked for him, too. According to Sharon, Dwayne has enough on her to cause real trouble. If he was arrested for something as petty as breaking and entering, he'd plea-bargain and give her up for dealing drugs, and *she'd* be the one who'd end up in jail."

Mia briefly closed her eyes. "Oh, no."

"Yeah."

"So what are we going to do?"

He found a pair of relatively clean shorts and came back to the bed. He sat down and pulled them on. "*We're* going to get you and Tasha out of here. Then *I'm* going to come back and deal with Dwayne."

Deal with Dwayne? "Alan—"

He was up again, slipping his shoulder holster over his arm and fastening it against his bare skin. "Do me a favor. Go into Tash's room and grab her bathing suit and a couple of changes of clothes." He bent down and picked up one of his empty duffel bags and tossed it to her.

Mia caught it, but she didn't move. "Alan..."

His back was to her as he searched his closet, pulling out a worn olive drab army fatigue shirt, its sleeves cut short, the ends fraying. He pulled it on. It was loose and he kept it mostly unbuttoned. It concealed his gun, but still allowed him access to it. He could get to it if he needed it when he "dealt with Dwayne." Unless, of course, Dwayne got to his own gun first. Fear tightened Mia's throat.

He turned to face her. "Come on, Mia. Please. And then go pack some of your own things."

She felt a flash of annoyance, hotter and sharper than the fear. "It's funny, I don't recall your *asking* me to come along with you. You haven't even told me where you're going."

"Lucky has a cabin in the hills about forty miles east of San Felipe. I'm going to call him, see if we can use his place for a few days."

Lucky. From Frisco's former SEAL unit. He was Frisco's friend—no, they were more than just friends, they were... what did they call it? Swim buddies.

"I'm asking for your help here," he continued, quietly. "I need you to come along to take care of Tash while I—"

"Deal with Dwayne," she finished for him with exasperation. "You know I'll help you, Alan. But I'm not sure I'm willing to go hide at some cabin." She shook her head. "Why don't we find someplace safe for Tasha to go? We could...I don't know, maybe drive her down to my mother's. Then I could come with you when you go to see Dwayne."

"No. No way. Absolutely not."

Her temper flared. "I don't want you to do this alone."

He laughed, but there was no humor in it. "What, do you really think *you're* gonna keep Dwayne from trying to kick my butt again? Are you going to lecture him on nonviolence? Or maybe you'll try to use positive reinforcement to teach him manners, huh?"

Mia felt her face flush. "No, I—"

"Dwayne Bell is one mean son of a bitch," Frisco told her. "He doesn't belong in your world—and you don't belong in his. And I intend to keep it that way."

She folded her arms across her chest, holding her elbows tightly so he wouldn't see that her hands were shaking with anger. "And which of those worlds do *you* belong in?"

He was quiet for a moment. "Neither," he finally said, unable to look her in the eye. "I'm stuck here in limbo, remember?"

Positive reinforcement. To use positive reinforcement to award positive behavior meant being as consistently blasé as possible when negative behavior occurred. Mia closed her eyes for a moment, willing herself not to fall prey to her anger and lash out at him. She wanted to shake some sense into him. She wanted to shout that this limbo he found himself in was only imagined. She wanted to hold him close until he healed, until he realized that he didn't need a miracle to be whole again—that he could be whole even if his knee gave out and he never walked another step again.

Wallowing in despair wouldn't do him a damn bit of good. And neither would her yelling at or shaking or even comforting him. Instead, she kept her voice carefully emotionless. "Well," she said, starting for the door with the duffel bag he'd tossed her. "I'll get Tasha's stuff." She turned back to him almost as an afterthought, as if what she was about to say to him didn't matter so much that she was almost shaking. "Oh, and when you call Lucky to ask about the cabin, it would be smart to tell him about all this, don't you think? *He* could go with you when you find Dwayne. He could watch your back, and *he* probably wouldn't resort to lectures on nonviolence as means of defense." She forced herself to smile, and was surprised to find she actually could. His insult had been right on target—and it wasn't entirely unamusing.

"Mia, I'm sorry I said that."

"Apology accepted—or at least it will be if you call Lucky."

"Yeah," Frisco said. "I'll do that. And I'll…" It took him a great deal of effort to say it, but he did. "I'll ask him for help."

He was going to ask for help. Thank God. Mia wanted to take one of the colorful medals from his dress uniform and pin it on to his T-shirt. Instead, she simply nodded.

"Then I'll stay with Tasha at Lucky's cabin," she said, and left the room.

13

Natasha pushed open the cabin's screen door, but then stopped, looking back at Frisco, who was elbow deep in dinner's soapy dishes. "Can I go outside?"

He nodded. "Yeah, but stay on the porch. It's getting dark." She was out the door in a flash, and he shouted after her, "Hey, Tash?"

She pressed her nose against the screen, peering in at him.

"Good job remembering to ask," he said.

She beamed at him and vanished.

He looked up to find Mia watching him. She was sitting on the couch, a book in her lap, a small smile playing about the corners of her mouth.

"Good job remembering to praise her," she told him.

"She's starting to catch on."

"Sure you don't want me to help over there?" she asked.

Frisco shook his head. "You cooked, I clean. It's only fair."

They'd arrived at Lucky's cabin just before dinnertime. It had been close to six years since Frisco had been up here, but the place looked almost exactly the same.

The cabin wasn't very big by any standards—just a living room with a fireplace and a separate kitchen area, two small bedrooms—one in the back, the other off the living room, and an extremely functional bathroom with only cold running water.

Lucky kept the place stocked with canned and dried goods—and enough beer and whiskey to sink a ship. Mia hadn't said a word about it, but Frisco knew she wondered about the temptation. She still didn't quite believe that alcohol wasn't a problem for him. But he'd been up here dozens of times with Lucky and some of the other guys from Alpha Squad, and he'd had cola while they made short work of a bottle of whiskey and a six pack of beer.

Still, he knew that she trusted him.

This afternoon, she'd followed his directions without so much as a questioning look as he'd asked her to leave the narrow back road and pull her car onto what was little more than a dirt path. They'd already been off the highway for what seemed like forever, and the dirt road wound another five miles without a sign of civilization before they reached an even smaller road that led to Lucky's cabin.

It was, definitely, in the middle of nowhere.

That made it perfect for SEAL training exercises. There was a lake not five hundred yards from the front porch, and countless acres of brush and wilderness surrounding the place.

It was a perfect hideout, too. There was no way on earth Dwayne Bell would find them here.

"How's your knee?"

Frisco glanced up to find that Mia had come to lean against the icebox, watching as he finished scouring the bottom of the pasta pot. He rinsed the suds from the pot by dunking it in a basin of clear, hot water, nodding his reply. "It's…improved," he told her. "It's been about eight hours since I've had to use the painkiller, and…" He glanced at her again. "I'm not about to start running laps, but I'm not in agony, either."

Mia nodded. "Good." She hesitated slightly, and he knew what was coming.

"When you spoke to Lucky…"

He carefully balanced the pot in the dish drain, on top of all the others. He knew what she wanted to know. "I'm meeting him tomorrow night," he said quietly. "Along with a couple other guys from Alpha Squad. The plan is for Thomas to come up in the afternoon and give me a lift back into San Felipe. You and Tash will hang out here.''

''And what happens when you actually find Dwayne?''

He released the water from the sink and dried his hands and arms on a dish towel, turning to look down into her eyes. ''I'm going to give him a thousand bucks and inform him that the other four thousand Sharon owes him covers the damages he caused by breaking into my condo. I intend to tell him that there's no amount of money in the world that would make retribution for the way he hit Natasha before she and Sharon moved out, and he's damned lucky that I'm not going to break him in half for doing that. I'm also going to convince him that if he so much as comes near Tash or Sharon or anyone else I care about, I will hunt him down and make him wish that he was dead.''

Mia's eyes were wide. ''And you really think that will work?''

Frisco couldn't resist reaching out and touching the side of her face. Her skin was so deliciously soft beneath his fingers. ''Yeah,'' he said. ''I think it'll work. By giving Dwayne some money—a substantial amount of money, despite the fact that it's only a fifth of what Sharon took—he doesn't walk away with nothing. He saves face.'' He paused. Unless this situation was more complicated than that. Unless there was something that Sharon hadn't told him, something she hadn't been quite honest about. But Mia probably didn't need to know that he was having doubts.

Unfortunately, she read his hesitation accurately. ''What?'' she asked, her gaze searching his face. ''You were going to say more, weren't you?''

He wanted to pull her close, to breathe in the sweet scent of her clean hair and luxuriate in the softness of her body pressed against his. He wanted that, but he couldn't risk touching her again. Even the sensation of her smooth cheek beneath his fingers had been enough to ignite the desire he felt whenever she was near—hell, whenever he so much as *thought* about her. If he pulled her into his arms, he would kiss her. And if he kissed her, he wouldn't want to stop.

"I got the sense Sharon wasn't one-hundred-percent honest with me," he finally admitted. Mia had been straightforward with him up to this point, sometimes painfully so. He respected her enough to return the favor. "I don't know— maybe I'm just being paranoid, but when I find Dwayne, I'm going to be ready for anything."

Mia's gaze dropped to his chest, to that hidden place near his left arm where his sidearm was snugly ensconced in his shoulder holster. Frisco knew exactly what she was thinking. He was going to go meet Dwayne with that weapon Mia disliked so intensely tucked under his arm. And it was that weapon that would help make him ready for anything.

She looked up at him. "Are you going to take that thing off when we make love tonight?"

When we make love tonight. Not if. When. Frisco felt the hot spiral of anticipation. Man, he'd hoped, but he hadn't wanted to assume. It was fine with him, though, if *she* wanted to assume that they were going to share a bed again tonight. It was more than fine.

"Yeah," he said, his voice husky. "I'll take it off."

"Good." She held his gaze and the air seemed to crackle around them.

He wanted to reach for her, to hold her, kiss her. He could feel his body's reaction to her nearness, to the soft curve of her lips, to the awareness in her eyes.

He wanted Mia now, but that wasn't an option—not with Tasha out sitting on the porch swing, rocking and singing a little song to herself. He tried to calculate the earliest he could get away with putting Tash to bed, tried to figure how long it would take her to fall asleep. Twilight was falling, and the cabin was already shadowy and dark. Even with no electricity, no bright lights and TV to distract the little girl, he had to guess it would be another hour at least before she'd agree to go to bed, another half hour after that before she was asleep.

He tried to glance surreptitiously at his watch, but Mia noticed and smiled. She didn't say a word, but he knew she was aware of everything he'd been thinking.

"Do you know where Lucky keeps the candles?" she asked, stepping away from him. "It's starting to get pretty dark."

He gestured with his head as he positioned his crutches under his arms. "In the cabinet next to the fireplace. And there's a kerosene lantern around here somewhere."

"Candles will be fine," Mia said, crossing to the cabinet. She threw him a very sexy smile over her shoulder. "I like candlelight, don't you?"

"Yeah," Frisco agreed, trying not to let his thoughts drift in the direction of candlelight and that big double bed in the other room. This next hour and a half was going to be the longest hour and a half of his entire life if he started thinking about Mia, with her long dark hair and her gorgeous, luminous eyes, tumbled onto that bed, candlelight gleaming on her satin smooth skin.

Mia found a box of matches on the fireplace mantel, well out of Tasha's reach, and lit one candle after another, placing them around the room. She looked otherworldly with the flickering candles sending shadows and light dancing across her high cheekbones, her full, graceful lips and her exotically tilted eyes. Her cutoff shorts were threadbare denim, and they hugged her backside sinfully snugly. Her hair was up in a braid. Frisco moved toward her, itching to unfasten it, to run his fingers through her silken hair, longing to see her smile, to hear her laughter, to bury himself in her sweetness and then hold her in his arms all night long. He hadn't had a chance to do that after they'd made love in the early hours of the morning, and now he found he wanted that more than he could believe.

She glanced at him again, but then couldn't look away, trapped for a moment by the need he knew was in his eyes.

"Maybe candlelight isn't such a good idea," she whispered. "Because if you keep looking at me like that I'm going to…"

"Oh, I hope so." Frisco moved closer, enough to take the candle from her hand and set it down on the fireplace mantel. "Whatever you're thinking about doing—I hope so."

Mia's heart was hammering. Lord, when he looked at her with such desire in his eyes, every nerve ending in her body went on red alert. He touched her lightly, brushing his thumb across her lips and she felt herself sway toward him, but he dropped his hand. She knew she shouldn't kiss him—not here, not now. Natasha was outside and she could come in at any moment.

She could read the same thoughts in Frisco's dark blue eyes. But instead of backing away as she'd expected, he lowered his head and kissed her anyway.

He tasted seductively sweet, like the fresh peaches they'd picked up at a local farm stand and sampled after dinner. It was a hard kiss, a passionate kiss, despite the fact that he kept both hands securely on the grips of his crutches, despite that the only place he touched her was her lips.

It was more than enough.

For now, anyway.

He pulled back and she found herself gazing into eyes the color of blue fire. And then she found herself reaching up, pulling his incredible lips down to hers again. She was wrong. Once was *not* enough.

"Are you gonna kiss again?"

Mia sprang away from Frisco as if she'd been burned.

She turned to see Natasha standing in the doorway, watching them. How long the child had been there, she couldn't begin to guess. She felt her cheeks flush.

Frisco smiled at Tasha. If he were the least bit perturbed, he was hiding it well. "Not right now."

"Later?"

His gaze flickered to Mia, and she could see genuine amusement lurking there. "I hope so."

Natasha considered this, head tilted to one side. "Thomas said if you broke Mia's heart, he was gonna kick you in the bottom." She sat down haughtily on the couch—the perfect

Russian princess. "He really said something else, but I don't say bad words."

The muscles in the side of Frisco's face twitched, but somehow he managed to hide his smile. "Well, Thomas and you don't have to worry. I have no intention of—"

"I made you a medal," Tash told him. "For not saying bad words, too. And for not drinking that smelly stuff," she added, almost as an afterthought, wrinkling her nose. She looked up at Mia. "Can I give it to him now?"

"Oh, Tasha, I'm afraid we left it back in my living room. I'm sorry..."

"It's beautiful," Tasha told Frisco, completely seriously. "You can have it when we go back. I'll give you the salute now, though, okay?"

"Sure..."

The little girl stood up and snapped off a military salute that would have impressed the meanest, toughest drill sergeant.

"Thanks, Tash." Frisco's voice was husky.

"Dwayne kissed Mommy and gave her a broke heart instead of getting married," she told them. "Are you going to get married?"

Frisco was no longer unperturbed. "Whoa, Tash, didn't we have this conversation already? And didn't we—"

"I would rather have a broke heart than Dwayne for a daddy," Tasha announced. "Why is it dark in here? Why don't we turn the lights on?"

"Remember that I told you there wasn't any electricity up here?"

"Does that mean that the lights are broke?"

Frisco hesitated. "It's kind of like that—"

"Is the TV broke, too?"

The little girl was looking up at Frisco, her eyes wide with horror. Frisco looked back at her, his mouth slightly open. "Oh, damn," he said, breaking her rule.

"Sweetie, there *is* no television up here," Mia said.

Natasha looked as if the end of the world were near, and Frisco's expression was nearly identical.

"I can't fall asleep without the TV on," Tasha whispered.

Frisco forced himself not to overreact as he went into Tash's bedroom for the third time in less than a half an hour. Yes, he'd seen Tasha in action on the night he'd accidentally turned off the TV set. She clearly depended on the damned thing to provide soothing background noise and light. She found it comforting, dependable and consistent. Wherever she'd been before this in her short life, there'd always been a television.

But she was a five-year-old. Sooner or later, exhaustion would win and she'd fall asleep. True, he'd hoped it would be sooner, but that was life. He'd have to wait a few more hours before Mia was in his arms. It wasn't *that* big a deal.

At least that's what he tried to convince himself.

As he sat on the edge of one of the narrow beds in the tiny back bedroom, Tasha looked up at him with wide, unhappy eyes. He kissed the top of her head. "Just *try* to sleep, okay?"

She didn't say a word. She just watched him as he propelled himself out of the room on his crutches.

Mia was sitting on one end of the couch that was positioned in front of the fireplace, legs curled up underneath her. Candlelight flickered, and she looked deliciously sexy. Carefully supporting his injured knee, he sat down, way at the other end of the couch.

"You're being very patient with her," she said softly.

He smiled ruefully. "You're being very patient with us both."

"I didn't come up here only for the great sex," she told him, trying to hide a smile. She failed and it slipped free.

"I had about two hours of sleep this morning, total," he said, his voice low. "I should be exhausted, but I'm not. I'm wide-awake because I know the kid's going to fall asleep, and I know that when she does, I'm going to take you into the other room, take off your clothes and make love to you, the way I've been dying to do again since you walked out of my bedroom this morning.''

He held her gaze. His own was steady and hot, and her smile quickly faded.

"Maybe we should talk about something else," she suggested breathlessly, and he forced himself to look away.

She was quiet for several long moments. Frisco could hear the second hand of her watch ticking its way around the dial. He could hear the cool night breeze as it swept through the trees. He heard the soft, almost inaudible creaking of the cabin as it lost the heat it had taken from the hot summer sun.

"I'm sorry I left the medal Tasha made for you at home," Mia finally said, obviously changing the subject. "We were in such a hurry, and I just didn't even think. She spent a long time on it. She told me all about what happened when you dropped the milk."

Frisco couldn't help but think about that new list that Mia had attached to his refrigerator—the list of things he could still do, even with his injured knee. He'd seen it for the first time as he'd been mopping up the spilled milk. It had taken the edge off his anger, turning his frustration into laughter and hot, sweet anticipation. Some of the things she'd written down were mind-blowingly suggestive. And she was dead right. He *could* do all of those things. And he intended to, as soon as he got the chance....

He forced himself to focus on their conversation. Tasha. The medal she had made for him. But the little girl had said it was for more than his recently cleaned-up language. "I didn't think she'd notice that I haven't been drinking," he confessed. "I mean, I haven't been making that big a deal about it. I guess it's kind of...sobering, if you'll pardon the pun, that she *did* notice."

Mia nodded, her eyes gentle. "She hasn't said anything to me about it."

He lowered his voice even further, so that if Tasha were still awake, she wouldn't hear. "I ordered that couch."

Mia looked confused, but then recognition flashed in her

eyes, and she clamped a hand over her mouth to keep from laughing out loud. "You mean the...?"

"Pink one," Frisco finished for her. He felt a smile spreading across his own face. "Yep. The other one was destroyed and I figured what the hell? The kid wants it so badly. I'll just make sure she takes it with her when she goes."

When she goes. The thought was not a pleasant one. In fact, it was downright depressing. And that was strange. When Tash first arrived, he could think of nothing but surviving, about making the best of a bad situation until the time that she would go. It hadn't taken long for that to change. It was true that having the kid around made life more complicated—like right now for instance, when he desperately wanted her to fall asleep—but for the first time in years he was forced to think about something other than his injury. He was forced to stop waiting for a chance to live again, and instead actually do some living.

The truth was, he'd adored Tasha from the moment she'd been born.

"I helped deliver her. Did you know that?" he asked Mia.

"Natasha?" she said. "I didn't know."

"Lucky and I were on leave and he drove out to Arizona with me to see Sharon. She was about to have the baby, and we were about to be shipped out to the Middle East for God knows how long. She was living in this trailer park about forty miles east of Tucson. Twenty minutes after we arrived, she went into hard labor. The nearest hospital was back in Tucson, so we got her into my truck and drove like hell."

He smiled. "But Sharon never does anything the easy way. She must've had the shortest labor in history. We had to pull off the road because Tasha wasn't going to wait."

As Mia watched, Frisco was silent for a moment. She knew he was reliving that event, remembering.

"It was incredible," he said quietly. "When that baby came out, it was... It was one of the high points of my life."

He shook his head, the expression on his face one of wonder and awe, even after all this time. "I'd never seen a miracle before, but I saw one that day. And when Lucky put that tiny baby in my hands… She was all red and wrinkly, and so *alive*—this little new life, only a few seconds old."

He glanced up at her, his smile tinged with embarrassment. "Sounds pretty corny, huh?"

Mia shook her head, unable to answer him, unable to speak. It wasn't corny. It was incredibly, heart-wrenchingly sweet.

"I held Tasha all the way to the hospital," he continued. "Sharon was out of it—which is pretty much her standard condition. So I wrapped that baby in my T-shirt and held her for what seemed like forever because she was crying, and Sharon was crying and the really stupid thing was that it was all I could do not to cry, too." He was quiet for a moment. "But I finally got Tasha quieted down. I sang to her and talked to her, promised her that the hardest part of her life was over. She'd been born, and that's always rough, but if I had anything to say about it, it was going to be a breeze for her from here on in. I told her I'd take care of her, and I'd take care of her mom, too.

"And then we got to the hospital, and the nurses came out to take her away, and I didn't want to let her go." He forced a smile, and it made him look impossibly sad. "But I did."

He looked down at his injured knee. "And three hours later, the CO called in all of SEAL Team Ten, and Alpha Squad shipped out on an emergency rescue mission."

"That's when you were wounded," Mia said.

It wasn't a question, but he glanced at her and nodded. "Yeah. That's when I was wounded." He was clenching his teeth and the muscle in the side of his jaw worked. "I didn't keep any of those promises I made to that little baby. I mean, I sent Sharon money, but…" He shook his head and forced another smile. "So I'm buying the kid a pink couch, hoping that'll make up for all those years I wasn't around." His smile became more genuine. "Lucky was going to go over with some of the guys and finish getting the place cleaned up. He'll be there to take delivery. I told him about the couch, but I'm not sure he believed me.'' He laughed. "He'll believe me when he sees it, huh?''

Mia didn't know whether to laugh or cry. Every flicker of emotion on Frisco's face, every glint of pain or sorrow or joy in his eyes, every word that he spoke, every word that he shared with her filled her heart with a feeling of longing so deep, she could barely breathe.

She loved him.

He was everything she didn't need. His wounds were so deep and so catastrophic. She could handle his physical limitations. For her own self, she didn't give a damn whether or not he needed a cane or crutches or even a wheelchair to get around. In her mind, his emotional limitations were far more crippling. It was his emotional baggage—the bitterness and anger he carried with him—that had the bulk and the weight to engulf her and drag her down, too.

Still, despite that, she loved him.

Mia felt her eyes flood with tears, and she turned away, not wanting him to see. But he did, and he leaned forward, his eyes filled with concern.

"Mia…?''

She silently cursed her volatile emotions as she wiped her eyes. "I'm sorry. I'm…being silly.''

He tried to make light of it. "It *is* pretty silly to cry over a pink couch.''

"I'm not crying about the couch. I'm crying…'' Mia made the mistake of glancing up into his eyes, and now she was trapped, unable to look away, held as much by the gentleness of his concern as by the fire and the intensity that was also in his gaze. "Because you've complicated my life beyond belief,'' she whispered.

He knew what she meant. He understood her unspoken message. Mia could see comprehension in his eyes, so she said the words aloud. "I'm falling in love with you, Alan.''

Frisco's heart was in his throat. He'd suspected that Mia cared, but there was a big difference between a vague suspicion and hearing the words directly from her mouth. Falling. In love. With *him*.

Dear God, was she blind? How could she possibly be falling in love with this dried husk of a man he'd become? How could beautiful, lighthearted, joyful Mia possibly love someone who wasn't whole?

Her words should have elated him. Instead, he felt only despair. How could she *love* him?

He could hear Mia's watch ticking, its second hand traveling full circle again and again.

Finally she stood and crossed to the screen door, gazing out into the night as if she knew how much her softly spoken honesty had thrown him.

He had to say something. He knew from the tight set of her back that she wanted him to say something, *any*thing, but he couldn't think of a single response. "You're crazy" seemed inappropriate, as did "You're wrong."

"Frisco?"

He turned to see Natasha standing in the hallway. Her nightgown was several sizes too large, and it hung almost all the way down to the ground. She was holding her stuffed bear by one of its raggedy arms. Her hair was tangled around her face, and her eyes were filled with tears.

"I can't sleep," she told him. "It's too quiet. Too *nothing.* I don't like it. I can't hear *any*thing at all."

Frisco glanced at Mia, who had turned back, but wouldn't meet his eyes. Man, she'd just spilled her guts to him, and he hadn't responded. He'd said nothing, done nothing. At least he had to tell her that her declaration had totally blown him away.

"Tash, go on back into bed," he said. "I'll be there in a sec, but I need to talk to Mia first—"

Mia interrupted him. "No, it's okay. Alan, we can talk later." She forced a smile, but her eyes looked so sad. "It was…bad timing on my part."

She looked away, and there was silence in the room. Frisco

could hear his own heart beating, and Tasha's slight snuffle and that damned ticking watch....

The idea came to him in a flash.

Frisco pulled himself to his feet. "Come on." He led the way back into Tasha's bedroom. The little girl followed, but Mia didn't move. He stuck his head back out the door. "You, too," he told her.

He could see uncertainty in her eyes. "Maybe I should just wait out here...."

"Nope, we need you. Come on." He went back into the bedroom. "Back in bed, Tash."

Mia stood in the doorway, letting her eyes get used to the dark. She'd been in this bedroom, helping Tasha put on her nightgown. Even though it was dark, she could identify the different shapes that were the furniture. The bed Tasha had climbed into was against one wall. Another bed was directly opposite it. There was a small table and a chest of drawers, and several long windows that were open to the soft breezes of the summer night.

Frisco was sitting on the other bed, his back against the wall. "Come here," he said to Mia quietly.

She stepped hesitantly into the room, and he gently took her arm and pulled her down in front of him on the bed so that she was sitting between his legs, her back leaning against his chest. He looped his arms around her waist, holding her firmly in place.

She fought him for all of a half a second before giving in to the decadently glorious feeling of his arms around her. She let her head fall back against his shoulder and allowed herself the luxury of enjoying the sensation of his rough chin against her temple.

She knew she'd surprised him with her statement of love. Shoot, she'd surprised herself. But when he'd failed to react in any way at all, she'd assumed that unless she could somehow explain her feelings, he was intending to push her away.

But right now, he was doing anything but pushing her away. He was holding her close.

His lips brushed her cheek and she fought the sudden urge to cry again. Maybe the fact that she was falling in love with him didn't frighten him quite so much as she'd imagined. Maybe now that he'd had several minutes to get used to the idea, he actually *liked* it. Maybe…

"Tasha thinks it's absolutely silent in here," he said, his voice raspy and warm in the cool darkness.

"It *is*." The little girl sat up in the other bed.

"Gotta lie down," Frisco told her. "This will only work if you lie down."

She obeyed, but then popped right up again. "What are we doing?"

"*You* are lying down in your bed," he told her, waiting as she did so, amusement in his voice. "*We* are here to check on this odd silence you claim is in this room. And it's odd because it's far from silent out in the living room. And it's sure as he—*heck* not silent outside the cabin."

"It's *not?*" Tasha sat up again. This time she caught herself, and lay back down before Frisco could scold her.

"No way. Shh. Lie *very* still and listen."

Mia found herself holding her breath as Frisco and Tasha fell silent.

"Man," Frisco said after a moment. "You're wrong, Tash. This is one of the noisiest rooms I've ever been in."

The little girl sat up. "Noisy…?"

"Lie down," he commanded. "And listen again."

Again the silence.

"Listen to the wind in the trees," Frisco said quietly. Mia closed her eyes, relaxing even farther into his embrace, loving the sensation of his arms around her and his breath against her ear as his voice floated out across the darkness. "Listen to the way the leaves whisper together when a breeze comes through. And there's a branch—it's probably dead. It keeps bumping against the other branches, trying to shake itself free and drop to the ground. Do you hear it?"

"Yeah," breathed Tasha.

Mia did, too. But just a moment ago, she hadn't even been

aware of the noise at all. Another gust swept by, and she heard the sound of the leaves in the wind. Whispering, Frisco had said. His descriptions were poetic in their accuracy.

"And the crickets," Frisco said. "Hear them? And there must be some kind of locust out there, too, making their music, putting on a show. But they'll hush right up if a stranger comes around. The story the insects tell is the loudest when their music stops."

He was quiet again.

"Someone must be camping around the other side of the lake," he said quietly. "I can hear a dog barking—whining, probably tied up somewhere. And—shhh! Listen to that rumble. Must be train tracks not too far from here. Freight's coming through."

Sure enough, in the distance, Mia could hear the faint, lonely sound of a train whistle.

It was amazing. Although she made her living teaching U.S. history, she considered herself an artist, raised around artists, brought up surrounded by artists' sensitivities and delicate senses of detail. She'd never be able to paint like her mother, but she wasn't a half-bad photographer, able to catch people's quirks and personalities on film. On top of being an artist, she considered herself a liberal feminist, in tune with her world, always willing to volunteer at the local church homeless shelter, sensitive to the needs of others. She was a modern, sensitive, artistic, creative woman—who had never taken the time to truly stop and *listen* to the sounds of the night.

Unlike this big, stern-faced, gun-carrying, flesh-and-blood version of G.I. Joe, who ignored physical pain as if his heart and soul were made of stone—who had the patience to listen, and the sensitivity to hear music in the sound of the wind in the trees.

Mia had been amazed at herself for falling for a rough, tough professional soldier. But there was so much more to this man besides the roughness and toughness. So much more.

"The night is *never* silent," Frisco said. "It's alive, always moving, always telling a story. You just have to learn to hear its voice. You've got to learn how to listen. And once you learn how to listen, it's always familiar, always like being home. At the same time, it's never boring. The voice might always be the same, but the story it tells is always changing.''

Another breeze shook the leaves, carrying with it the sound of that distant dog barking. It was remarkable.

''And that's only *outside* the cabin,'' he told them. ''Inside, there's a whole pile of noises, too. Inside the cabin, *you* become part of the night's story.''

''I can hear you breathe,'' Tasha said. Her voice sounded sleepy and thick.

''That's right. And I can hear *you* breathing. And Mia, too. She keeps holding her breath, thinking that'll help her be more quiet, but she's wrong. Every time she exhales and then sucks in another big breath, it's ten times as loud. If you don't want to be heard, you need to breathe slowly and shallowly. You need to become part of the night, breathing along with its rhythms.''

Mia could hear the distinct sound of his lips curving up into a smile. She didn't need to see his face to know it was one of his funny half smiles.

''Every now and then I can hear Mia's stomach rumble. I don't know, Tash—maybe we didn't feed her enough at dinner,'' Frisco continued. ''And I can also hear the second hand on her watch. It's making a hell—heck—of a racket.''

''Maybe it's *your* watch that you hear,'' Mia countered softly, feeling much too noisy. Her breathing, her stomach, her watch...next he was going to tell her that he could hear her heart beating. Of course, due to her present position, pressed firmly against him, her heart was pounding loudly enough to be heard across the entire state.

''My watch has LED's,'' he breathed into her ear. ''It's silent.''

She had to ask. ''Where did you learn to listen like this?''

He was quiet for a moment. ''I don't know. I did a lot of

night details, I guess. When it's just you and the night, you get to know the night pretty well."

Mia lowered her voice. "I've never known anyone like you."

His arms tightened around her. "The feeling is...very mutual."

"Are you gonna kiss?" Tasha's voice was *very* drowsy sounding.

Frisco laughed. "Not in front of you, kid."

"Thomas told me if you and Mia had a baby, it would be my cousin."

"Thomas is certainly full of all kinds of information, isn't he?" Frisco released his hold on Mia, giving her a gentle push up and off the bed. "Go to sleep now, Tash. Remember, you've got the night keeping you company, all right?" He picked his crutches up off the floor.

"All right. I love you, Frisco."

"Love you, too, Tash."

Mia turned away as Frisco bent over the little girl's bed and gave her a quick kiss.

"Sit with me for a minute?" the little girl asked.

Mia heard Frisco sigh. "All right. Just for a minute."

Mia went into the living room, listening to wind in the trees, listening to the sound of her own breathing, the ticking of her watch. She stood at the screen door, looking out into the night, aware of the flames from the candles leaping and flickering behind her.

It may have been one minute or ten, but when she finally heard Frisco follow her out into the living room, she didn't turn around. She was aware of him watching her, aware that he didn't move any closer, but instead stopped, not even crossing to sit down on the couch.

She felt nervous at his silence, and she kicked herself for letting her feelings slip out the way they had. She hadn't been thinking. If she *had* been, she would've remembered that love wasn't on his agenda.

Still, the way he'd held her as they'd sat together in Tasha's room...

She took a deep breath and turned to face him. "I didn't mean to scare you. You know... Before."

"You didn't." He shook his head, as if he were aware he wasn't telling her the truth. "You *did*. I just... I don't..." It was his turn to take a deep breath. "Mia, I don't understand."

"What part are you having problems with?" she asked, taking refuge in her usual cheekiness. "The part where I said I love you, or... Well, no, that was the only part, wasn't it?"

He didn't laugh. He didn't even crack a smile. "A few days ago, you didn't even like me."

"No. A few days ago, I didn't like the person I thought you were," she told him. "I was wrong, though—you're incredible. I meant it when I said I've never met anyone like you. You're funny and smart and—"

"Dammit, stop," he said, pushing himself forward on his crutches, but then stopping in the middle of the room as if he were unsure of where to go, what to do. He ran one hand through his hair, leaving it messy—a visual testament to his frustration.

"Why? It's true. You're wonderful with Tasha. You're gentle and patient and kind, yet at the same time I don't doubt your ability to be anything *but* gentle in more aggressive situations. You're a soldier with an absolute code of honor. You're sensitive and sweet, yet you've got a willpower that's made of stone. You're—"

"Physically challenged," Frisco ground out through clenched teeth. "Don't leave *that* out."

14

"Yes, you're physically challenged, but you're also strong enough to deal with it." Mia took a step toward Frisco, and then another and another until she was close enough to touch him, until she *was* touching him.

When Mia touched him, it was so easy to forget about everything. When she touched him, the entire world went away. He pulled her toward him, needing the sanctuary of her kiss, but afraid she might take his silence for agreement. He stopped himself and forced himself to pull back.

"Mia, you don't understand. I—"

She kissed him. She kissed him, and he was lost. He was lost, but he was also suddenly, miraculously found.

She was fire in his arms, fire beneath his lips. She was an explosion of all that he wanted—only she wasn't out of reach. She was right here, well within his grasp.

Frisco heard himself groan, heard his crutches clatter to the floor, heard her answering sound of satisfaction as he kissed her harder now—deeper, longer, hotter kisses filled with all of his need and desire.

And then she pulled back. "Make love to me."

It wasn't an entreaty he needed to hear twice. "I'll check on Tash," he said hoarsely.

She slipped out of his arms. "I'll take some candles into our bedroom."

Candles. Candlelight. Yes. Frisco picked up his crutches and moved as silently as he could toward the room where

Tasha was sleeping. He could hear the child's slow and steady breathing before he even reached the doorway.

She was asleep.

For how long, he couldn't say. She might wake up in an hour or two. In fact, she'd *probably* wake up in an hour or two and be scared and confused. But for right now, she was asleep. For right now, he had the freedom to lock himself in that other bedroom with Mia and indulge in physical pleasures the likes of which he'd gotten a taste of early this morning.

For Mia, their joining would be more than mere physical satisfaction. Mia loved him. She actually believed that she loved him.

But sooner or later, just like Tasha, Mia would wake up, too. And then she'd see him without those rose-colored glasses that she always wore. She'd realize that he had been lying—lying both to her and even to himself.

His knee wasn't going to get any better. Steve Horowitz was right. Frisco had come as far as he could. He'd fought hard and long, but to keep fighting would only damage his joint further. It would be counterproductive. It would put him back into a wheelchair—maybe even for the rest of his life.

It was time to accept that which he'd denied for so many years.

He was permanently disabled. He wasn't going to be a SEAL ever again.

The truth crashed down around him, crushing him, squeezing him, and he nearly cried out.

He had to tell Mia. She said she loved him, but would she love him if she knew the truth?

He wasn't Lt. ''Frisco'' Francisco of SEAL Team Ten. He was Alan Francisco, disabled civilian. He didn't even know who Alan Francisco was. How could she possibly love him if he no longer knew who he was?

He had to tell her. Yet at the same time, he didn't want her to know. He couldn't bear the thought of her looking at him with pity in her beautiful hazel eyes. He couldn't bear to say the words aloud. It was hard enough to admit he was temporarily disabled. But *permanently* disabled...

Mia's hair was down loose around her shoulders and she was smiling as she came toward him. He closed his eyes as she began unbuttoning his shirt, tugging him toward the bed at the same time.

She took his crutches and laid them on the floor. Then she gently pushed him down so that he sat on the bed, and swept his shirt off his shoulders.

"Mia..." he rasped.

"Get rid of the gun, will you?" she murmured, pressing feathery light kisses against his neck.

He unbuckled his shoulder holster and slipped it and his sidearm into the top drawer of a rickety old bedside table. He tried again, and again his voice sounded hoarse and strained. "Mia. About my knee..."

She lifted her head, gazing directly into his eyes. "Does it hurt?"

"No, it's all right. It's not—"

"Shh," she whispered, covering his mouth with hers. "We've already talked enough tonight."

She kissed him again and he let himself drown in her sweetness. He'd tried to tell her, but she didn't want to talk. And he really didn't want to say any of those awful truths aloud.

She was offering him a temporary escape, and he reached for it eagerly. He grabbed it with both hands and held on tight to the magic of right here and right now. In Mia's arms, reality vanished, leaving only sheer perfection, only pure pleasure.

The outside world, with all of its problems and harsh truths disappeared.

But only for an hour or two.

He rolled back with her onto the bed, covering her with his body, kissing her, determined to take that hour or two and use it to its fullest.

He pulled her shirt up and she helped get it over her head. She was wearing a bra, and the black satin and lace against her skin was enticingly sexy, but not nearly as sexy as the candlelight would be, flickering across her bare breasts. He unfastened the front clasp, freeing her from its restraints.

He made a sound, deep in his throat as he touched her, and she pushed herself up onto her elbows. "Is your knee all right? Maybe I should be on top."

Her eyes were a swirl of yellow and brown, flecked with bits of green and concern.

"No," he murmured, lowering his mouth to where his hands had been just moments before, lightly encircling one hard bud of a nipple with the tip of his tongue.

He heard her sudden inhale of pleasure, felt her legs tighten around him and her hips rise to meet him. But just as quickly as she'd reacted, she released the pressure of her legs. "Alan, please, I don't want to accidentally hurt you...."

He was balancing on his left leg. It was awkward, but with practice, he knew he would become more graceful. "You're not going to hurt me," he told her.

"But what if—"

"Mia, you're going to have to trust me on this, okay? Trust me enough to know that I'll tell you if I'm in pain. Right now, I'm not in pain." He pressed himself against her, fitting his arousal to her most intimately, to prove his point.

She moaned, arching up against him. "I *do* trust you."

Her words broke through the many layers of his desire—a pinprick of reality breaking through to this dreamworld. She trusted him. She *loved* him. His stomach tightened with remorse and despair, into a solid, cold block of deceit.

But her fingers were unfastening his shorts and her mouth covered his in a breathtaking kiss, warming him, melting him—at least a little bit, at least for a little while.

He awkwardly moved back, pulling her shorts and panties down her smooth, silky legs. She lay back against the pillows, her long dark hair fanning out across the white sheets, her eyes on fire as she gazed unsmilingly up at him. She was naked and so vulnerable in that position, yet she didn't try to cover herself. She didn't even move. She just waited. And watched as he pushed down his own shorts, as he released himself from his briefs.

She smiled then, gazing first at his arousal and then up into his eyes.

She watched, unmoving, as he covered himself, the heat in her eyes growing stronger, even more molten. She shifted her hips, opening herself even further to him, her invitation obvious.

Frisco inched himself forward, brushing the inside of her ankle with his mouth, trailing kisses up the smoothness of one calf while he caressed the soft inside of her other leg with his hand. He lifted his head when he reached her knees. She was up on her elbows again, her breasts rising and falling with each rapid breath. Her lips were parted and her hair tumbled down around her shoulders. As he met her eyes, she smiled a hot, sweet smile.

"Don't stop there," she told him.

Her smile was contagious and Frisco found himself grinning back at her before he lowered his head and continued his journey.

He heard her gasp, heard her soft cry of pleasure as he reached his destination. Her hands were in his hair, the softness of her thighs against his face as he tasted her sweet pleasure.

Maybe this would be enough.

The thought flashed through his mind as he took her higher, as he brought her closer to the brink of release.

Maybe he could find contentment or even happiness spending the rest of his life as Mia's lover. He could live forever in her bedroom, waiting for her to return from work, ready and willing to give her pleasure whenever she so desired.

It was, of course, a ridiculous idea.

How could she love a man who did nothing but hide?

Yet, hide was exactly what he'd been doing for the past few years. The truth had been there to see if he hadn't been so damn busy hiding from it.

Yeah, he was a real expert at evading the truth.

"Alan, please..." Mia tugged at his shoulders, pulling him up.

He knew what she wanted, and he gave it to her, filling her completely with one smooth thrust.

She bit down on her lip to keep from crying out, rising up to meet him.

His own pleasure was so intense, he had to stop, resting his forehead against hers while he struggled to maintain control.

"We fit together so well," she whispered into his ear, and when he lifted his head, he could see all of her love for him shining in her eyes.

And he knew at the moment that there was no way he could continue to deceive her. He had to tell her the truth. Not now. He couldn't tell her now. But soon. Very soon.

She began to move slowly underneath him and he matched her pace, watching her eyes, memorizing the pleasure on her face. He knew that once she knew the truth, she was as good as gone. How could he expect her to stay? He'd walk away from himself, if only he could.

"You're so serious tonight," she murmured, reaching up to touch the side of his face.

He tried to smile, but he couldn't, so he kissed her instead.

Her kiss was like magic, carrying him away to a place where there was only pleasure and light, where darkness and despair were set aside, if only temporarily.

They moved together faster now and even faster, bodies slick with heat and desire. There was no room between them for anything but the giving and taking of pleasure. Or love.

Frisco felt Mia's body tighten around him, felt her muffle her cries of passion with a deep, searing kiss. His body responded instantly to the sounds and sensations of her release, and he exploded with a fireball of pleasure that flared with a white-hot light behind his closed eyes.

The brilliant light brought clarity, and clarity brought another unwanted truth. He loved her.

He loved her.

Oh, Lord, he didn't love her. He *couldn't* love her.

His emotions were confused, and that, combined with the chemicals his body released at his climax, had given him this odd sensation that he had mistaken for love. It was nothing, and it would no doubt fade the same way his intense feelings of satisfaction and pleasure would eventually diminish.

Frisco slowly became aware of the soft hissing sounds of the candles' flames, of the ticking of Mia's watch from where it lay across the room on the dresser, of Mia's slow and steady breathing.

Damn, he was twice as big as she—he was crushing her. He rolled off of her, gathering her into his arms and cradling her close.

She sighed, opening drowsy eyes to smile up at him before she snuggled against his shoulder.

"Mia," he said, wondering how to tell her, how to begin. But she was already asleep.

It was not a big surprise that she was asleep—she'd been up all of the previous night, helping him take Tasha to the hospital. Like him, she'd probably only had around a two-hour nap in the morning. And then she'd had to endure the upset of Dwayne Bell's destructive visit to his apartment....

He gazed down at her, curled up against him, her hand pressed against his chest, covering his heart.

And that odd feeling that was surely just a strange chemical reaction made his heart feel tight and sore.

But that didn't mean that he loved her.

It didn't mean anything at all.

"Where's Tash?"

Frisco came out of the bathroom with his hair still wet from his shower, dressed only in a pair of shorts slung low on his lean hips, a towel around his neck. His question was phrased casually, but Mia couldn't miss the undercurrent of tension that seemed to flow from the man.

He looked tired, as if he hadn't slept well last night. He hadn't been in bed with her when she'd awoken this morning.

She had no idea how early he'd gotten up. Or why he'd gotten up at all.

She'd fallen asleep in his arms last night. She would have loved to have awakened that same way.

Mia set her book down on the end table, first marking her page with a leaf Natasha had brought inside to show her.

"Tasha's outside," she told him. "She asked, and I told her she could play right out front. I hope that's all right."

He nodded, sitting down across from her on the couch. He looked more than tired, Mia realized. He looked worn-out. Or burned-out and beaten down. He looked more like the grim angry man she'd first met. The glimpses of laughter and good humor and joy he'd let her see over the past several days were once again carefully hidden.

"I wanted a chance to talk to you while Tash was outside," he said, his voice uncommonly raspy. But then he didn't say anything else. He just cleared his throat and gazed silently into the cold fireplace.

"Well, Tasha's outside," Mia finally murmured. "And I'm listening."

He glanced up at her, briefly meeting her eyes and flashing one of his crooked smiles. "Yeah," he said. "I know. I'm just…you know, trying to find the right words." He shook his head and the flash of pain in his eyes nearly took her breath away. "Except there are no right words."

Mia couldn't believe what she was hearing. What had happened between last night and this morning? Last night they'd made love so perfectly, hadn't they? Or maybe it had only been perfect for her. He'd been quiet, almost subdued—she'd even commented on it. She leaned forward, wanting to reach for him, but suddenly, horribly afraid of his rejection.

He'd been honest with her, and told her he didn't love her. She in turn had told herself she didn't care, but that had been a lie. She *did* care. She wanted him to love her, and she'd foolishly hoped that the sex they shared would at least hold his attention until she could somehow, some way, make him love her, too.

She couldn't bear to know the answer, but still, she had to ask. "Are you trying to dump me?"

His blue eyes flashed as he looked up at her. "Hell, no! I'm... I'm trying to figure out how to tell you the truth." He held her gaze this time, and Mia was nearly overpowered by the sadness she saw there, mixed in among his quietly burning anger.

She wanted to reach for him, but his anger held her back. "Whatever it is, it can't be *that* bad, can it?"

"My knee's not going to improve," he said quietly, and she realized there were tears in his eyes. He gestured to his crutches. "This is as good as it's going to get. Hobbling around on crutches or with a cane."

Alan was finally facing the truth. Mia felt her own eyes flood with tears. Her heart was in her throat, filling her with relief. This wasn't about her, wasn't about *them*. It was about him.

She was so glad. He was facing the truth, and once he looked it in the eye, he could finally move forward.

At the same time, she grieved for him, knowing how hard it must've been for him to reach his conclusion.

He looked away from her, and his voice dropped even lower. "I'm not going to be a SEAL again. That's over. I have to accept the fact that I'm...permanently disabled."

Mia wasn't sure what to say. She could see the anger and bitterness beneath the pain in his eyes, and she realized that by telling her this, he was probably uttering these words aloud for the very first time. She decided to keep her mouth shut and simply let him talk.

"I know I told you that I was going to work past this," he said. "I know I made that list that's on my refrigerator, and if wanting something badly enough was all I needed to make it happen, damn, I'd be doing wind sprints right now. But my knee was destroyed and all the wishing and wanting in the world isn't going to make it better. This is it for me."

He looked up at her as if he wanted her to comment. Mia said the only thing she possibly could in the circumstances.

"I'm sorry."

But he shook his head. "No," he said tightly. "*I'm* sorry. I made you think that there would be something more. I let you believe that I had some kind of future—"

She couldn't let that one pass. "You *do* have a future. It's just not the one you thought you'd have back when you were eleven years old. You're strong, you're tough, you're creative—you can adapt. Lucky told me there's an instructor job waiting for you. If you wanted, you could choose to teach."

Frisco felt a burning wave of anger and frustration surge through him, devouring him. Teach. Man, how many times had he heard *that?* He could teach, and then watch his students graduate out of his classroom and do the things he would never do again. "Yeah, I'll pass on *that* barrel of laughs, thanks."

But Mia didn't let up. "Why? You'd be a *great* teacher. I've seen how patient you are with Natasha. And Thomas. You have an incredible rapport with him. And—"

His temper flared hotter, but the anger didn't succeed in covering up his hurt. There was nothing about this that didn't hurt. He felt as if he were dying. Whatever part of him that hadn't died back when his leg was nearly blown off, was dying now.

"Why the hell do *you* care what I do?" It wasn't exactly the question he was burning to ask her, but it would do for now.

She was shocked into silence, and gazed at him with her luminous eyes. "Because I love you—"

He swore, just one word, sharp and loud. "You don't even know me. How could you *love* me?"

"Alan, I *do* know—"

"*I* don't even know who I am anymore. How the hell could you?"

She nervously moistened her lips with the tip of her tongue, and Frisco felt his rage expanding. Dear God, he wanted her. He wanted her to stay. He wanted her to love him, because, dear Lord, he was in love with her, too.

The tight, uncomfortable feeling in his chest had never faded. He'd awakened repeatedly throughout the night to find it burning steadily, consuming him. It wasn't going to go away.

But she was. She was going to go away. Because, really, how could she love him? She was in love with a phantom, a shadow, an echo of the man he used to be. And sooner or later, even if he didn't tell her, she'd figure it out. Sooner or later she'd realize he was scamming her—that he'd been scamming her all along. And sooner or later, she would realize that she'd made a mistake, that he wasn't worth her time and laughter, and she would leave.

And then he'd be more alone than ever.

"Why should I bother to teach when I can sit home and watch TV and collect disability pay?" he asked roughly.

"Because I know that would *never* be enough for you." Her eyes were hot, her voice impassioned. How could she possibly have such faith in him?

Frisco wanted to cry. Instead he laughed, his voice harsh. "Yeah, and teaching's right up my alley, right? I certainly fit the old adage—'Those who can, do. Those who can't, teach.'"

She flinched as if he had struck her. "Is that *really* what you think about teachers? About *me?*"

"It wouldn't be an adage if there weren't some truth to it."

"Here's another adage for you—'Those who are taught, do. Those who teach, shape the future.'" Her eyes blazed. "I teach because I care about the future. And children *are* the future of this world."

"Well, maybe I *don't* care about the future," he shot back. "Maybe I don't give a damn about *any*thing anymore."

She raised her chin. "I know that's not true. You care about Tasha. And I know, even though you won't admit it, that you care about me."

"You're as hopeless as I was when it comes to wishful thinking," he lied, wanting to push her over the edge, needing her to get mad enough to walk away, wanting her to stay forever, and knowing that she never would. How could she? He was nothing now, nobody, no one. "It's typical. You only see what you want to see. You moved to San Felipe from Malibu, thinking you're going to save the world by teaching underprivileged kids all about American history, when what those kids *really* need to learn is how to get through another day without some kid from the rival gang gunning them down when they walk to the store.

"You took one look at me and figured maybe I was worth saving, too. But just like the kids in your school, I don't need what you're teaching."

Her voice shook. "You're so wrong. You need it more than anyone I've ever met."

He shrugged. "So stick around, then. I guess the great sex is worth putting up with your preaching."

Mia looked dazed, and he knew he'd dealt their relationship the death blow. When she stood up, blinking back a fresh flood of tears, her face was a stony mask.

"You're right," she said, her voice trembling only slightly. "I don't know who you are. I thought I did, but..." She shook her head. "I thought you were a SEAL. I thought you didn't quit. But you have, haven't you? Life isn't working out exactly the way you planned it, so you're ready to give up and be bitter and angry and collect disability pay while you drink away the rest of your life, sitting on your couch in your lousy condominium, feeling sorry for yourself."

Frisco nodded, twisting his lips into a sad imitation of a smile. "That's right. That just about sums up my big plans for my exciting future."

She didn't even say goodbye. She just walked out the door.

15

"Yo, Navy, was that Mia I saw heading west, driving like she was behind the wheel of the Batmobile?"

Frisco looked up grimly from the peanut butter and jelly sandwich he was making for Natasha as Thomas King pushed open the screen door.

"Hey, Martian girl," the lanky teenager greeted Tash with one of his rare smiles.

"Thomas!" Tasha launched herself at the kid and immediately burst into tears. "Frisco yelled and yelled at Mia, and she went away!"

Thomas staggered back under the sudden unexpected weight of the little girl, but he managed to shift her into a position easier to hold on to. His dark eyes sought confirmation from Frisco over the top of Tasha's head. "Is that right?"

Frisco had to look away. "In a nutshell."

"I didn't want Mia to go," Tasha wailed. "And now she'll never come back!"

Thomas shook his head in disgust. "Oh, perfect. I come up here thinking *I'm* the one bearing bad news, and it turns out you guys have already done yourselves in without any outside help." He turned to the little girl still wailing in his arms. "You. Martian. Turn off the siren. Stop thinking only about yourself, and start thinking about Uncle Navy over here. If Ms. S. doesn't come back, *he'll* be the big loser, not you."

To Frisco's surprise, Tasha actually stopped crying.

"And you, Navy. Check yourself into a hospital, man. It's

time to get your head examined." Thomas lowered Tasha to the floor and picked up the plate that held her lunch. "This yours?" he asked her.

She nodded.

"Good," Thomas said, handing it to her. "Go sit on that funny-looking swing on the porch while you eat this. I need to talk to Uncle Crazy here, all right?"

Tasha's lips were set at heavy pout, but she followed the teenager's order. As the screen door closed behind her, Thomas turned back to Frisco.

But instead of berating him about Mia's AWOL status, Thomas said, "Your friend Lucky gave me a call. Apparently something came up. Said to tell you he's out of the picture until 2200 hours tomorrow night—whenever the hell *that* is. I mean, ten o'clock is ten o'clock—there's no need to get cute."

Frisco nodded. "It's just as well—I'm going to need to find someone to take care of Tash, now that…" Mia's gone. He didn't finish the sentence. He didn't need to.

"I don't know what went down between you two," Thomas said, reaching into the bag of bread and pulling out two slices and laying them directly onto the counter. He pulled the peanut butter jar closer and began spreading the chunky spread onto the bread, "but you oughta know that Ms. S. doesn't hang out with just anyone. I've known her for four years, and as far as I know, there's only been one other guy besides you that she's said good-night to after breakfast, if you know what I mean. She's been selective, Uncle Fool, and she's selected *you*."

Frisco closed his eyes. "I don't want to hear this."

"Plugging your fingers in your ears so that you can't hear it doesn't change the truth, my man," Thomas told him, adding a thick layer of sweet, sticky strawberry jam to his sandwich. "I don't know what she told you, but she wouldn't't've let you get so close if she didn't love you, with a capital *L*. I don't know what the hell you did to make her fall for you, but you'll be the biggest ass in the world if you don't take advantage of—''

Frisco's temper frayed. "I'm not going to stand here and be lectured by some kid!"

Thomas took a bite of his sandwich and chewed it thoughtfully as he gazed at Frisco. "Why are you always so angry, Navy?" he finally asked. "You know, I used to be just like you. I used to live and breathe anger. I thought it was the only way to stay alive. I was the meanest son of a bitch on the block. I didn't join a gang because I didn't *need* a gang— everyone was scared of me. I was tough enough to go solo. And I was on an express bus straight to hell. But you know what? I got lucky. I got the new teacher for history the year I was fifteen. I was six months away from dropping out, and Ms. S. did something no one ever did before. She looked me in the eye and somehow saw through all that anger, down to who I was underneath.''

Thomas gestured at Frisco with his sandwich. "I remember, it was the day I pulled a knife on her. She told me to put the blade away and never bring it back to school again. She said I hid behind anger because *I* was the one who was scared— scared that everyone was right, that I was worthless and good for nothing.

"I mocked her, but she just smiled. She told me that she'd seen some of my test scores, and from what she saw, not only was I going to graduate from high school, but I was going to be valedictorian." He shook his head. "She didn't give up on me, and when I turned sixteen, I kind of just kept putting off dropping out. I kept telling myself that I'd stay for another week, 'cause of the free lunches." He looked at Frisco. "If I hadn't lucked out and had Ms. Summerton for a teacher, I would've ended up in jail. Or dead.''

"Why are you telling me this?"

"Because you don't seem to realize what was directly under your nose, Uncle Blindman.''

Frisco used his crutches to propel himself away from the

kitchen counter, his movements jerky. "I *do* know. You're wrong."

"Maybe. But one thing I'm right about is whatever it is you're scared of, whatever you're hiding under your anger, it's nothing compared to the fear you *should* be feeling about losing Ms. Mia Summerton. Be afraid of that, Navy, be *very* afraid."

Frisco sat on the couch, with his back to the cabinet that held enough whiskey to sink a ship.

It wouldn't take much. All he had to do was pull himself to his feet, set his crutches in place and then he'd be standing in front of that very same cabinet. The door would pop open with a pull of one hand...

Thomas and Natasha were down at the lake, not due to return until late afternoon, when they were all scheduled to leave for San Felipe. But right now there was no one around to protest. And by the time they returned, it would be too late. By then, Frisco wouldn't give a damn what anyone thought, what anyone said.

Not even little Tasha with her accusing blue eyes.

He closed his eyes. He would welcome the oblivion that a bottle of whiskey would bring. It would erase the picture he had in his mind of Mia's face right before she walked out the door.

He'd needed to tell her the truth. Instead he'd insulted her avocation and made it seem as if their relationship had been based purely on sex.

Why? Because he was so damned afraid that she would leave.

In fact, he *knew* Mia would leave. So he'd pushed her away before she could leave on her own initiative.

Very clever. He prophesied his own doom, and then went and made damn sure it happened. Self-sabotage, it was called in all the psychology textbooks.

Savagely Frisco pulled himself to his feet and set his crutches underneath his arms.

* * *

Mia pulled her car over the side of the road, swearing like a sailor.

She couldn't believe that she'd allowed herself to fall into such a classic trap. It had been *years* since she'd made this kind of mistake.

For the past few years, she'd been successful—she'd been able to work with and get through to the toughest, hardest cases in the high school. And she'd been able to do that by being thick-skinned.

She'd looked countless angry, hurt, and painfully frightened young men and women in the eyes. She'd let all of their harsh, insulting, sometimes shockingly rude words bounce off of her. She'd met their outbursts with calm and their verbal assaults with an untouchable neutrality. They couldn't hurt her if she didn't let them.

But somehow she'd let Alan Francisco hurt her.

Somehow she'd forgotten how to remain neutral in the face of this man's anger and pain.

And, God, he was in so much pain.

Mia closed her eyes against the sudden vision of him on the night they'd taken Tasha to the hospital. She'd seen him sitting on his bed, bent over from pain and grief, hands covering his face as he wept.

This morning Alan's darkest fears had been realized. He'd admitted—both to himself and to her—that he wasn't ever going to get his old life back. He wasn't going to be a SEAL again. At least not a SEAL on active duty. He'd come face-to-face with a harsh reality that had to have shattered the last of his dreams, crushed out the final flicker of his hope.

Mia knew Alan didn't love her. But if ever there was a time that he needed her, it was now.

And she'd let his angry words hurt her.

She'd run away.

She'd left him alone and on the edge—with only a five-year-old child and several dozen bottles of whiskey for comfort.

Mia turned her car around.

* * *

Frisco stared at the bottle and the glass he'd set out on the kitchen counter.

It was a rich, inviting amber color, with an instantly familiar aroma.

All he had to do was pick up the glass and he'd crawl into that bottle for the rest of the afternoon—maybe even for the rest of his life. He'd forget everything that he wasn't, everything that he couldn't be. And when he woke up, dizzy and sick, when he came eye to eye with what he'd become, well, he'd just have another drink. And another and another until once again he reached oblivion.

All he had to do was pick up that glass and he'd fulfill his family legacy. He'd be one of those good-for-nothing Francisco boys again. Not that they'd know any better, people had said, the way the father sits around drinking himself into an early grave....

That was his future now, too. Angry. Alcoholic.

Alone.

Mia's face flashed in his mind. He could see her beautiful hazel eyes, her funny smile. The hurt on her face as she walked out the door.

He gripped the edge of the counter, trying to push the image away, trying not to want what he knew he couldn't have.

And when he looked up, there was that glass and that bottle, still sitting on the counter in front of him.

Hey, why fight destiny? He was pegged to follow this path right from the start. Yeah, he'd temporarily escaped by joining the Navy, but now he was back where he'd started. Back where he belonged.

At least he'd had the integrity to know that Mia didn't deserve to spend her life in his personal hell. At least he had *that* much up on his old man.

Man, he loved her. Pain burned his stomach, his chest—rising up into his throat like bile.

He reached for the glass, wanting to wash away the taste, wanting not to care, not to need, not to feel.

I thought you were a SEAL. I thought you didn't quit.

Mia might as well have been standing in the room with him, her words echoed so loudly in his head.

"I'm not a SEAL anymore," he answered her ghostly presence.

You'll always be a SEAL. You were when you were eleven years old. You will be when you die.

The problem was, he'd already died. He'd died five years ago—he was just too stubborn and stupid to know it at the time. He'd lost his life when he'd lost his future. And now he'd lost Mia.

By choice, he reminded himself. He'd had a choice about that.

You do have a future. It's just not the one you thought you'd have back when you were a boy.

Some future. Broken. Angry. Less than whole.

I know you're going to do whatever it takes to feel whole again. I know you'll make the right choices.

Choices. What choices did he have now?

Drink the whiskey in this glass. Polish off the rest of the bottle. Kill himself slowly with alcohol the way his old man had. Spend the rest of his miserable life in limbo, drunk in his living room, with only the television for company.

He didn't want that.

You're strong, you're tough, you're creative—you can adapt.

Adapt. That's what being a SEAL had been all about. Sea, air or land, he'd learned to adapt to the environment, adapt to the country and the culture. Make changes to his method of operation. Break rules and conventions. Learn to make do.

But adapt to *this?* Adapt to forever walking with a cane? Adapt to knowing he would remain forever in the rear, away from the front lines and the action?

It would be so hard. It would be the hardest thing he'd ever done in his entire life. Whereas it would be so damn easy just to give up.

It would've been easy to give up during Hell Week, too, when he'd done the grueling training to become a SEAL.

He'd had the strength to keep going when all around him strong men were walking away. He'd endured the physical and psychological hardships.

Could he endure this, too?

I know you'll make the right choice.

And he *did* have a choice, didn't he? Despite what he'd thought, it came down to the very basic of choices.

To die.

Or to live.

Not just to be or not to be, but rather to do or not to do. To take charge or to lie back and quit.

But dammit, Mia was right. He *was* a SEAL, and SEALs *didn't* quit.

Alan Francisco looked down at the whiskey in his hand. He turned and threw it into the sink where the glass shattered and the whiskey trickled down the drain.

He chose life.

Mia's car bounced as she took the potholed dirt road much too fast.

She wasn't far now. Just another few miles until the turnoff that would lead directly to the cabin.

Determinedly, she wiped the last traces of her tears from her face. When she walked back in there, when she looked Alan in the eye, he was going to see only her calm offer of comfort and understanding. His angry words couldn't hurt her because she wouldn't let them. It would take more than that to drive her away.

She slowed as she rounded a curve, seeing a flash of sunlight on metal up ahead of her.

It was another car, heading directly toward her, going much too fast.

Mia hit the brakes and pulled as far to the right as she could, scraping the side of a tree as the other car went into a skid.

She watched it plunge down a sloping embankment, plowing through the underbrush and coming to a sudden jarring stop as it hit a tree.

Mia scrambled to unfasten her seat belt, fumbling in her haste to get out of her car and down to the wreck.

It was almost entirely hidden in the thick growth, but she could hear someone crying. She pushed away branches to get to the driver's side door, yanking it open.

Blood. There was blood on the man's forehead and face but he was moving and…

Dwayne Bell. The man in the driver's seat was Dwayne Bell. He recognized her at the exact moment she recognized him.

"Well, now, it's the girlfriend. Isn't *this* convenient," he said in his thick Louisiana drawl. He reached up to wipe the blood from his eyes and face.

Natasha. The crying sound came from *Natasha*. What was *she* doing here…?

"Dammit, I think I must've hit my head on the wind shield," Dwayne said.

Mia wanted to back away, to run, but Natasha was belted into the front seat. Mia couldn't simply just leave her there. But maybe Dwayne had hit his head hard enough to make him groggy…. Maybe he wouldn't notice if…

Mia quickly went around to the other side of the car. Tasha already had her seat belt unfastened and was up and in Mia's arms as soon as the door was opened.

"Are you okay?" she asked, smoothing back Tasha's hair from her face.

The little girl nodded, eyes wide. "Dwayne hit Thomas," she told Mia, tears still streaming down her face. "He fell down and was all bloody. Dwayne made him dead."

Thomas…? Dead? No…

"I screamed and screamed for Thomas to help me—" Tasha hiccuped "—but he wouldn't get up and Frisco couldn't hear me and Dwayne took me in his car."

Thomas was unconscious maybe, but not dead. Please God not dead. Not Thomas King….

Moving quickly, Mia carried Natasha around the car and up the embankment, praying Dwayne was too dizzy to notice, hoping that if she didn't turn around to check, he wouldn't—

"Where you going in such a hurry, darlin'?" Dwayne drawled.

Mia froze. And turned around. And found herself staring down the muzzle of a very big, very deadly-looking gun.

Dwayne held a handkerchief to his forehead, but his gun hand was decidedly steady as he hefted his bulk out of the car.

"I think we'll take your car," he told her with a gap-toothed smile. "In fact, you can drive."

Frisco knew something was wrong. The woods were too quiet. There was no echo of laughter or voices from the lake. And he'd never known Tasha to be silent for long.

The footpath down to the water wasn't easy to navigate on crutches, but he moved as quickly as he could. And as he neared the clearing—out of force of habit—he drew his side-arm from his shoulder holster. He moved as silently as he could, ready to drop his right crutch should the need arise to use it.

He saw Thomas, crumpled on the beach, blood on his face.

There was no sign of Tasha—or anyone else. But there were fresh tire tracks at the boat drop. Whoever had been here had gone.

And taken Tasha with them.

Frisco holstered his weapon as he moved quickly toward Thomas.

The kid stirred as Frisco touched him, searching for a pulse. He was alive, thank God. His nose was bleeding and he had a nasty-looking gash on the back of his head. "Tasha," he gasped. "The fat man took Tash."

The fat man.

Dwayne Bell.

Took Tasha.

Frisco had been at the cabin, wrestling with his demons

while Dwayne had been down here kicking the living daylights out of Thomas and kidnapping Tash. Guilt flooded him
but he instantly pushed it aside. He'd have time to feel guilty
later. Right now he had to move fast, to get Tasha back.

"How long ago?" Frisco tore a piece of fabric from his
shirttail and used it to apply pressure to the back of Thomas's
head as he helped the kid sit up.

"I don't know. He hit me hard and I went down." Thomas
let out a stream of foul language that would've made a SEAL
take notice. "I tried to fight it—I heard Tasha screaming for
me, but I blacked out. Dammit. Dammit!" There were tears
in his eyes. "Lieutenant, she's scared to death of this guy.
We gotta find her and get her back."

Frisco nodded, watching as Thomas forced away his dizziness and crawled to the lake to splash water onto his face,
washing away the blood. The kid probably had a broken nose,
but he didn't so much as say ouch. "Can you walk, or should
I get your car and bring it around?"

Thomas straightened up, wobbling only slightly. "I can
walk." He felt his pockets and swore again. "The fat man
took my car keys."

Frisco started up the path that led back to the cabin. "So
we'll hot-wire it." He looked back. "Tell me if I'm going
too fast for you." Now *that* was a switch, wasn't it?

"*You* know how to hot-wire a car?"

"It's something we're taught in the SEAL teams."

"Shoot," Thomas said. "I could be a SEAL."

Frisco looked back at him and nodded. "Yeah, you could."

16

"**I** need your help."

Frisco looked out the open car window, up at Lt. Joe Catalanotto, the Commanding Officer of SEAL Team Ten's Alpha Squad. Cat looked like he was ready to ship out on some high-level security training mission. He was dressed in fatigues and a black combat vest and wore his long dark hair back in a ponytail.

"Right now?" Cat asked, bending slightly to look inside the car, his sharp gaze taking in Thomas's battered appearance and bloody T-shirt.

"Yeah," Frisco said. "My sister's kid's been snatched. Sharon got herself in too deep with a drug dealer. He's the one that took the kid. I need help finding him and getting her back."

Joe Cat nodded. "How many guys you need?"

"How many you got?"

Frisco's former CO smiled. "How's all seven of Alpha Squad?"

Seven. Those seven were the six guys Frisco had served with—along with his own replacement. That was one man he *wasn't* looking forward to working with. But he nodded anyway. Right now he needed all the help he could get to find Natasha. "Good."

As Frisco watched, Cat slipped a microthin cellular phone from the pocket of his vest and dialed a coded number.

"Yeah, Catalanotto," he said. "Cancel Alpha Squad's flight out. Our training mission has been delayed—" he glanced up at the cloudless blue sky ''—due to severe weather conditions. Unless otherwise directed, we'll be off base as of 1600 hours, executing local reconnaissance and surveillance training.'' He snapped the phone shut and turned back to Frisco. ''Let's pay a visit to the equipment room, get the gear we need to find this guy.''

''Whoa, Frisco, nice couch!''

With the exception of the glaringly pink couch, Frisco's apartment was starting to look like command central.

Lucky had finished cleaning the place up and had moved the sofa in yesterday. Now, under Joe Cat's command, Bobby and Wes—Bob, tall and built like a truck; Wes, short and razor thin, but inseparable since BUD/S training had made them swim buddies—had moved aside all unessential furniture and set the small dining room table in the center of the living room.

''You've gotta do the rest of the room in pink, too—it suits you, baby!'' Six and a half feet tall, black and built like a linebacker, Chief Daryl Becker—nicknamed Harvard—possessed an ivy league education and a wicked sense of humor. He carried a heavy armload of surveillance gear, which he began to set up on the table.

Blue McCoy was the next to arrive. The blond-haired SEAL brought several large cases that made the muscles in his arms stand out in high relief. Assault weapons—God forbid they'd need to use them. Even the normally taciturn executive officer and second in command of Alpha Squad couldn't resist commenting on the pink couch.

''I'm dying to meet this new girlfriend of yours,'' Blue said in his soft Southern drawl. ''Please tell me that sofa there belongs to her.''

Mia.

Where the hell was she? She should have been back long before him.

But her apartment was still locked up tight. Frisco had gone out to check at least five times since he'd arrived. He'd even left a message on her answering machine, thinking she might phone in. He hadn't apologized—he'd need to do that in person. He'd simply told her that he was looking for her. Please call him.

"Okay," Harvard said, finishing hooking the computers and other equipment to Frisco's phone line. "We're all set. When this Dwayne calls, you keep him talking and we'll pinpoint his location in about forty seconds."

"*When* Dwayne calls. *If* Dwayne calls." Frisco couldn't keep his frustration from buzzing in his voice. "Dammit, I *hate* waiting."

"Gee, I forgot how much fun it was to work with the King of Impatience," Lucky said, coming in the door. Another man followed him. It was Ensign Harlan Jones, aka Cowboy—the hotheaded young SEAL who'd replaced Frisco in the Alpha Squad. He nodded a silent greeting to Frisco, no doubt subdued both by the seriousness of a kidnapped child and the strangeness of being in the home of the man whose place he'd taken for his own.

"Thanks for coming," Frisco said to him.

"Glad to be able to help," Cowboy replied.

Frisco's condo had never seemed so small. With eight large men and Thomas there, there was barely room to move. But it was good. It was like old times. Frisco had missed these guys, he realized. He just wished Natasha hadn't had to be kidnapped to bring them all together again.

And that had entirely been up to him. *He'd* been the one keeping his distance, pushing the squad away. Yeah, the fact that he wasn't one of them anymore stuck in his throat. Yeah, it made him jealous as hell. But this was better than nothing. It was better than quitting....

"You got anything to eat?" Wes asked, heading for the kitchen.

"Hey, Frisco, mind if I crash on your bed?" Bobby asked, also not waiting for an answer before he headed down the hall.

"Who hit *you* in the face with a baseball bat?" Lucky

asked Thomas, who'd remained silent and off to one side until now.

The kid was leaning back against the wall and he looked as if he should be sitting if not lying down. "Dwayne," he answered. "And it was the barrel of his gun, not a baseball bat."

"Maybe you should go home," Lucky suggested. "Take care of that—"

Thomas turned to give the other man a cool, appraising look. "Nope. I'm here until we get the little girl back."

"I think Alpha Squad…"

"I'm *not* leaving."

"…can probably handle—"

Frisco cut in. "The kid stays," he said quietly.

Blue stepped forward. "Your name's Thomas, right?" he said to the boy.

"Thomas King."

Blue held out his hand. "Pleased to meet you," he drawled. The two shook. "If you're going to be helping us, why don't I show you how some of this equipment works?"

Frisco sat down on the pink sofa next to Joe Cat as Blue and Harvard began giving Thomas a crash course in tracing phone calls. "I can't just sit here waiting," he said. "I've got to do something."

Wes came back out of the kitchen, having overheard Frisco's remark. "Why don't you make yourself a nice cup of hot tea," he teased in a lispingly sweet voice, "and curl up on your nice pink couch with your favorite copy of *Sense and Sensibility* to distract you?"

"Hey," Harvard boomed in his deep, subbass voice. "I heard that. I *like* Jane Austen."

"I do, too," Cowboy interjected.

"Whoa," Lucky said. "Who taught *you* to read?"

The room erupted in laughter, and Frisco restlessly stood up, pushing his way out the door and onto the landing. He knew that humor was the way the men of Alpha Squad dealt with stress and a tense situation, but he didn't feel much like laughing.

He just wanted Natasha back.

Where was she right now? Was she scared? Had Dwayne hit her again? Dammit, if that bastard as much as *touched* that little girl...

Frisco heard the screen door open behind him and turned to see that Joe Cat had followed him.

"I want to go talk to my sister again," Frisco told the CO. "I think there's more to this than she's told me."

Cat didn't hesitate. "I'll drive you over. Just let me tell the guys where we're going." He stepped back into Frisco's condo, then came back out, nodding to Frisco. "Let's go."

As they headed down to the parking lot, Frisco glanced back one last time at Mia's lifeless condo. Where *was* she?

Mia carried Tasha across the well-manicured lawn to the front door of the big Spanish-style house.

This was ludicrous. It was broad daylight, they were in the middle of a seemingly affluent, upper-middle-class suburb. Down the street, several landscapers cleaned up a neighbor's yard. Should she scream for help, or try to run?

She did neither, well aware of that very large gun Dwayne Bell carried concealed in his pocket. If she had been alone, she might have risked it. But not with Natasha in her arms. Still, it gave her a chill to know that she could clearly identify the address where they'd been brought, and the man who'd brought them here.

"Shouldn't you have blindfolded us?" she asked as Dwayne opened the door.

"Can't drive if you're blindfolded. Besides, you're here as my guests. There's no need to make this more unpleasant than it has to be."

"You have a curious definition of the word *guest,* Mr. Bell," Mia said as Dwayne shut the door behind her. The inside of the house was dark with all the shades pulled down, and cool from an air conditioner set well below seventy degrees. She could hear canned laughter from a television somewhere in the big house. Tasha's arms tightened around her neck. "I've never held someone at gunpoint simply to invite them into my home. I think *hostage* is a more appropriate term."

"Actually, I prefer the word *collateral*," the overweight man told her.

A man appeared, walking toward them down the hall from a room that might've been a kitchen. His jacket was off and he wore a gun in a shoulder holster very similar to Frisco's. He spoke to Dwayne in a low voice, glancing curiously at Mia and Natasha.

"Have Ramon take care of it," Dwayne said, loudly enough for Mia to overhear. "And then I want to talk to you both."

There were at least two other men in the house—at least two of them carrying weapons. Mia looked around as Dwayne led them up the thickly carpeted stairs, trying to memorize the layout of the house, determined to gather any information that would be valuable for Frisco when he came.

Frisco would find them. Mia knew that as surely as she knew that the late-afternoon sun would soon slip beneath the horizon.

And then he would come.

"The stakes are higher than I thought," Frisco said tightly, coming out into the drug-and-alcohol rehab center's waiting room. Joe Catalanotto rose to his feet. "Sharon didn't steal five thousand from Bell—she stole *fifty* thousand. She fudged his bookkeeping—didn't think he'd notice."

He headed for the door, toward the parking lot and Joe Cat's jeep.

"Can she pay it back?" Cat asked.

Frisco snorted. "Are you kidding? It's long gone. She used most of it to pay off some gambling debts and blew the rest on drugs and booze." He stopped, turning to Cat. "Let me borrow your phone. Sharon gave me the address where she used to live with Bell," he told Cat as he dialed the number of the cellular phone link they'd set up back at his apartment.

The line was picked up on the first ring.

"Becker here." It was Harvard.

"It's just me, Chief," Frisco said. "Any calls?"

"Nothing yet. You know we would have relayed it directly to you if there were."

"I've got an address I want to check out. It's just outside of San Felipe, in Harper, the next town over to the east. Have Lucky and Blue meet me and Cat over there, all right?" He gave Harvard the street address.

"I've got that location on my computer," Harvard told him. "They're on their way, soon as I print them out a map. You need directions?"

Cat was listening in. "Tell H. to send a copy of that map to the fax in my jeep."

Frisco stared at Joe Cat. "You have a *fax* machine in your *jeep?*"

Cat smiled. "CO privileges."

Frisco ended the call and handed the phone back to Cat. But Cat shook his head. "You better hold on to it. If that ransom call comes in…"

Frisco met his friend's eyes. "If that ransom call comes in, we better be able to trace it," he said grimly.

"And pray that we're not already too late. Sharon told me Dwayne Bell has killed in revenge for far less than fifty thousand dollars."

"No one's home," Lucky reported as he and Blue McCoy silently materialized alongside Cat's jeep, down the street from the house Sharon had lived in with Dwayne Bell.

"I went through a basement window," Blue told Frisco and Joe Cat. "From what I could see from just a quick look around, Dwayne Bell doesn't live there anymore. There were kids' toys all over the place, and there was mail on the kitchen counter addressed to Fred and Charlene Ford. Looks like Bell moved out and these other folks moved in.''

Frisco nodded, trying not to clench his teeth. It would've been too easy if Bell had been there. He'd known that coming out here was a long shot to start with.

Cat was looking at him. ''What do you want to do?''

Frisco shook his head. Nothing. There was nothing they *could* do now but wait. ''I want the phone to ring.''

''He'll call and we *will* get Natasha back,'' Lucky said with far more confidence than Frisco felt.

Mia tried the window of the tiny bedroom where she and Tasha were being held. It was sealed shut. They wouldn't get out that way, short of breaking the glass. And even if they *could* break it without Dwayne and his goons hearing them, there was a *long* drop down to the ground.

Tasha sat on the bed, knees hugged tightly to her chest, her blue eyes wide as Mia made her way around the room.

The closet was minuscule—there was no way out there.

There were no secret doors, no hidden passages, no air ducts in the walls or crawl spaces underneath the throw rug. There was no hidden telephone with which she could make a furtive call for help, no gun in the dresser drawer that she could use to defend them.

The door was locked with a bolt on the outside.

They weren't going anywhere until Dwayne or his goons unlocked it.

There was nothing to do now but wait.

The phone rang.

They were halfway back to the condo, when the cell phone in Frisco's pocket chirped and vibrated against his leg. Joe Cat quickly pulled the jeep over to the side of the road as Frisco flipped the phone open.

''Frisco.''

It was Harvard. ''Call's coming in,'' he reported tersely.

"I'm linking it directly to you. Remember, if it's Bell, keep him talking."

"I remember."

There were several clicks, and then the soft hiss of an open line.

"Yeah," Frisco said.

"Mr. Francisco." It was Dwayne Bell's lugubrious voice. "You know who I am and why I'm calling, I assume."

"Let me talk to Tasha."

"Business before pleasure, sir," Bell said. "You have twenty-four hours to return to me the money that your charming sister stole. Fifty thousand, plus another ten in interest."

"It's going to take me longer than twenty-four hours to get together that kind of—"

"I'm already being very generous out of sentimentality for what Sharon and I once shared. It's nearly 6:00. If I don't have cash in hand by 6:00 p.m. tomorrow, I'll kill the girl. And if I don't have it by midnight, then I'll kill the child. And if you go to the police, I'll kill them both, and take your sister to prison with me."

"Whoa," Frisco said. "Wait a minute. What did you say? Both? The girl, *then* the child…?"

Bell laughed. "Oh, you don't know? Your girlfriend is a guest in my house as well as the brat."

Mia. Hell, Bell had Mia, too.

"Let me talk to her," Frisco rasped. "I want proof they're both still all right."

"I anticipated that." He must have turned away from the phone because his voice was suddenly distant. "Bring them in."

There was a pause and a click, and then Mia's voice came on the line. "Alan?"

The sound was boomy and Frisco knew Bell had switched to a speaker phone. "I'm here," he said. "Are you all right? Is Tash with you?"

Lucky appeared silently outside Joe Cat's car window. As

Frisco glanced at him, he pointed to his own cellular phone and signaled a thumbs-up.

Harvard had gotten the trace. They had a location.

"Yes," Mia was saying. "Listen, Alan. My parents have money. Go to them. Remember I told you they live near the country club in Harper?"

No, she'd told him her parents lived in Malibu.

"Just be careful of my dad—he's a little nuts, with all those guns he has in his collection, and his two bodyguards."

Harper. Guns. Two bodyguards. Damn, she had the presence of mind to tell him where they were and how many men there were guarding them.

"That's enough," Bell cut in.

"My parents have the money you want," Frisco heard Mia say sharply. "How is Alan going to get it if I don't tell him where to go?"

"I have the address," Frisco told her. "I'll take care of the money, you take care of Tasha. Tash—are you okay?"

"I wanna go home." Natasha's voice was wobbly.

"She doesn't have her medicine, so if her temperature goes up again, put her in the bathtub and cool her down. Do you understand?" Frisco said to Mia as quickly as he could. "Stay with her in the bathroom. And talk to her so she's not scared. You know how she gets when it's too quiet. I know she's too little to listen to the sounds of the night the way I can."

Man, he hoped she understood. If Mia and Tasha kept talking, the SEALs would be able to use high-tech, high-powered microphones to help pinpoint their location inside of the house. Frisco would need that information before he could figure out the best way to launch their attack against Bell and his men.

"Mia, I'll get that money soon. Right now, in fact, all right?"

"All right. Alan, be careful." Her voice shook slightly. "I love you."

"Mia, I—"

The line went dead. Frisco clicked off the telephone, cursing Dwayne Bell, cursing himself. But what, exactly, had he intended to say?

I love you, too.

God, the words had been right on the tip of his tongue. Forget about the fact that Cat and Lucky and Blue were listening in. Forget about the fact that a relationship with him was the last thing Mia needed.

But if after all he'd said and done she could still love him... No, she didn't *need* a relationship with him, but maybe, just maybe she wanted it.

God knows he did, despite the fact that he may well have burned his bridges with the awful things he'd said to her. Burned? Damn, he'd bombed the hell out of them.

Still, she'd told him that she *loved* him.

"We got it—273 Barker Street in Harper," Lucky leaned in the window to say. "Harvard's faxing a map and leaving Thomas at headquarters to relay any other calls. He and the rest of the squad will meet us over there."

Frisco nodded, hope flooding through him as he turned to Joe Cat. "Let's move."

Mia's stomach hurt as one of Dwayne Bell's cohorts followed her and Natasha back up the stairs.

Take care of Tasha, Frisco had told her. He'd given her as much carefully disguised information in his message as she'd tried to give him. *Stay with her in the bathroom. Put her in the bathtub.* If bullets started to fly, bullets like the ones that could be fired from Dwayne's enormous gun, bullets that could pass through walls and still have enough force to kill, then the bathtub, with its hard enamel, would be the safest place.

He'd told her to talk to Tasha. Why? *Talk to her so she's not scared.* Why would he want them to talk? It didn't make sense. But it didn't have to make sense. He'd asked—she'd do it.

Right now, Frisco had said. *I have the address.* Mia knew without a doubt that he was on his way. Somehow he'd found them. He'd be here soon.

She stopped in front of the open bathroom door, turning to look back at the man with the gun. "We need to use the bathroom."

He nodded. "Go ahead. Don't lock the door."

Mia drew Tasha inside the tiny room, closing the door behind her, taking a quick inventory.

Pedestal sink, grimy tub with a mildewed shower curtain, a less-than-pristine-looking toilet.

The window was tiny and sealed shut, the same as the window in the bedroom.

There was a narrow linen closet that held a few paper-wrapped rolls of toilet paper and several tired-looking washcloths and towels.

Mia took one of the washcloths from the closet and turned on the warm water in the sink, holding the small square of terry cloth underneath. "Okay, Tash," she said. "We're going to try to fool Dwayne and his friends into thinking that you're really sick, and that you might throw up, okay?"

The little girl nodded, her eyes wide.

"I need you to take a deep breath and hold it in for as long as you can—until your face turns *really* red, all right?"

Tasha nodded again, drawing in a big breath as Mia wrung out the washcloth.

"Now, this is going to be warm against your face, but we want you to feel kind of warm and sweaty so Dwayne will believe you've got a fever, okay?"

The little girl stood staunchly as Mia pressed the warm cloth against her forehead and cheeks. By the time Tasha exhaled, she was flushed and quite believably clammy.

"Can I get a drink?" she asked, turning on the cold water.

"Sure," Mia said. "But remember to look sick, okay?" She waited until Tash was done at the sink before she opened the bathroom door. "Excuse me. I think we better stay in here. Tasha's got a fever and—"

Behind her came the awful sound of retching, and Mia

turned to see Tasha leaning over the toilet, liquid gushing from her mouth.

"Oh, hell!" the man with the gun said in disgust, backing away and closing the bathroom door.

"Natasha," Mia started to say, alarmed.

But Tasha turned to look at Mia with a wicked light in her eyes. "I put lots of water in my mouth and spit it out," she whispered. "Do you think we fooled him?"

There was a sound from outside the door, and Mia opened it a crack. It was the man with the gun.

"I'm putting a bolt on the outside of this door," he said gruffly. "You're gonna have to stay in here. Dwayne don't want no mess. Can I get the kid some blankets or something?"

Mia nodded. "Blankets would be great."

She closed the door and turned back to Natasha, giving the little girl a big thumbs-up.

Now she had to keep talking. For some reason, Frisco wanted her to keep talking.

And she prayed that after this was all over, he'd still be alive to explain exactly why.

17

"**I**'ve got something," Harvard said, fine-tuning the dials of the ultrasensitive microphone that was aimed at the Barker Street house. "Sounds like a woman and a kid singing—I think it's 'The Alphabet Song.'"

He held out his padded earphones and Frisco slipped them on, staring out the darkened glass window in the side of Harvard's van at the house they were watching.

It was them. It had to be them. And then the song ended, and he heard Tash speak.

"Mia, why are we sitting in the bathtub?"

"Because your uncle thought we'd be safest here."

"'Cause Dwayne wants to make us dead, like he did to Thomas?"

"Honey, Frisco's not going to let that happen."

"Because he loves us?" the child asked.

Mia hesitated. "Yes," she finally said. "Because he loves...us."

Frisco knew she didn't believe what she was telling Tash. And why should Mia think he loved her after the terrible things he'd said? The thought of it made his chest ache. He handed the headphones back to Harvard. "It's them, Chief," he said. "Can you pinpoint their location?"

"Back of the house," Harvard told him, turning his dials. "I've got a TV up much too loud in the front of the house, along with sounds of someone eating."

Frisco nodded. That was a start. He'd have a better idea of Mia and Tash's exact location after Blue, Cowboy and Lucky checked in from their sneak and peek. In the early hours of the dusk, the three SEALs were checking over the yard and exterior of the house, looking for alarms or booby traps—anything that would tip Bell off as to their presence.

And Wes and Bobby were scanning with an infrared device that would help place the locations of Mia and Tash and their kidnappers. Bell and two others—that's what Mia had managed to tell him. All armed.

Three lowlifes against eight SEALs. There was no way the SEALs could lose.

Except for the fact that Frisco was determined that the SEALs would not open fire. Not with Mia and Tasha in the house, even despite the fact that they were protected by the bathtub. Because God help him if something went wrong and one of the two people he loved most in all of the world wound up in the cross fire.

No, they were going to have to do this by stealth—which currently was not one of his strengths. There was no way in hell he could climb up the side of the house silently.

"Hey! I found an extra headset and vest in the back of my jeep." Joe Catalanotto climbed into the van, tossing both in Frisco's direction.

"Man, do you know how long it's been since I've worn one of these?" Frisco asked, holding up the vest and lightweight headphones.

Cat nodded. "Yeah," he said. "I *do* know. Put 'em on. Blue and Lucky are starting to report in. You're gonna want to hear what they're saying."

Frisco slipped on the black combat vest. It was a newer version of the heavy-duty vest he'd damn near worn out during his five years as a SEAL. It was made from lighter fabric than his old vest and was more comfortable.

It felt good. He slipped on the headset and adjusted the lip microphone, plugging the wire into the radio unit in the vest. He adjusted the frequency and—

"...ly nothing in the yard." It was Blue McCoy, speaking in a low voice. "No extra alarms or movement sensors—

nothing. The alarm on the house is Mickey Mouse—Lucky already overrode it. There's also a trellis in the back—it's perfectly placed. Like an engraved invitation to the second floor.

"I'm already up there." This was Cowboy's voice. "Windows seem tight. But there's a third floor—probably an attic. Windows there look good and loose. Easy access."

"I got movement on the infrared," Bobby's deep voice reported. "Two are still stationary on the second floor, and three are downstairs, in the front of the structure, although one is moving now toward the back."

"That's Cliff," Harvard reported. "He just told his home-boy Ramon that he's going into the kitchen to get more salsa for his corn chips. They're watching something on an adults-only channel. Not much dialogue but lots of cheesy music."

Blue's voice again. "The house has seven rooms down-stairs. A living room in the southeast corner. A dining room to the immediate west, and a kitchen and some kind of rec room stretches along the entire back of the house."

Frisco grabbed paper and pen and sketched a rough floor plan as Blue continued to describe the layout, and the location of all doors and windows.

"Cat, you want me to insert through the attic?" Cowboy asked.

"It's Frisco's show," Cat replied, turning to look at him.

Frisco looked up from his drawing and shook his head. "Not yet. Report back to the van," he said, speaking into his mike for the first time in five years. "Everyone but Bobby. I want you to stay on the infrared, Bob. I need to be dead sure that Mia and Tash aren't moved from that upstairs room."

"You got it," Bobby replied.

It only took a few minutes for the rest of Alpha Squad to appear from the shadows and gloom of the early evening.

Frisco's plan was simple.

"I want Cat and Lucky to go in through the attic windows and work their way down to the second floor where Mia and Tash are held. The rest of us will make a silent entry through this back door." He pointed down to his drawing. "Except for Bobby, who's going to stay glued to the infrared and Harvard who's gonna keep listening in."

"Bor-ring," Bob's voice sounded over their headsets from somewhere out in the yard.

"Someone's got to do it," Joe Cat told him.

"Yeah, but why me? I mean, come on, a damn paraplegic in a wheelchair could handle *this* job...."

There was a sudden silence in the van. Nobody looked at Frisco or his crutches. Nobody so much as moved.

Bobby realized what he'd said and he swore softly. "Frisco, man—I didn't mean that the way it sounded.... I wasn't thinking."

"As usual," Wes added.

Frisco sat down, looking up at the uncomfortable expression on the faces of his friends.

"It makes sense for me to switch places with Bob," he said quietly. "Doesn't it?"

Joe Catalanotto was the first to look up and into his eyes. "This isn't going to be a difficult operation," he said. He glanced over at Blue. "We figured—"

And suddenly it was all clear to Frisco. "You figured you could let me play soldier one last time, huh?" he said, knowing that he spoke the truth. "You figured you could baby-sit me, and the fact that I can't run and can barely walk without crutches wouldn't put the squad in that much danger."

Cat respected him enough not to try to lie. But he couldn't bring himself to agree, either. So instead, he said nothing. But the answer was written plainly on his face.

"But still, my being there is going to put the squad in some danger," Frisco said.

"It's nothing we can't handle—"

"But if I'm not part of the team that goes in the back door, the chances of a snafu happening decreases."

"It's not that big a deal—"

Frisco pulled himself to his feet. "Bob, when we get ready to go, I'll switch with you."

Bob sounded as if he were in agony. "Frisco, I didn't mean to—"

"You'll have to wait until I get out there, because I want eyes on that infrared scanner at all times."

Lucky stepped forward. "Hey, buddy, we know how important it is for you to go in there and—"

"Working in a team means recognizing individual team members' strengths and weaknesses," Frisco told him evenly. "As much as I want to be the one to protect Mia and Natasha, I know I can't climb in the attic window. And the fact is, I have no business trying to sneak in that back door, either. I'll man the infrared." He took a deep breath. "Blue, you've got the point. You're in command once you're inside the house." He knew he could trust Blue McCoy to make the right decisions to apprehend Dwayne and his two men with the least amount of gunplay. "Okay, let's get into position."

One by one, the SEALs slipped out of the van, fading into the darkness of the night.

Frisco turned to Joe Cat. "Don't move Mia and Tash downstairs until you receive an all clear."

Cat nodded. "We'll wait for your signal."

Frisco clumsily swung himself out of the van and started toward the shrubs at the edge of the yard where Bobby and the infrared scanner were hidden. But Joe Cat stopped him.

"You know, it takes a real man to put others' welfare and safety before his own pride," Cat said.

"Yeah, right. I'm one hell of a hero," Frisco said. "Excuse me while I go hide in the bushes while the rest of you guys risk death to rescue my niece and my girlfriend."

"We both know that what you just did was impossibly hard and incredibly heroic," Cat countered. "If that were Ronnie in that house, I'm not sure I would've been able to assign myself out of the action."

"Yes, you would've," Frisco said quietly. "If you knew that putting yourself in the assault force would not only risk the lives of your men, but risk Ronnie's life…" He shook his head. "I had no choice. You would've had no choice, too."

Joe Cat nodded. "Maybe." He paused. "I'd like to think so."

"I'm counting on you to take care of Mia and Tash," Frisco said.

"These guys aren't going to hear us coming. If we do this right, the risk is minimal."

And doing it right meant that he wasn't in the way. Damn, as much as Frisco hated that, he knew it was true.

"Hey, you said it yourself. Working as a team means recognizing team members' strengths and weaknesses," Joe said as if he could read Frisco's mind. When Frisco would have nodded and turned away, Joe Cat stopped him again. "You can still be part of SEAL Team Ten, Lieutenant. God knows we need your strengths. I've got one hell of a shortage of dependable instructors and way too many raw recruits coming into the SEAL Teams to be able to teach 'em properly. You have a wealth of information to pass on to these kids. You could virtually have your pick of subjects to teach."

Frisco was silent. Teach. *Those who can, do. Those who can't, teach.* Except, what was it that Mia had said? *Those who are taught, do. Those who teach, shape the future.*

"And as for your weaknesses..." Joe Cat continued. "Do you remember the very end of Hell Week? You weren't in my boat team, but I know you probably heard the story. I was a half a day away from the end of the ordeal, and I got a stress fracture in my leg. Talk about pain. It was hell, but I wouldn't quit. I wasn't gonna quit after I'd come that far. But I was *damn* close to being taken out. One of the instructors— a real bastard nicknamed Captain Blood—was about to call for the medics and have me removed."

Frisco nodded. "I remember hearing that."

"But then Blue and the other guys who were left in my boat team told Captain Blood that I was okay, that I could make it. In fact, they said I'd run a mile down the beach to prove it. And the captain looked at me and told me if I could run that mile, he'd let me stay in 'til the end.

"There was no way in hell I could *walk,* let alone run, but

Blue and the other guys picked me up, and they ran that mile carrying me.''

Frisco *had* heard that story. With their incredible show of unity and loyalty, Cat and Blue and the rest of their boat team were rewarded by having the hard-nosed instructor announce them secure nearly six hours before the official end of Hell Week. It was unprecedented.

Joe Cat reached out and squeezed Frisco's shoulder. ''Right now you're letting us carry *you*. But don't think there's no way you can carry us in return, my friend. Because you can. By teaching those recruits who are going to back us up someday, you'd be shouldering more than your share.''

Frisco was silent. What could he say?

''Think about it,'' Cat said quietly. ''At least think about it.''

Frisco nodded. ''I will—after you get Mia and Natasha safely out of that house.''

''I know you meant after *we* get them out of there. All of us—working as a team.''

Frisco smiled. ''Right. Slip of the tongue.''

From where he sat, Frisco could see the light coming from an upstairs window. This window was smaller than the others—it had to be the bathroom.

Mia and Natasha were on the other side of those panes of glass. So close, yet so damn far.

As he watched the infrared scanner, the reddish-orange spots that were the Alpha Squad moved closer to the house. Two who had to be Lucky and Cat moved up onto the house.

The other four—Blue, Bobby, Wes and Cowboy—were motionless now, waiting for Frisco's command.

Inside the house, according to his scanner, nothing had changed. Dwayne and his men were still in the living room. Mia and Tash were still upstairs.

Mia and Tash.

Both of them had given him unconditional love. Funny, he had no problem accepting it from the kid, but from Mia…

Frisco hadn't believed it was possible. It still seemed much too good to be true. She was filled with such joy and life while he was the poster model for despair. She had such strength of purpose while he was floundering and uncertain.

He hadn't told her he loved her. He could have. But instead he'd attacked her, attacked her avocation. He'd pushed her away. Yet still she loved him.

Was it possible that she'd somehow seen the desperate, frightened man that hid beneath the anger and pain of his verbal attack? Thomas had told him she'd done the same with him, making a critical difference in his life, altering his destiny, shaping his future.

Those who are taught, do. Those who teach, shape the future.

Frisco could picture Mia telling him that, her eyes blazing with passion and fire. She believed it so absolutely.

And right then, as Alpha Squad waited for his signal to move into Dwayne Bell's house, Frisco knew just as absolutely that he wanted a second chance.

His entire life was full of second chances, he realized. Another man might have died from the wounds he'd received. Another man would never have made it out of that wheelchair.

Another man would let Mia Summerton get away.

He thought of that list that she'd posted on his refrigerator—all the things he could still do. There *was* so much he could still do, although some of it was going to be extremely hard.

Like not being an active-duty SEAL. That was going to be damned hard. But it was going to be damned hard whether he spent the rest of his life drinking in his living room, or if he signed on as an instructor. His disappointment and crushed hopes would be a tough weight to carry, a rough road to walk.

But he was a SEAL. Tough and rough were standard operating procedure. He'd come this far. He could—and he would—make it the rest of the way.

"Okay," Frisco said into his lip microphone. "The three

targets haven't moved. Let's get this done. Quietly and quickly, Alpha Squad. Go.''

There was no response over his headset, but he saw the shapes on the infrared scanner begin to move.

Blue clicked once into his lip mike when the downstairs team were all inside.

"Moving slow in the attic," he heard Joe Cat breathe. "Beams are old—don't want 'em to creak."

"Take as long as you need," Frisco told him.

It seemed to take an eternity, but Frisco finally heard Cat report, "In place."

He and Lucky were outside the upstairs bathroom door. That was Blue's signal to move.

Frisco heard the flurry of movement and the sound of four automatic weapons being locked and loaded. That was when the noise started.

"Hands up," Blue shouted, his normally smooth voice hard and clipped. "Come on—let me see 'em. Hands on your heads!"

"Come on, get 'em up!" It was Cowboy. "Come on—*move!*"

"What the…" Frisco could faintly hear Dwayne's voice as he was picked up over all four microphones.

"Move it! Down on the floor, faces against the rug. Let's *go.*" That was Bobby, along with an accompanying crash as he helped someone down there.

"Who the hell are you?" Dwayne kept asking. "Who the hell are you guys?"

"We're your worst nightmare," Cowboy told him, and then laughed. "Hell, you don't know *how* many years I've been waiting to say that line!"

"We're Alan Francisco's friends," Frisco heard Blue tell Dwayne. "Okay, Frisco, Mr. Bell and his associates have all been relieved of their weapons."

"Take 'em out into the front yard and tie 'em up, Blue," Frisco ordered. He had already moved across the yard and was nearly inside the house. "H., use that fancy equipment of yours to dial 911. Let's get the police garbage removal squad to take away the trash. Cat, this is my official all clear. Let's get Mia and Tasha out of there."

The bathroom door swung open, and Mia stared up into the face of an enormous dark-haired stranger carrying an equally enormous gun.

He must've seen the surge of panic in her eyes because he quickly aimed the gun down toward the floor. "Lt. Commander Joe Catalanotto of the Alpha Squad." He identified himself in a rather unmistakable New York accent. "It's all right now, ma'am, you're safe."

"Dwayne's been detained—permanently." Another man poked his head in the door. It was Lucky O'Donlon. Both men were wearing army fatigues and some kind of black vest.

"Are you okay?" the dark-haired man—Joe—asked.

Mia nodded, still holding Tasha close. In the distance, she could hear the sound of sirens. "Where's Alan? Is he all right?"

Lucky smiled, coming forward to give them both a hand out of the bathtub. "He's downstairs, waiting for the police to arrive. They're not going to be real happy to see us here, doing their job for them, so to speak."

"I pretended to throw up so the bad man would lock us in the bathroom," Natasha told Lucky proudly.

"That's very cool," he told her, perfectly straight-faced. But when he looked up at Mia, there was a glint of amusement in his eyes. "Barfing kid as weapon," he said to her under his breath. "The thought makes the strongest man tremble with fear. Good thinking."

"I want to see Alan," she said.

The man named Joe nodded. "I know he wants to see you, too. Come on, let's go downstairs."

"How many SEALs are here?" she asked Joe as Lucky, Tasha in his arms, led the way down the stairs.

"All of Alpha Squad," he told her.

"How did you ever get him to agree to let you help?"

"He asked us."

Mia stared at Joe. Alan asked *them* for help? They didn't volunteer and he grudgingly accept? God, she'd been so afraid he'd come here on his own and get himself killed....

"It's hard for him, but he's learning," Joe said quietly. "Give him time. He's gonna be okay."

"Frisco!" Tasha shouted.

Mia stopped halfway down the stairs, watching as the little girl wriggled free from Lucky's arms and launched herself at Alan Francisco.

He was dressed similarly to the other SEALs, complete with black vest and some kind of headphone thing. His crutches clattered to the living room floor as he caught Tasha in his arms.

From across the room, over the top of Tasha's head, Alan looked up at Mia. Their eyes met and he smiled one of his sad, crooked, perfect smiles.

Then, God help her, she was rushing toward him, too—as shamelessly as Natasha had.

And then she was in his arms. He held her as tightly as he could with Tasha still clinging to him, too.

"I'm sorry," he whispered into her ear. "Mia, I'm so sorry."

Mia wasn't sure if he was apologizing for his angry words or Dwayne's abducting them. It didn't matter. What mattered was they were safe and he was safe and he had actually *asked* for help....

Flashing lights marked the arrival of police squad cars, and Frisco loosened his hold on Mia and let Tasha slide down to the floor.

"Can we talk later?" Frisco asked.

Mia nodded. "I was coming back, you know," she told him. "To the cabin. To talk to you—talk, not fight. That was when Dwayne nearly ran me off the road."

Her beautiful hazel eyes were shining with unshed tears. She had been coming back to the cabin. She loved him enough to swallow her pride.

And suddenly later wasn't good enough. Suddenly there were things he had to tell her, things that couldn't wait.

Frisco knew in that moment that even if right then and there, in a miraculous act of God, he suddenly regained full use of his injured leg, he would still be less than whole.

He knew with a certainty that took his breath away that it was only when he was with this incredible woman that he was truly complete.

Oh, he knew he could live without her—the same way he knew he could live without ever running again. It would be hard, but he could do it. It wasn't as if she'd saved him. She hadn't—he'd done that himself. With a little help. It had taken Natasha to nudge him back to the world of the living. And once there, Mia's warmth and joy had lit his path, helping him out of his darkness.

Frisco knew he'd probably never run again. But he also knew that he didn't have to live without Mia.

That was something he had at least a small amount of control over.

And he could start by telling her how he felt.

But there wasn't any time. The police had arrived, and the uniformed officers were less than pleased that the SEALs had taken matters into their own hands. Joe Cat had intercepted the officer in charge and was trying to calm him down, but back-up had to be called along with the police captain.

And instead of telling Mia that he loved her, Frisco turned to Lucky. "Do me a favor, man, and walk Mia and Tash out to Harvard's van. I want to get them out of here, but I've got to set one thing straight with the police before we leave."

"Absolutely."

Frisco picked up his crutches, positioning them under his arms as he looked back at Mia. "I'll try not to take too long."

She gave him a tremulous smile that added so much weight and meaning to her words. "That's okay. We'll wait."

Frisco smiled back at her, suddenly almost ridiculously happy. "Yeah," he said. "I know. But I don't want to keep you waiting any longer."

* * *

"I told the police captain that Sharon was willing to testify against Bell," Frisco told Harvard and Mia as they climbed out of the van and started toward the condo courtyard. "With her help, they can ID Bell as the perpetrator in a number of unsolved robberies and possibly even a murder."

"Sharon saw Dwayne *kill* someone?" Mia asked Frisco in a low voice.

He nodded, glancing at Harvard who was carrying a drowsy Tasha. But her five-year-old ears were as sharp as ever and she lifted her head. "I saw Dwayne kill someone, too," Tasha told them, her eyes filling with tears. "I saw him kill Thomas."

"Thomas isn't dead," Frisco said.

"Yes, he is," Tasha insisted. "Dwayne hit him and made him bloody, and he didn't get back up."

"Thomas is waiting for you, princess, up in the condo."

"Oh, thank God," Mia said. "Is he really all right?"

"A little shaky, maybe," Frisco said, "but, yeah. He's okay."

All signs of her drowsiness gone, Tasha squirmed free from Harvard's arms. Like a flash, she ran up the stairs. But the condo door was locked, and she pounded on it.

As Mia watched, it swung open, and sure enough, there was Thomas King, looking a little worse for wear. Tasha launched herself at him, and nearly knocked the teenager over.

"Hey, Martian girl," Thomas said casually and matter-of-factly, as if they'd run into each other on the street. But he held the child tightly. That and the sudden sheen of tears in his eyes gave him away.

"I thought you were dead," she told him, giving him a resounding kiss on the cheek. "And if you were dead, then you couldn't marry me."

"*Marry* you?" Thomas's voice slipped up an octave. "Whoa, wait a minute, I—"

"A Russian princess has to marry a king," Tasha told him seriously.

"You're kind of short," Thomas told her. "I'm not so sure I want a wife who's that *short*."

Tasha giggled. "I'll be taller, silly," she told him. "I'll be sixteen."

"Sixteen…" Thomas looked as if he were choking. "Look, Martian, if you're still interested when you're *twenty*-six, give me a call, but until then, we're friends, all right?"

Natasha just smiled.

"All right," Thomas said. "Now, come on inside and see what Navy bought for you."

They disappeared inside the house, and Mia could hear Tasha's excited squealing. She turned to Frisco, who was painstakingly pulling himself up the stairs. "Is it the couch?"

Frisco just shook his head. "Man, I forgot all about it."

"I didn't," Harvard said, laughter in his voice.

Curiosity overcame Mia, and she hurried to Frisco's door. And laughed out loud. "You got it," she said. "The couch. Dear Lord, it's so…"

"Pink?" Frisco volunteered, amusement and chagrin glinting in his eyes as he followed her inside.

Tasha was sitting in the middle of the couch, her ankles delicately crossed—the perfect Russian princess, despite the fact that her hair was tangled and her face dirty and tear streaked.

Harvard started packing up the array of equipment, and Thomas moved to help him.

"This stuff is so cool," Mia heard Thomas tell Harvard. "What do I have to do to become one of you guys?"

"Well, you start by joining the Navy," Harvard said. "And you work your butt off for about three years, and maybe, just maybe, then you'll be accepted into the BUD/S training."

"Hey," Frisco said to Natasha. "Don't I get a hug? Or any thanks?"

Tasha looked at him haughtily. "Russian princesses *don't* say thank you or give hugs."

"Wanna bet?" He sat down on the couch next to the little girl and pulled her into his arms.

She giggled and threw her arms around his neck. "Thank you, thank you, thank you, thank you, thank you—"

Frisco laughed. Mia loved the sound of his laughter. "Enough already," he said. "Go wash your face and get ready for bed."

Tash stood up, casting a look of longing back at the sofa.

"Don't worry," Frisco told her. "It'll be here in the morning."

"You bet it will," Harvard interjected. "And the morning after that, and the morning after *that*…"

"I don't know," Mia said. "It's starting to grow on me." She held out her hand to Tasha. "Come on. I'll help you."

Frisco watched them disappear into the bathroom. Tasha was dragging, clearly exhausted. It wouldn't be long before she was sound asleep. He turned back to Harvard. "Need help getting that stuff together?"

Harvard grinned, reading his mind. "All done. We're out of here. Gee, sorry we can't stay."

Frisco held out his hand, and Harvard clasped it. "Thanks, man."

"It was good seeing you again, Francisco. Don't be a stranger."

"I won't be," Frisco told his friend. "In fact, I'll probably be coming over to the base in a few days to talk to Cat."

Harvard smiled, his powerful biceps flexing as he easily lifted pounds and pounds of heavy equipment. "Good. See you then."

He followed Thomas outside and closed the door behind them.

The sudden silence and stillness was deafening. Frisco started toward Tasha's room, but stopped short at the sight of Mia quietly closing the little girl's door.

"She's already asleep," she told him. "She was exhausted."

Mia looked exhausted, too. Maybe this wasn't a good time to talk. Maybe she just wanted to go home.

"Do you want a cup of tea?" Frisco asked, suddenly horribly uncertain.

She took a step toward him. "All I want right now is for you to hold me," she said quietly.

Frisco carefully leaned his crutches against the wall and slowly drew her into his arms. She was trembling as she slipped her arms around his waist. He pulled her closer, held her tighter and she rested her head against his chest and sighed.

"Did you really ask the Alpha Squad for help?" she asked.

"Is that so hard to believe?"

Mia lifted her head. "Yes."

He laughed. And kissed her. She tasted so sweet, her lips were so soft. He'd been crazy to think he could ever give her up.

"Were you really coming back to the cabin?" he asked her.

She nodded.

"Why? You said damn near all that there was to say pretty concisely. Your vision of the way my future might've been was pretty accurate—although I'm willing to bet you didn't picture me drinking myself to death on a pink couch."

"The way your future might've been...?"

There was such hope in her eyes, Frisco had to smile. "That's not my future, Mia," he told her. "That was my past. It was my father who drank himself into oblivion every night in front of the TV set. But I'm not my old man. I'm a SEAL. You were right. I'm still a SEAL. And it's only my knee that got busted, not my spirit."

"Oh, Alan...."

"Yeah, it hurts to know I'm not going to go on the active-duty list, but that's the hand fate dealt me. I'm done wallowing," he told her. "Now I'm going to get on with my *true* future. I'm going to talk to Joe Cat about that instructor position. And I've got Tash to think about, because Sharon's gonna have to do time on those DUI charges even if the man she hit lives...."

Mia was crying. She was crying *and* she was laughing.

"Hey," Frisco said. "Are you all right?"

"I'm great," she told him. "And so are you. You made it, Alan. You're whole again." Her eyes filled with a fresh flood of tears. "I'm so happy for you."

He was whole? Frisco wasn't quite so sure. "I'm going to look for another place to live," he told her, searching her eyes. "I figure if I sell this place, I can maybe get something a little closer to the base, maybe something on the water—something on the ground floor. Something big enough for me and Tash and maybe…you, too…?"

"Me?" she whispered.

He nodded. "Yeah, I mean, if you want to…."

"You want me to live with you…?"

"Hell, no. I want you to *marry* me."

Mia was silent. Her eyes were wide and her lips slightly parted. She didn't say a word, she just stared at him.

Frisco shifted his weight nervously. "I know you're probably speechless with joy at the thought of spending the rest of your life with a man who owns a pink couch and—"

"Do you love me?"

Frisco could see from her eyes that she honestly didn't know. How could she not know? Well, he realized, because for starters, he'd never actually said the words….

"You know, up at the cabin, when I said all those horrible things…?"

Mia nodded.

"What I *really* meant to say was that I'd fallen absolutely in love with you, and that I was terrified—both of what I was feeling, and of the thought of you ruining the rest of your life by spending it with me."

She was indignant. "How could you have thought that?"

He smiled. "I still think it—I just figure I'll work really hard to keep you happy and smiling, and you won't even notice. You also won't notice that when we vote, we cancel each other out."

"Democracy in action," Mia said.

"And maybe, someday—if you want—we could add 'making babies' to that list you started on my refrigerator," he told her. "What do you say?"

"Yes," Mia told him, emotion making her voice tremble. "I say oh, yes."

Frisco kissed her.

And he was whole.

New York Times Bestselling Author

DIANA PALMER

With her undeniable flair for giving readers what they love most, Diana Palmer delivers a searing, explosive story in which one man and one woman confront their splintered past and walk a precarious tightrope between life and death.

This is a novel readers will not soon forget.

DESPERADO

"A gripping story...Palmer's compelling suspense and beautiful visuals keep the reader interested."
—*Publishers Weekly*

Available the first week of June 2003 wherever paperbacks are sold!

MIRA®

From *USA TODAY* bestselling author

EMILIE RICHARDS

comes the story of a woman who has played life by the book, and now the rules have changed.

Faith Bronson, daughter of a prominent Virginia senator and wife of a charismatic lobbyist, finds her privileged life shattered when her marriage ends abruptly. Only just beginning to face the lie she has lived, she finds sanctuary with her two children in a run-down row house in exclusive Georgetown. This historic house harbors deep secrets of its own, secrets that force Faith to confront the deceit that has long defined her.

PROSPECT STREET

Available the first week of June 2003 wherever paperbacks are sold!

MIRA®

USA TODAY
Bestselling Author

KAREN HARPER

Early one morning Claire Malvern awakes to an empty bed—and her husband missing. There is no trace of Keith Malvern—only an eyewitness who claims a man jumped off the bridge at Bloodroot Falls in the middle of the night.

It is the spectacular waterfall that first drew Claire and Keith to pursue the dream of opening a bed-and-breakfast in the rustic lodge above Bloodroot River. But the dream becomes a nightmare when Keith's body is found snagged in the river rapids, his death ruled a suicide.

Claire knew her husband would never take his own life. But local sheriff Nick Braden thinks her suspicions of foul play are unfounded. Despite his skepticism, Nick and Claire start digging into her husband's past...and what they uncover paints a shocking portrait of what really happened that September night....

The Falls

"...deft juxtaposition of the cast of creepy characters and a small-town setting...makes for a haunting read."
—*Publishers Weekly* on *The Stone Forest*

Available the first week of June 2003 wherever paperbacks are sold!

SUZANNE BROCKMANN

66680	FOREVER BLUE	___ $5.99 U.S.	___ $6.99 CAN.
66948	PRINCE JOE	___ $5.99 U.S.	___ $6.99 CAN.

(limited quantities available)

TOTAL AMOUNT	$_____
POSTAGE & HANDLING	$_____
($1.00 for one book; 50¢ for each additional)	
APPLICABLE TAXES*	$_____
TOTAL PAYABLE	$_____

(check or money order—please do not send cash)

To order, complete this form and send it, along with a check or money order for the total above, payable to MIRA® Books, to: **In the U.S.:** 3010 Walden Avenue, P.O. Box 9077, Buffalo, NY 14269-9077; **In Canada:** P.O. Box 636, Fort Erie, Ontario L2A 5X3.

Name:_____

Address:_____ City:_____

State/Prov.:_____ Zip/Postal Code:_____

Account Number (if applicable):_____

075 CSAS

*New York residents remit applicable sales taxes.
Canadian residents remit applicable GST and provincial taxes.

MIRA®